"Are you in a bad place now, William?"

"What do you mean?"

Annie shrugged. "Breezing back into town and then readying to leave again... What haven't you told me?"

He paused, his hands grazing over hers before pulling away. "Nothing."

Her wide eyes slowly narrowed. *"Something."*

"You and I haven't gotten off on the right foot, Annie, and I'd like to make a fresh start with you."

"I don't really know what to say."

"Consider this gift a peace offering for all the times I should have been with you staring up at the moon. I really wish you would."

"You missed a lot, William. And to suddenly start a friendship now..."

"I'm sorry. I should have been here."

"No. You should have called me, instead of dropping off the face of the earth. I didn't know what had happened to you. I assumed you didn't care about me anymore."

"I always cared," William whispered. "I *care*."

Dear Reader,

A long time ago, I heard the adage "Friends are the family you choose," and as I have friends I embrace as sisters, I believe this to be true. As far as families go, sometimes they hurt us and sometimes we lose our way.

In *A Promise Remembered*, I wanted to imagine a community that would become family for Annie and William, who loved each other once upon a time but think a second chance at happiness is out of their reach. As Annie fights to protect her family and William runs from past mistakes, they might think they're each too broken to choose a new life, a happier life. And yet, they have a cast of supportive friends—from Dan and Earl, to Margie and Joe—who love Annie and William enough to nudge them along to the happily-ever-after they both deserve. Because we all deserve friends who love us as family and a family that pulls us closer to love.

I wish that for us all.

I'd love to connect with you. Find me on Facebook on my author page or visit my website, elizabethmowers.com.

Wishing love to you and yours,

Elizabeth

HEARTWARMING

A Promise Remembered

———

Elizabeth Mowers

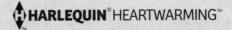

HARLEQUIN® HEARTWARMING™

Recycling programs
for this product may
not exist in your area.

ISBN-13: 978-1-335-51058-7

A Promise Remembered

Copyright © 2019 by Elizabeth Mowers

This edition published by arrangement with Harlequin Books S.A.

For questions and comments about the quality of this book,
please contact us at CustomerService@Harlequin.com.

Printed in U.S.A.

Elizabeth Mowers wrote her first romance novel on her cell phone when her first child wouldn't nap without being held. After three years, she had a happy preschooler and a hot mess of a book that will never be read by another person. The experience started her down the wonderful path of writing romances, and now that she can use her computer, she's having fun cooking up new stories. She's drawn to romances with strong family connections and plots where the hero and heroine help save each other. Elizabeth lives in the country with her husband and two children.

To Mom, who always knew I'd be a writer.

To Dad, who was proud of me no matter what.

To Danielle, my moon baby.

To Michaela, my water baby.

And to Kevin, who won my heart in Marquette
all those years ago.

CHAPTER ONE

WILLIAM KAUFFMAN CLUTCHED his right hand in his lap, rubbing a thumb over the tops of knuckles that still carried the scabbed gash from the latest in his line of regrets. Slouched in the driver's seat of his rusted-out Chevy truck, he carefully examined the wound. It was the only one visible to the world.

It wouldn't be a long visit. Quite brisk in fact. Chinoodin Falls, Michigan, was the last place he wanted to be, but he owed it to his mother to make one last visit before hightailing it west and possibly out of the country. The thought of rescuing the 1981 Indian motorcycle rusting away in her shed, which should have passed directly to him, was highly motivating, too. If he could sell his truck for a few bucks, he could travel farther on his true father's wheels—undetected.

Parked along the street, with the Chevy's engine gently idling, William eyed the illuminated windows of the greasy spoon where he'd been trapped most evenings and weekends as a child. A bland storefront with a faded green awning over the entrance, the dimly lit Pop's Place sign hung crookedly over the front door. The sight, so long forgotten, now aroused in him a giddy fantasy of the words coming unfastened and crashing to the ground. He silently wished it to happen. If it did, perhaps he'd know in his heart that burying his ugly past spent there was somehow genuinely possible.

As the early summer sun sank beneath the Lake Superior shoreline, casting hues of oranges and purples over the charming downtown Main Street, William grimaced at patrons shuffling through the diner's open doors. The only thing slower than their moseying walk was their drawn-out Upper Peninsula accent, a mimic of folks from Northern Wisconsin and Minnesota. They carried on into Pop's Place as if they hadn't a care in the world: he despised them. His eyes darted along the storefront window, straining for a glimpse of his mother and some sign that returning to Chinoodin Falls after a twelve-year absence wasn't the terrible mistake he feared it to be. He was an older version of the angry kid who'd taken off years ago, but as he shook out his aching right hand to turn off the ignition, he didn't feel any wiser.

He pulled his grease-stained baseball cap down snugly over his forehead and shoved his fists in the front pockets of his worn-out blue jeans before jutting across the street. He reminded himself that nobody in this little town knew what he had done, and they wouldn't find out unless he was foolish enough to tell them. All he had to do was make a quick visit to appease his mother, persuade her to give him the motorcycle and then sell his truck. He'd only have to invest two to three days tops before he could be on his way. If he kept his head down and stuck to the plan, no one could stop him from escaping west.

ANNIE CURTIS WIPED perspiration from her brow with the top of her shoulder while carrying a tray of dinners to table four. She slid the plates to each patron with a brief nod before noticing the lone straggler sauntering through the front door.

"Take a seat anywhere, honey," she called, as he had seemed to miss the Seat Yourself sign. Without acknowledging her, he sidled up to the end of the counter and stood a menu in front of him, partially shielding his face from view. Annie refilled soda glasses for table three before cruising along the counter, order pad in hand.

"What can I get you?" she asked the cracked menu cover as the stranger ducked behind it.

"Joyce," he said in a barely audible grumble.

Annie frowned, cocking her head closer. "Excuse me?"

"Send Joyce out, would ya?"

"Joyce isn't working the dining room tonight. You're stuck with me. What can I get you to drink?"

The stranger readjusted the menu and peered over the top of it, the whites of his eyes darkened by the shadow of his baseball cap.

"I need to see Joyce *now*."

Annie hesitated, narrowing her eyes to study him. He was tall with a broad frame and a muscular build, but if she was pressed to give a detailed description to the police, she wouldn't be able to manage more than "gray T-shirt and faded Levi blue jeans."

"What do you want with her?"

The stranger dipped his head and grumbled, "It's important."

Annie tapped a pen on the top of her order pad for a moment before sauntering back to the office for her boss.

"A fellow at the end of the counter wants you," she called. Joyce, a round woman well into retirement age, hoisted herself out of her desk chair and scurried past Annie to the dining room, trying to catch her breath along the way.

"Miles," Annie whispered, slipping back to the kitchen's order window. The young cook craned his bandana-covered head to see her. "Grab me a frying pan. There's some weirdo out there asking for Joyce."

"What's he want with her?"

"I don't know, but he's acting dodgy."

Miles raised a discerning eyebrow. "What do you wanna do?"

"*Miles,*" Annie said, holding out her hand. *"Come on."*

"Annie Curtis, you're gonna hit a guy with a frying pan?"

"No..." she said as her subconscious protested. "Maybe."

Miles paused. "Seriously?"

"There's something about him that's very familiar, but I can't put my finger on it. Did a convict escape from the prison?"

"How would *that* be familiar?"

"Miles, sometimes you see a story on the news, but it doesn't register in your consciousness until later."

"You're going to need more than a frying pan if there's a convict sitting out there."

"I don't know if it's a convict, Miles. That was just one theory. Something about him reminds me of…" Annie gasped and touched her fingertips to her lips.

"Oh."

"Annie?" Miles's eyebrows pinched together. "Are you okay?"

"Keep the pan on standby," she muttered before scooting to the kitchen door and peeking out the porthole window. A cool sweat pricked every dainty hair down her neck as if someone had opened the door and let in a draft. It had been almost a dozen years since she'd waited anxiously on her mother's back porch for that man to come for her, and now that he had finally returned home, he'd brushed her off. Sitting coolly behind the counter and hiding under the shadow of his cap, he was merely yards away and yet still so distant.

Annie watched Joyce spring into his arms and clutch him in a bear hug. His profile was an aged, heavier version than the boyish one she'd hopelessly spent hours admiring so many years ago. She had run her fingers along the scruff of his chin and nipped at his mischievously curled lips for an entire summer, back when she'd been young and careless. It had been the last summer of her youth, the last summer of innocence, the last summer before…

Annie drew a sharp breath and thrust open the kitchen door with a surge of adrenaline she didn't yet know how to expel. Storming up behind the counter to size up the heartless cad who basked in his mother's enthusiastic affection, she clenched her jaw and squared off in front of him. Joyce had quickly worked herself into a tizzy, clasping William's face between her palms and shrieking with joy as patrons jumped in equal parts amusement and alarm.

"Baby boy, where have you been? I can hardly breathe. Look. Look! My hands are shaking." Joyce turned to nearby patrons and announced for all to hear that her son was home from the Navy, and her prayers had finally been answered. Folks nodded and smiled politely, turning attention back to their Salisbury steaks and Reuben sandwiches.

"Did you decide?" Annie asked in a strained voice, attempting to interrupt Joyce's hysterics.

"A coffee, please. Decaf, if you have it," William said without casting his eyes in her direction. Annie scowled as he squeezed Joyce's tear-stained face into his chest. He had a lot of nerve showing up with that easy grin plastered across his face. For a moment she imagined smacking it clear off him with the frying pan, tiny white teeth scattering to the ground like it happened in cartoons.

"William," Joyce said, slightly releasing the death grip she had on him. She retrieved a tissue tucked between her bosom, dabbed her eyes and scowled up at him. "Dontcha recognize who this *is*?" William paused and studied Annie for a moment as she reciprocated with a cold glare. She had no desire to supply any word of help to the self-centered jerk. Joyce finally filled the awkward silence. "It's *Annie*."

Annie waited as recognition fell over William's sun-kissed face. There had been a time when Joyce would have described her to William as *"your* Annie," but those days had long passed. Though as she stood before him, memories thundering toward her like a freight train, she doubted they would be long buried.

"Annie Curtis?" he said, his smile fading to a wince. "H-how are you? I didn't know you worked here."

"Obviously," she said, pouring his coffee with a jerk to splash it over the rim of his cup. "How long's it been now?"

William faltered, raising the brim of his hat

to reveal those pool-blue eyes in which she had once swum laps. They were the one thing that hadn't aged a day and were still just as hypnotizing. If the rest of his weathered face blurred so all she could see were those eyes, she might as well be peering at the eighteen-year-old boy she'd once called "*her* William."

Joyce hugged William again and pulled his face down for another smooch, snapping his gaze away and releasing Annie from the spell. Pressing her round nose against William's, Joyce giggled.

"Oh, shucks, sweetie, I'm so excited to see you. I almost had a heart attack when I saw that face. Can you drop dead from pure happiness?"

Annie glanced up at the ceiling as she turned to place the coffeepot back onto its burner. The prodigal son appeared, and Joyce was itching to throw him a ticker tape parade. Between running the diner, worrying about losing business and…well…other problems, times had been hard on Joyce. Annie wanted to be happy for her friend. She wanted to make Joyce's joy her joy, because she loved that old woman as much as she had loved her own mother. Instead, she flexed the muscles in her clenched jaw.

Perhaps Joyce was eager to forgive and forget, but Annie had a long memory and wasn't about to pretend William Kauffman had done anything other than abandon his mother when she had needed him most. Besides, Joyce hadn't been the only person William had bailed on; her own pride suddenly felt very tender and bruised, recalling the memory. She had stood there for hours and hours…

Joyce patted William on the arm. "Whatcha hungry for? You musta been eat'n junk on the road. Let me wrap some things up real quick while Miles fixes you anything you want. And when we get home we'll celebrate with some-tin' fancy."

"What's good?" William asked, finally focusing on Annie as Joyce hurried to the back.

"Everything," Annie said. She pursed her lips to bite back every scathing remark for William she'd dreamed up when she was crying into her pillow all those nights ago.

"I'll have that," he said with a smirk, flashing his baby blues at her. Annie mocked his reply under her breath as she strolled back into the kitchen to place the order.

"Egg salad on rye, Miles," she called, strumming her fingers on the wall and shaking her head in disgust. Maybe William thought he could act the part and simply charm people into forgiving him, but she certainly wasn't going to fall for it. She'd had one too many men fool her in the past to be made a fool of ever again, and he had been the first.

Miles leaned into view. "It'll take me a few minutes to whip up a new batch of egg salad. The carton in there is past its peak."

"Ripe, is it?"

"It needs to be tossed."

"Even better," Annie said with a shrug, walking to the refrigerator to fix the sandwich herself.

"I was listening for shouts of attack, you know," Miles said, directing his attention to the grill. "Who was looking for Joyce?"

"Nobody worth mentioning."

"So, you don't need the frying pan?"

Annie's mouth turned into a smile, though her eyes had darkened. "Nope. I'm taking care of it." She scooped out a heaping portion of egg salad and flicked the spoon over a slice of bread with a plop. "Perfect," she said before waltzing out to the dining room.

WILLIAM DEVOURED HIS sandwich, his ravenous appetite suddenly apparent as he sized up his old stomping ground. At first glance it had all the basic amenities of a greasy spoon: heavy white mugs with varying degrees of coffee stains; slices of pie displayed attractively in a countertop dessert case; and tables adorned with ketchup bottles, sugar packets and coffee creamer. But unfortunately it hadn't changed much since he'd left, and the wear and tear, which had been noticeable years ago, was now grossly evident.

The tiny entryway was cluttered with empty vintage gumball machines he'd once kicked over as a kid. A large, opaque glass-globe light fixture hung awkwardly low at the entrance, caked with a heavy film of dust and dated 1960s' appeal. The three perimeter walls of the long, narrow diner had large bay windows to catch the warm, cheery glow of the morning sun, but by nightfall, the fluorescent overhead lights, sterile and intrusive, made William shudder. He tried to ignore the childhood memory of being forced to work in the restaurant most evenings as his stepfather, Dennis, disapprovingly scrutinized his every move.

Elbows planted firmly on the counter, William distracted himself with the sight of Annie as she hustled in and out through the swinging doors that led to the kitchen. With each push of the aluminum door, he caught a whiff of the sizzling, steaming engulfment of grease just beyond it. Even the momentary sniff of it made his stomach churn. That kitchen had seemed like a humid prison, caking his skin and hair in a grimy film. He took a swig of coffee and turned to inspect the dining room.

The scuffed sand-colored tabletops were still sandwiched between vertical vinyl booths of spruce green and chestnut. Most seats were torn, with faded spots where thousands of patrons had plopped their derrieres over the years. As Annie seated a couple in their fifties, William grimaced as he waited for the *thwart* sound the seat cushions always made. The couple crouched over to manipulate their bodies into the booth, and—*thwart*—their weight pushed the air out of the giant rips in the vinyl. He used to find it amusing as a kid, the sound playing into his adolescent sense of humor, but now it, along with all the other sights, was beginning to be too much.

William slowly swiveled his barstool, also grossly cracked and fading. Running his hand along the long L-shaped counter with a cream laminate and two-inch metal banding, he forced a few deep breaths. The counter still comfortably sat twelve people and provided a perch at the far end to view the entire diner and all its happenings.

It was from this perch William sipped his coffee and studied Annie as she served her customers, occasionally fidgeting with the waist of her apron whenever her eyes shifted his way. It wasn't busy for a dinner rush, leaving her time to chat with patrons as she breezed by him, nose tilted ever so slightly in the air. By the time she slapped his bill on the counter, he concluded she had developed a serious attitude problem.

William's inner monologue finally found his lips. "Refill on your coffee? Sure, sounds great, Annie. Thanks so much for offering," he said. From across the countertop, she gritted her teeth and poured him another cup, stopping short at least an inch and a half from the rim. "A little more, thanks," he told her with a sweet smile before glancing at the bill. "That's awfully steep for a lousy sandwich and a pickle, don't you think? Are you highballing me here?"

Annie shrugged and cleared his plate before he could finish his pickle or protest further. She was a far cry from the vivacious girl he had known in high school who had been hard to miss with her natural good looks and vibrant laugh. As she hustled back and forth behind the counter, the heavy polyester uniform couldn't mask her thin frame and bony elbows, while her hair, tied up in a ratty knot, framed dark circles shadowed beneath her eyes.

"How long have you been working here?" he asked, eyeing her intently. He hadn't been prepared to see her again, not after all this time. But as she scooted here and there, her eyes focused only on the task at hand, he found himself yearning for her to look at him. "I said, how long have you been—"

"I heard you."

"Do you like it here?"

Her mouth twisted. "I suppose."

"Don't be too enthusiastic," he said. "It's only my mom's place."

Her chin jerked up. "What was that?"

"I wouldn't want you to hurt yourself, Annie."

A flush crept up her face as she stopped short in front of him. He braced himself, waiting for a reaction of any kind, even if it was an outburst. Anything had to be better than the silent treatment.

"Can I get you something else, sir?" she asked. William's stomach lurched at the coldness in her voice. At how forced it was, as if she were straining for control.

"Grab me a water, would you?" he said, holding a fist to his mouth to try to calm his upset stomach. Seeing Annie had thrown him for a loop, that was for sure, but he never expected he would have such a physical reaction to it. "I'm feeling a bit queasy."

Annie's eyes slowly widened as William groaned and leaned heavily against the counter, tiny dots of perspiration percolating on his forehead.

"Oh," she said, her voice no louder than a whisper. "Oh, William."

"What?" He motioned for the water. Annie slinked backward to fetch an ice water and crept closer again, hesitating before handing it to him.

"I've done something…" She winced. "Awful."

"What?" William asked, although he wasn't really listening. A wave of nausea propelled him to his feet.

"The restroom is over by the—"

"I know," he gulped, racing to its sanctuary.

"I'm sorry!" Annie called after him, but he didn't have time to wonder what she meant.

ANNIE HURRIED TO the kitchen, grabbed the carton of remaining egg salad and slammed it into the trash. She paced, or rather hid behind the kitchen door, periodically peeking out the porthole to see if William had ventured back out among the living. As each minute ticked by, her own stomach clenched tighter as if in a vise.

"Is everything okay, dear?"

Annie jumped at Joyce's warm voice, homey and inviting like a crackling fire. Immediately, a pang of guilt slammed her. Joyce was her dearest friend, and she might have killed her only son. As much as she wanted to throw herself at Joyce's feet and offer a dramatic confession, she decided it might be best not to mention what she'd done until all the facts shook themselves out in their own good time.

"William's sick," she blurted.

"Sick?" Joyce said, her face contorting into a mass of wrinkles in the blink of an eye.

"He's been in the bathroom for a while now."

Joyce scurried off as Annie found Miles staring at her.

"What?" she said, popping her hands to her hips like a hen rearing to peck.

"Annie Curtis," Miles reprimanded her. "Do I even want to know why?"

"I'll take the blame, Miles, so I'll stop you

right there," Annie replied, sneaking a peek out the porthole window again.

"Joyce could lose her license."

"Nah, he won't call the health inspector on his own mother."

"What about on you?"

Annie scrunched her face. "Don't you have something to fry back there?" She furiously slammed the top of his order bell several times and shooed him back to the kitchen. "Order up, order up, *order up*, Miles."

He shook his head. "Call me before you tell Joyce you poisoned her baby. I sure don't want to miss that."

Annie returned to the porthole window and heaved a sigh of relief when William finally emerged, though staggering and green.

She ventured out to the dining room. "Are you okay?" she asked him softly. William turned and glared at her, making her recoil slightly.

"Annie, what exactly did you mean before when you said you were sorry?"

Annie paused, grazing a finger over her lips as she scrambled for an explanation. She had yelled the words like a reflex, without thinking, without predicting the consequences. But now, as William's eyes narrowed, she knew they were a tragic mistake.

She winced. "Hmm?"

A deep growl vibrated behind his lips. "That's what I thought."

"I pulled the car around to the front, dear," Joyce said, hurrying over to them. "I can take you straight to the emergency room."

William put a hand over his stomach. "Take me back to the house."

"But you got sick so suddenly and so violently. They should check you over to find out what's wrong. You're dehydrated at the very least."

William shot Annie a scowl. "I *know* what happened."

Annie's eyes pleaded with William to not give her away. She couldn't bear to imagine the look of disappointment and hurt in Joyce's eyes when she learned what Annie had done. It would be too awful.

"Was it something you ate here?" Joyce asked, turning to Annie to help supply the answer. As Annie clasped her hands in a prayer and was about to explain, William shook his head.

"You can't trust sushi from a gas station, Mom."

Annie's mouth dropped open as Joyce took her son's arm and patted it.

"Golly, no. It had probably been sitting out for days, William."

William allowed his mother to squeeze him in a long hug, but his body was rigid, eyes boring holes into Annie. Several moments passed before he finally responded. "Something like that."

"I'll bet you won't do that again," Annie said, cringing, knowing full well she was pressing her luck. William huffed at her as Joyce led him to the door.

Perhaps their long-awaited reunion hadn't gone completely as Annie would have predicted, but she took satisfaction in William Kauffman knowing where she stood.

CHAPTER TWO

ANNIE POKED HER head into her children's shared bedroom as Marjorie, her neighbor, helped them fumble into pajamas.

A nurturing widow in her sixties, Marjorie had proved to be a reliable confidante and babysitter in recent years. While Annie was prone to overreaction, nothing ever seemed to rile serene Marjorie. Her auburn hair had peppered to white over the years, and her face, a road map of heavy wrinkles and lines, was radiant because of the loving expressions it constantly displayed. A transplant from Tennessee, she carried a Southern hospitality and charm. Between Joyce and Marjorie, Annie was certain her own mother was in heaven, sending surrogates to stand by her side.

"Are you okay, honey?" Marjorie asked in her sweet, charming lilt.

Annie managed a negligent shrug, the day hanging heavy around her neck as she leaned against the doorway.

Marjorie kissed her tenderly on the cheek. "We'll have a cup of tea on it another time. They've been watching the clock, waiting for you. I'll let myself out."

Annie climbed onto her daughter's bed and sighed with satisfaction. Despite all her failures over the course of her adult life, the two little people tumbling over themselves to embrace her were certainly not included in the list. They were the only reason that the last few years had been tolerable.

Betsy was an outspoken eight-year-old with a round, expressive face and big brown eyes like hers. She had a goofy expression to match any occasion and had certainly gotten herself into trouble by an inappropriately timed raised eyebrow. James, on the other hand, was as fair and gentle as a light summer rain. With storm-gray eyes and moppy brown hair, he moved delicately through the world, examining it from his owl perch before cautiously dipping in a toe and joining the action.

While they didn't share a father, the two were thick as thieves, and Annie, who had no siblings of her own, took solace in the fact that what she couldn't give them in extended family, she had made up for by giving them each other.

James, following Betsy's flailing pantomime directions, selected a Rapunzel storybook from the cupboard and sandwiched himself between Annie and Betsy on his bed.

"Wasn't it your turn to pick?" Annie asked as James snuggled into her side. He shrugged as Betsy yanked the book from his hands and flipped open the cover.

"I love this book so much," Betsy said, shuddering with excitement.

Annie tucked a pillow behind her back and prepared to read Rapunzel for the hundredth time. "Why?"

Betsy tipped her head back against her pillow before replying with a whimsical look, "I love how the prince saves Rapunzel and carries her off to his palace."

"That isn't how life works, Bets."

"I know. I know," her daughter grumbled, aware she had heard this talk before. "But I still like this story the best, and I want to read it a hundred more times. A *thousand* more times!"

"Well, I'm not so sure about that," Annie said. She pulled the covers over the three of them. "But I'll read it once tonight." As her children melted deeper against her, she understood the allure of getting lost in a little fantasy now and again, especially a romantic one. Her children didn't need to be privy to the disappointing ways of the world yet. Unfortunately, that was her job.

WILLIAM THRUST OPEN the rickety shed door and stood back to admire how everything inside was still meticulously placed just as Dennis had left it. It was a clear indicator his mother had not been inside since Dennis's death three years ago. As the early-morning sun filtered in from behind him, thousands of dust particles glittered and swirled around his first hesitant step. The air inside hung heavy and musty. With his eyes closed, the stale scent of cedar chips, rusted-out gas cans and motor oil wafted over him. It engulfed his nostrils with a nostalgia he had long tried to bury. Only one whiff and he was back to the day his life veered off course.

Right on the threshold of this shed, when William hadn't had any proof that he was the true victim and not the violent juvenile Dennis had claimed, his stepfather had tried to have him arrested. For as many times as he had recalled the altercation, the details had slowly begun to fade. Perhaps it was a way to cope with his anger and soften the hard edges, but standing in the shed again, the details came back to him: the dueling sawhorses Dennis had made him sand until his fingertips were raw and bleeding; Dennis's applered tool chest he'd once innocently scratched and paid hell for later; and the wooden pallet he'd punched a fist through minutes before the cops arrived and Dennis had falsely accused him of assault. It took all his restraint to not boot the nearest thing just for the satisfaction of hearing it shatter and break against the wall.

Heaving a sigh, he jerked the corner of a dust-covered drop cloth to reveal one of his teenage fantasies in all its chrome glory: the classic 1981 Indian motorcycle. Fully restored, practically fawned over daily by the old man, it was a thing of pure beauty. And now it was finally his.

He gingerly ran his fingers over the smooth cinnamon-colored paint that had inspired him to nickname the motorcycle Old Red. He carefully swung his leg over the leather seat and firmly gripped the handlebars. The bike had been sitting cold for several years in the harsh Lake Superior winters, so he drew a breath and hoped for the best.

He shifted the transmission to Neutral and carefully set his choke. After pulling in the clutch, he pressed the starter button and waited for the crackle of the engine to tear through every corner of the tiny shed.

Nothing.

William double-checked that his kill switch wasn't set at Off and tried again, but the engine was silent.

Perfect.

"Call *The Chinoodin Chronicle*! Hell hath officially frozen over."

A grin leaped to William's face at the familiar voice. "How are you doing, man?" His buddy Brandon Rodriguez strode into the shed and embraced him in a bear hug. "How'd you know I was back?"

"Son, please. I know everything happening in this town." Brandon slung his suit jacket over a chair and loosened his tie. He stopped short to admire the vintage bike. "Are you fixin' up Old Red?"

"It looks like I have to. I can't get it started."

"I'd love to buy it off you, but the hours I work at the mayor's office wouldn't leave me enough time to make it worthwhile."

"Are you at the mayor's office now?"

"Two years in August," Brandon replied, sitting back on a dusty sawhorse. "What are you doing in town?"

William shook his head. "Hard to say right now."

Brandon nodded and held out a grocery bag. "A homecoming gift of sorts."

William glanced in the bag. "Pabst Blue Ribbon beer?" He chuckled. "Are you still drinking that?"

"Nah. Only for you, man," Brandon said. "Rocky's was my first stop when I heard you were back. I had to help you stock the fridge. Have you been by the diner yet?"

"Unfortunately," William said, his empty gut still raw from the restless night.

"Did you catch a glimpse of Annie?"

"I caught more than that."

"She's still a good-looking woman, eh?"

"Annie? Annie Curtis? Are you two…?" William couldn't quite get the words out, but his meaning was clear.

"Oh, no. Annie's great, but I'm already seeing someone. How long are you staying?"

"Just passing through."

Brandon surveyed the shed. "Well, I know things ended on a sour note before."

"That's an understatement."

"Yeah, it sure is. It's been a long time." He focused on William. "If you're interested, I could always put in a good word for you with Annie. Maybe help mend some of the…"

William waved off the idea immediately.

"Not worth my time or hers, Brandon."

"Did you tell her you're just passing through?"

William snorted. "Why would I? It's none of her business. Besides, she wouldn't be interested."

"No?"

William angled his chin. "Am I missing something?"

Brandon looked confused just as the shed door swung wide with a loud creak.

"I thought I heard you out here." Joyce carefully stepped inside before stopping short and studying the two men. "Back together again," she mused. "My, oh, my, has it been a long time. Brandon, did you know William surprised me?"

Brandon waggled his eyebrows. "I can imagine."

"I'm sure they heard me hollering with joy all the way in Munising."

"It didn't take him long to find that bike."

Joyce rolled her eyes. "William, should I feel honored you at least came to see me first?"

William shrugged. "Who can say for certain that that's what I did?" Joyce swatted him playfully on the arm as he grinned. "I had to make sure we were still on good terms. It needs more tender loving care than I'd hoped, though."

"Don't we all," Joyce said. "We need to leave in ten minutes, Will. We can get coffee at the diner."

"The diner?"

"Our shift begins in half an hour." Joyce shuffled outside and headed to the house as William squeezed past the motorcycle and scratched his chin.

"Helping at the diner, eh?" Brandon said, collecting his suit jacket.

"I wasn't planning on it."

"What better things do you have to do?"

"Get this engine running for one."

"Ah, there's time."

But that was exactly what William didn't have much of and wanted to avoid—spending more time in Chinoodin Falls than he could afford.

ANNIE SPED INTO the diner. Her purse dangled from her wrist and a sweater was slung haphazardly over her shoulder as she swirled her hair into a messy bun. After calling hello to

Joyce and playfully hip checking Karrin, her fellow waitress, on her scramble to begin her shift, she sprinted to the office. Beads of sweat were already perspiring on her lip when she stopped short at the sight of William carelessly rummaging through her desk as if he owned the place. The scene caught her so completely off guard, it took a moment for her to piece together a coherent sentence.

"What…what…what on earth do you think you're doing?" she finally stammered, charging toward him and slamming her purse onto the desk. Her eyebrows shot up as she waited for an explanation, but William made no effort to answer her. He leaned comfortably back in *her* chair and a satisfied grin curled his lips. "That's my desk, you know," she pointed out.

"Good morning to you, too."

"What are you doing here?"

"Well, I'll tell you if you wouldn't mind easing up a bit."

"You tell me right now," she commanded, her shadow darkening his handsomely chiseled jaw. She avoided looking directly into his eyes, hoping to avoid the mesmerizing pull of those blue pools. William stretched his hands, clasped them behind his head and leaned farther back in her chair.

"Seriously, Annie, I can practically see up your nose from this angle."

Annie pursed her lips and looked around for the nearest thing to knock the easygoing smile off his face. She snatched the papers he was reading from the desk in one crinkled wad and smacked his shoulder with them.

In an instant, William was on his feet. "*Hey.* What's the matter with you?"

"What are you snooping through?" She flipped through the papers with such speed, she couldn't read or register what they were. The last few years she had tried her best to keep the paperwork for the diner organized— invoices, tax forms, payroll—but it was nearly impossible between working the floor and hurrying home to her children after each shift. As she eyed the evidence of her miserable bookkeeping abilities, it was his scent that finally made her turn her head. She caught her breath at its charming appeal and found William studying her. His gaze sending a series of tickles like butterfly kisses down her spine.

She didn't know what was going on here, but she wasn't going to stand around and twiddle her thumbs while he slowly pieced together an explanation. She could table this matter for later, after she had collected herself and put more distance between them. As she tossed the papers at him in a flurry, William sat back on the edge of the desk and crossed his arms.

"I was searching for your letter."

"My letter?" she said with a sputter.

"Mmm-hmm. I know I missed your voice mail."

"Voice mail?"

"Unless… Were you planning to apologize in person, Ms. Curtis?" William rubbed his stomach. "I was up all night, you know. It's a wonder I didn't have to go to the hospital after all."

Annie scoffed. "I saw you when you left. You weren't that sick."

"No? Have you ever been poisoned before?"

"Are you accusing *me* of poisoning you?"

"Didn't you?"

"I don't know what you're talking about," Annie said, tipping her nose in the air on her way out of the office.

"What goes around comes around, Annie."

"Remind yourself of that fact!" she called. Desperate for an outlet to funnel complicated feelings she'd ignored since she was seventeen years old, Annie attempted to start the coffee maker with a series of pointedly timed clangs and clanks. After a moment of telling it off in vulgarities muttered under her breath, she noticed a shadow behind her.

"Are you okay?" Miles was cautiously peeking from around the corner.

"I'm a little mad."

He carefully pried a glass coffeepot from her whitened fingertips. "At my kitchen?"

"At you know who."

"Do you want to talk about it?"

"Nope."

"Do you think revving yourself up on caffeine is gonna make things better?" Annie reluctantly smiled, snatching back the pot and shoving it into the coffee maker with a final clank. "You know, Annie, he seems like a decent guy. I talked to him earlier and…" Annie's eyes narrowed as the husky college student hurriedly backpedaled. "I mean…he's a total jerk, and I guess I don't like him, eh?"

Annie jerked a nod of approval as she waited for the coffee to percolate.

"Too bad you can't hide out in the kitchen with me today," Miles suggested before chugging a soda.

"You know I'd love to, kid, but the farthest point from you know who happens to be the dining room." Impatient for her jolt of caffeine, she stole a swig of Miles's soda and rolled her eyes at the fact that that wasn't nearly far enough.

WILLIAM GNAWED ON a piece of bacon while sizing things up from the end of the counter. Between observing the morning regulars and quietly recounting his youth slaving away in the diner, he had enough to occupy his attention. Though nothing was as fascinating as the way Annie Curtis could work the dining room. She carried food trays with ease and chatted to all like a long-lost friend. She winked at her regulars, anticipated their requests and bubbled with laughter until, that is, she had to walk within three yards of him. He had categorized himself as the black sheep over the years, depending on the situation, but Annie now helped him experience it at a more personal level.

"That's it. Keep ignoring me," he whispered under his breath. She'd marched past him into the kitchen, her face etched in a stern glare.

It was a figure at the entryway that finally drew his attention. A tall, hefty man with a commanding presence and pressed suit, who looked out of place in the small, folksy diner.

William could feel the energy in the room shift as others followed the man's arrogant saunter.

"Hello, Sean," Joyce said. Her voice rang brittle with forced politeness.

William did a double take, recognizing the dressy brute as Sean Butler, a fellow Chinoodin High alumnus who had graduated a year ahead of him. He had been a smug jerk in high school, and judging by his demeanor, he hadn't changed much except for putting on a few pounds and splurging on polished designer shoes.

Sean halted, his eyes on William. William calmly sipped his coffee and waited for Sean to lose interest in his presence. He generally didn't engage others in conversation, choosing to keep to himself as much as possible. Besides, if he remembered correctly, Sean's conversational skills were akin to a wrecking ball.

"Hey," Sean grunted, screwing up his face to place William. "Chinoodin High?"

"A year behind you."

"That's right, that's right. Heh. You're Joyce's son, eh?"

"Will."

Sean leered at him. "I know who you are. You're not moving back, are you?"

William had no desire to stay in Chinoodin

Falls longer than the time it took to eat his breakfast, but the disgust in Sean's voice rubbed him the wrong way.

"Hard to say."

Sean snorted. "Why's that?"

"I haven't decided."

"Are you holding up the counter and weighing your options?"

"Do you need a second-by-second commentary, or can't you fill in the blanks on your own?"

Sean jutted his chin before what sounded like a forced chuckle. "You're a plethora of knowledge, ain't ya?"

William took another sip of his coffee and turned his attention to what was behind the counter. He knew when he was being baited and couldn't afford to lower himself to Sean Butler's level. "So, it's back from the Navy, is it? Are you gonna help your mother clean up this dump? Lord knows it needs it. I hate just being seen in this place."

William was surprised Sean knew he had been in the Navy. Suddenly Annie burst through the swinging doors, a tray of breakfasts teetering in her hands. Sean straightened and lumbered toward her as she hurriedly passed out the plates before trying to slip around him.

"I'm in the middle of the morning rush, Sean. I'll talk to you later," she said before hustling into the kitchen, but Sean barreled through the kitchen doors after her like a pit bull fixated on a scrap of meat.

Joyce hovered nearby, wringing her hands fitfully. When her frightened eyes found William's, his spine stiffened in alarm. A quick glance around the dining room proved that Joyce wasn't the only one on edge with Sean's arrival. The collective murmur of folks' conversations had momentarily hushed. A few customers had put down their newspapers. Two women exchanged a worried glance. They were a herd of antelope at the watering hole, and a lion had just been seen on the savannah. They knew something he didn't, and he hated surprises.

The seconds ticked by as he decided whether or not to investigate. He had no sooner mulled the thought over when Sean's voice boomed from the kitchen, startling several customers and jarring William to his feet. He wasn't sure what he'd find waiting for him on the other side of those doors, but he had every intention of finding out.

As he braced himself to throw his full weight against the swinging aluminum doors, Sean emerged with a snarl donning his upper lip. Being confronted with William, he stopped short, the two men mirroring each other's expressions, standing toe to toe.

"*Whoa*. Call off your son, Joyce," Sean finally spat without tearing his eyes from William.

"You're the one hollering in there," William said in a deep tone.

"True," Sean replied in a hushed voice as he hoisted his belt higher on his waist. "The wife still needs to be told from time to time. You know how that goes, *swabbie*."

William's jaw tightened as Sean sauntered around him and stopped to grab a few mints on his way out the front door. The little wife? If Annie had married Sean Butler, it was no wonder she looked as harried and worried as she did. Losing a Miss Congeniality award was the very least of her problems if Sean had weaseled, or more likely bulldozed, his way into her life.

ANNIE HUNG BACK until she was sure Sean had left. She detested his unannounced visits. They were manipulative confrontations she worried would escalate into public scenes. Every so often, like clockwork, he'd fabricate an excuse about how she was doing a poor job mothering James just so he could come by and unleash verbal jabs in front of her friends and coworkers. But as much as she hated it, they were the witnesses she preferred. On occasion he had stumbled onto her porch steps, sweating whiskey sours and moaning profanities. Any humiliation she tolerated at work was better than scurrying the children off to hide in their bedrooms.

She knew Sean delighted in the power he wielded over her. He was James's father, so she wanted to believe that underneath the verbal jabs, he loved the little guy, but she really couldn't vouch for it with any certainty. Most days, James's welfare was an excuse Sean used to make her life miserable.

Annie bit the inside of her cheek and refused to cry. It wouldn't solve anything except make her eyes puffy and solicit questions from her friends. She held firmly to her mantra: no emotional breakdowns except in the shower.

After forcing a few deep, calming breaths, she smoothed the front of her dress and stepped out into the dining room with the resolve of a royal diplomat.

"Are you okay, honey?" Joyce whispered, looping an arm through hers.

Annie feigned a smile. "Of course." But when she read pity in William's gaze, a sinking pit in her stomach quaked open. Pity was something she absolutely could not take.

She'd had her fair share of it over the years. The pitiful stares after Julian ran out, leaving her pregnant with Betsy and practically destitute, still haunted her.

There had been a pity party disguised as a wedding reception when, out of pure desperation to provide for Betsy and herself, she had married Sean. Oh, how she had wanted to escape from the hall after Sean got drunk with his buddies and forgot her during their first dance.

She was still paying the price for those bad decisions, and she didn't need anyone's pity *or judgment*, especially William Kauffman's. Perhaps if he hadn't bailed on her in the first place, things would have been different somehow. But instead, here he was, standing in front of her as the aftershock of Sean's visit rattled her.

"Are you okay?" His voice aimed to soothe, but Annie wouldn't allow it. She paused, fiddling with her apron strings as William leaned closer, the heat from his strong build warming her skin, making goose bumps prickle up her neck.

"Never better," she said.

"I heard the way he talked to you."

"So?"

"Does he do that often?" Annie shrugged in dismissal, but he quickly continued. "You don't deserve that, Annie."

She met his gaze, ready to defy his pity, but found only grave concern instead. His center of gravity seemed to shift, and she thought he was about to reach out and touch her. How she had ached for him to touch her when it had been another man cozied up beside her in bed and all that truly comforted her was the memory of his gentleness.

Annie pulled away. "Unless you want to place another order, I have paying customers to see to. Excuse me."

She breezed past him. She hated that she still longed for him to touch her. And she hated that he was witnessing how her life had fallen apart these last twelve years without him in it.

WILLIAM SLID A For Sale sign onto his dashboard in one swift movement. Once he sold his truck, he'd have enough money to gas up

Old Red and head for the Pacific Northwest for the summer. Who knew where things would lead him after that? He'd travel on the wind, no ties to anyone, and decide next steps as opportunities arose.

"Are you selling your truck?" Joyce frowned at him, having just locked up the diner for the night. William nodded, opening the passenger door and helping her up into the cab. "What's wrong with it?"

"I can't drive a motorcycle and a truck at the same time."

Joyce clutched her handbag on her lap and fiddled with the straps as William climbed into the driver's seat.

"I don't see why you can't have both. There's room in the garage and shed."

He stalled before answering as Joyce's eyes bored holes in the side of his face. She had assumed he was home to stay, and he knew he had to correct her. At some point. After firing up his Chevy, he offered a reply.

"I need to sell her while she's still running."

"On her last legs, is she?"

"Something like that," he said, tuning the radio to a classic-rock station. Joyce nodded before yanking a handkerchief from her purse and hacking into it with such force, William nearly swerved off the road. "Ma, are you okay?"

Joyce attempted a nod as her cheeks swelled to a patchy rouge. With each gasp for breath between coughing fits, William was more alarmed, his eyes darting back and forth between her and the road.

After several agonizing seconds, she finally heaved a sigh, clutching her chest in relief. "Oh, goodness," she breathed. "I'm glad that's over. Don't look so worried, sweetie. It comes and goes."

"What exactly?" William said, resting his hand tenderly on her shoulder.

"It's a little respiratory infection I'm still shaking. My immune system is building itself up again after my being sick last winter. I could do with a nap before dinner." Joyce blotted her mouth with her handkerchief before carefully tucking it into her purse. She smiled reassuringly. "Really, honey, I'm fine."

"Have you seen a doctor?"

"Of course, of course. My seasonal allergies aggravate it. Plus it's been a long day."

William finally eased back into his seat and put both hands on the wheel. "It was an interesting day."

"How so?"

"Does Sean Butler come into the diner often?"

Joyce rolled her eyes. "Define *often*."

"He hasn't changed a lick since high school, you know."

"Did you know him, dear?"

Bullies like Sean hardly went unnoticed in a school as small as Chinoodin High. "Unfortunately. How long have they been married?"

"They divorced three years ago, but he's as awful an ex-husband as he was a husband." William tensed, imagining Annie married to Sean Butler. He was a class-A creep. "Annie's had a rough time of it," Joyce continued, tilting her head back to rest.

"Why? What's happened?" William frowned. A soft hum vibrated behind Joyce's cute smile as she lovingly patted his leg. *"What?"* he blurted, shoulders jerking in defense.

"Some things don't fade with time, I suppose."

"Never mind," he said, turning up the radio volume. The less he knew about Annie and her troubles, the better. She'd be a dot in his rearview mirror in a matter of days anyway.

CHAPTER THREE

SITTING ON HER porch steps, Annie wrapped her arms around herself. Summer evenings like this one reminded her of her youth, riding her bicycle around the neighborhood and down to the lake. She hadn't had a care in the world back then except a scolding and a cold dinner if she didn't get home before dark.

But as she admired James tenderly coaxing a caterpillar onto his hand, she regretted that he had bigger problems at the tender age of six than she had ever had.

"Look, Betsy," he said, carefully crouching closer to his sister, his eyes fixated on his prize. "He was on the flowers."

"Can I hold him?" she said, examining his discovery. "We can build him a little house or bed out of these sticks."

Annie knew they could be a happy little family if they could just get away, but the informal arrangement with Sean kept her from pressing her luck. He was content to let her have sole custody of James and she didn't want to jeopardize that. Besides, it would be difficult to leave good friends. They were the closest thing to family she and the children had.

Although she had just glanced at the clock on her phone, she obsessively checked it again. Each minute dragged them that much closer to Sean's arrival. His visits were better than sharing a home, but their arrangement was far from great for her and the children.

She closed her eyes briefly when she heard Sean's BMW roll up the street. He swung wide into the driveway and sat for a minute, letting the car idle while issuing orders at someone on the other end of his cell phone. Annie was not in the mood to draw out their exchange any longer than necessary, but each second he spent on the phone was one less second he had with James.

The children, having spotted Sean's car racing from down the block, had fled behind the shrubs along the side of the house. The tips of their visible sneakers the only giveaway of their position.

"The movie starts in a few minutes. Where is he?" Sean asked, finally emerging from the car.

"James!" Annie called. "Your father is waiting!"

Sean sneered. "Is he hiding again?"

"He doesn't want to go," Betsy said, stepping out from behind the shrubs, a hand propped on each hip. "He doesn't feel good."

"Ugh, come on! I don't have time for this." Sean clipped his phone to his hip and charged toward the bushes.

"Wait, Sean," Annie said, jogging to intercept him. "Give me a second first." Hurrying past him and around the shrubs, she knelt in front of James. His big gray eyes peered up at her, pleading to be left alone. Annie's heart sank as she stroked a wisp of hair off his face and summoned the most pleasant voice she could muster. "Your father is going to take you to a movie, and then he'll bring you straight home."

"I don't wanna go."

"He'll probably buy you a popcorn," Annie reminded him, but James shook his head. "I know you want to stay here, kiddo, but your dad really wants to spend time with you. You'll be home before you know it. We'll stay up later than usual tonight, so we can squeeze in a few books before bed, okay?"

Betsy wrapped him in a hug and placed a white pebble in his hand.

"Here, James. This lucky stone will make you brave."

"Don't you want candy?" Sean yelled impatiently from the driveway.

Annie gently took James's small hand and led him out from behind the bush.

"Are you hungry?" Sean asked, grasping James. The little boy attempted to slink away from his father's firm grasp. "Well, are ya or aren't ya?" Sean demanded.

"He just ate dinner, but perhaps a treat at the movie would be nice," Annie said, kneeling to hug James and kiss him sweetly on the ear. It was all she could do to refrain from scooping him up in her arms, running into the house and locking the door behind her.

"We're going to have to fly to make it there on time. Those dinosaurs start fighting in ten minutes."

"Wait," Annie said as James buckled himself into the back seat. "I thought you were going to see a cartoon."

"Cartoons are for wussies, right, kid?"

"Nothing scary, Sean. He's only six."

Sean gave Annie the once-over. "Maybe I should take you out instead, huh? I kind of regret letting you get away when you still look like that."

"Stop it, Sean," Annie warned, clutching Betsy against her side. Sean squinted down at the little girl.

"You can't go 'cause you're not invited," he taunted in singsong. Betsy scowled up at him, her fierceness impressive for a girl her age. "Nice attitude you have there, princess. You're taking after your mother in that department, I'm sorry to see." He strolled back to the car, flipping sunglasses down onto his face. "Rude little brats like you don't get popcorn and candy."

"I wouldn't want to go even if he invited me," Betsy told her. "But I'd go to be with James."

"I know, baby," Annie replied, squeezing Betsy without tearing her eyes from the top of James's head slunk in the back seat.

Sean would never physically endanger James, but she knew how easily a mean-spirited man could wound a tender little heart.

WILLIAM PERKED UP at the sound of voices. Because the diner closed early on Friday nights, he thought he'd have the place to himself to scavenge the fridge after spending the afternoon working on Old Red. Poking his head through the swinging doors, he discovered Annie and a pint-size replica in the dining room.

Annie's head shot up as he drifted toward their table. He knew he was a sight, still covered in motor oil and grime, but Annie's frown appeared more intense than usual as she crossed her arms over her chest and glowered. The little girl sitting across from her shoveled a large forkful of chocolate cake into her mouth and stuck her hand out when William introduced himself. He instantly decided he liked Betsy, chocolatey grin and all.

"What are you doing here tonight?" he asked, sliding into the booth next to Betsy as Annie had made no effort to accommodate him.

"Why?" Annie asked suspiciously.

"I didn't expect to see you here. The place is closed, and I didn't know you had a key."

"Of course I have a key," she said. "Who do you think has been opening and closing around here for the past few years?" William leaned back defensively. He knew his reaction registered when Annie paused, took a deep breath and started again. "We had a craving for cake."

"We needed to get out of the house for a little while," Betsy clarified, grinning up at him.

"Is everything okay?" he asked. Annie nodded before pressing a glass of milk to her lips and taking a sip, but she was far from convincing.

"Mom says we need to drown our sorrows in chocolate cake."

"Cake is good for that," he said without breaking his gaze from Annie. Something big was weighing on her, and although he knew he wasn't her favorite person, he felt inclined to help.

"For my birthday I want a giant pink cake with hearts all over it. What's your favorite kind of cake, William?" Betsy scooted onto her knees to peer up at him. Her chocolatey breath and puppy-dog eyes were so endearing, and so innocently invading his personal space, William couldn't help but grin before answering.

"Chocolate, I suppose."

"With icing?"

"Yes."

"And sprinkles?"

"Sure."

"And candy?"

"Betsy…" Annie said, her voice low and

strained. Betsy sat back on her heels and eyed her mother for any indication she was in trouble. When Annie winked at her, she immediately relaxed and returned to her chocolate cake. "If you'll excuse me a minute, William," Annie said.

William nodded as Annie quickly slid out of the booth, her eyes already reddened with tears. She ducked into the ladies' restroom, and he turned his attention to his chatty companion. She was a lively child. The joy she drew from a single slice of chocolate cake, her eyes goggling with excitement with each sugary lick, made him hard-pressed to recall the last time he had enjoyed one of life's simple pleasures with such gusto.

"Betsy, how are *you* doing?"

She considered this. "Happy and sad," she said.

"Why?"

"Happy I get to eat cake, but sad James isn't here."

"Is James your brother?"

She nodded solemnly. "We get sad when James has to go with his dad."

"Oh."

"We want him to stay with us *all* the time."

"How old is James?"

"He's six, and I'm eight."

"So you're the big sister, huh?"

Betsy beamed with pride. "I protect him when mom argues with Sean. She says I'm going to be a good mommy one day."

"I'll bet you will be." The stress in Annie's home became clear. Sending your child off with the likes of Sean Butler would put anyone in a bad mood. "What's up, kid?" he asked as Betsy had hesitated. She had all but finished a couple bites of cake.

"Maybe mom wants the last of it," she said, hovering her fork over the shared plate.

"Nah. I think you should finish it off, and we'll get her a fresh piece."

Betsy's eyes brightened with delight. "Good idea, William!"

William stood and lingered near the table, waiting for the little girl to lick the plate clean.

"We're getting you a fresh slice," he told Annie, who'd marched out of the bathroom.

"No, thank you," she replied, motioning for Betsy to join her. The little girl hustled out of the booth to stand beside her mother.

"*Okay,*" William redirected. "How about a drive down to the lake, then? I thought I'd cruise around the peninsula if you'd like to join me."

Annie vigorously shook her head and put her hand on Betsy's shoulder to silence the little girl's enthusiastic squeal of approval.

"We have to get back."

"But mom, couldn't we, please?" Her mother shot her a stern look as a final warning.

"Another time." William winked at Betsy, escorting them to the entrance. As he exited ahead of them and held open the door, he could feel Annie hesitate.

"Thank you," she said, briskly scooting by him.

"Thank you," Betsy echoed cheerfully.

"Annie," William called. She turned as Betsy bounded ahead of her to the car. "Is there anything I can do for you? For the both of you?"

Annie seemed to scrutinize his words.

"Why?"

"You seem like you've got the world on your shoulders."

Her face fell. She studied him for a few moments, her wide brown eyes drawing him further in with each slow blink. She was guarded from what he assumed was a direct result of years spent with Sean. And while he knew he shouldn't care, seeing her again made him feel like a hint of the man he'd been in high school. A man he had long forgotten.

As he moved closer, she shook her head and turned to her car. Her quick dismissal reminded him that a lot of time had passed and that she'd most likely forgotten the man he once was, too. Still, before he left Chinoodin Falls, he'd need some assurance that she was going to be okay.

ANNIE JOGGED THROUGH the back door of the diner and snatched her apron just as Mia, a fellow waitress with a spirited disposition, handed her a cup of coffee.

"Thanks, M," she breathed between gulps. "I feel like I'm always running from one thing to the next."

"How's the little guy?" Mia asked, her clumpy mascara-coated lashes batting with concern.

"I can't tell if he really has a tummy ache or if it's anxiety."

"Girl, your ex-husband gives *me* a tummy ache. I covered your tables."

Annie softened in appreciation as she caught her breath. She'd taken James to the doctor for the first appointment of the day before dropping him at school. His temperature was a little above normal, but the doctor believed he was fine. It was nearly summer, and not wanting him to miss end-of-the-year festivities, she'd said goodbye to him with an extra hug and kiss.

She and Sean had argued the night before, as per usual, and she knew James internalized it. He had zero control in a stressful relationship with his father, so a sudden tummy ache probably had more to do with his emotional health than physical. She couldn't blame him. She felt like she couldn't fix things either, and she was an adult.

"How's my favorite lady?" Miles called from the kitchen.

"I can hear you, you know!" Mia said, her bottom lip turning down in a pout.

"Mia," Miles said, poking his head around the corner. "You know I have nothing but love for you, but my heart will always belong to Annie. What can I make you?"

"I'll stick with coffee."

Mia pointed at Annie's waist. "You need some sustenance, A. Miles, scramble her some eggs."

"Coming right up!"

Annie scrunched up her face. "I can't eat right now, Mia."

"You have to eat something good. I can't

have you skinnier than me on my wedding day."

"What I need is to drop two hundred pounds of ex-husband."

"Maybe he'll get amnesia."

Annie laughed. "A girl can dream," she said, but her face fell once she spotted William sitting at the end of the counter. She had mulled over his comment from the other night, trying to decipher what it meant. *Is there anything I can do for you?* He'd had some nerve telling her he loved her, running out on her without any explanation and then showing up more than a decade later as if she hadn't meant anything to him in the first place. *Now* he wanted to know if there was anything he could do for her? He was too late.

She greeted the Old Timers, a name she'd coined for a group of retired men who were her favorite regular customers. All born and raised in Michigan's Upper Peninsula, their friendly banter was as charming as their thick, Fargo-sounding accents. Heavily reminiscent of the Finnish and German influence on the area, some native speakers sounded like they were conversing in another language once they really got going. But Annie had lived in the Upper Peninsula since she was a child, so deciphering was old hat.

"Dare she is!" Joe declared, slapping the table. "How ya doin' now, Annie?" With his sparkling blue eyes and puffy red nose, he could have walked straight out of a quaint, small-town pub.

Danny winked at her, fluffy white eyebrows fluttering above large, thick glasses. "Mia had to bring us our coffee, and she don't pour it right, dontcha know."

Annie smiled and pulled out her order pad. "Are you eating this morning or just shooting the breeze and holding my tables hostage?"

Joe pointed a calloused finger at her. "Now don't start! I need a refill on my coffee first."

Annie tapped her pen on the table in feigned anger. "I'm never gonna retire if you only order coffee, Joe."

He took a sip and peered at her over the top of his cup. "But it's such *good* coffee."

"I brew it myself." She winked before turning to the others. "How about you, Earl? Do you want the Early Riser breakfast, like usual?"

Earl flipped the corner of his newspaper down to contemplate her suggestion. He'd ordered the same breakfast every day for three years. He purchased *The Chinoodin Chronicle* newspaper and read it cover to cover at the table every morning. And even if the temperature reached eighty degrees, he'd worn the same red Kromer hat with fleece-lined flannel and earflaps. His eyes darted around the room before he flipped the corner of his paper back up, shielding his face. "Yah," he answered in his usual gruff way.

The Old Timers had been coming into the diner occasionally long before Annie had started working there. But when Dennis passed away and Annie began full-time, as Karrin told it, the Old Timers quickly took notice. They had begun arriving every morning since like clockwork.

Annie hustled to grab the coffeepot, aware that William's eyes were following her.

"Good morning, Annie," he said, his voice soft and easy like a swaying oak. She nodded curtly before returning to the Old Timers. The ones without coffee flipped over their cups, but kept right on talking about the newcomer.

"What's *his* story?" Joe asked. Annie caught William's eye. His look deepened from over the top of his coffee mug, making her nerves tingle.

"I couldn't tell you," she said, turning back to Joe. "He's Joyce's son."

"Is he single?"

"Why, Joe? Are you interested?"

"You're really in a mood today, ain't ya, Annie?" Joe said. "He's a good-lookin' kid is all."

"Kid? He's my age." She scoffed.

"You're still a kid, you know."

"Joe, I haven't been a kid in ages."

"Bah, I'd snap you up if I were forty years younger."

Danny piped up. "If only I were *thirty* years younger, Annie. Do you like older men?"

She huffed. "Men are more trouble than they're worth."

"I take offense to that," Joe added playfully.

"You would!" Annie didn't feel young enough to even consider dating again. She had had her fair share of worries over recent years to zap her youthful glow and energy for any kind of social life. Maybe someday, when she was older and wiser, she'd meet some- one sweet like Danny or Joe. They were good guys, although she'd had three years of daily interaction to vet them.

"So, like I said," Joe continued. "He's a good-lookin' kid, Annie."

"He's not my type."

Danny howled. "Ya? You go for the ugly fellows, eh?"

She grinned. "Really ugly is more like it."

William was still handsome, though she'd never admit it to anyone other than herself. He'd traded his boyish looks for the mature face of a man. His voice had deepened to a husky bravado, except for the other night, when it had drawn her in with its warm gentleness. But it was his gaze that sent her heart skipping. Those eyes had remained unchanged. They'd studied her the other night in the parking lot, admired her with such a fierceness, her knees had nearly buckled. She'd forgotten what it felt like to have a man see her, truly see her, and want to know her. She'd had no choice but to hurry off. It took every ounce of her being to glue herself together every day and get by for the sake of her children. But the way he had looked at her that night and the way his eyes followed her now…

Annie took down an order for another pair of customers before whisking behind the counter to fill two sodas. She angled her chin, aware William had been waiting for her to make eye contact.

"How's Betsy?" he asked.

"Fine."

"She's a great kid. You should be really proud."

"I am."

William searched her face. "I got a kick out of talking to her. She's spunky."

"Spunky?"

"Yeah."

"Okay."

"She is. She reminds me of you when we were in high school."

Annie paused, waiting for more explanation. "Is that how you remember me, William? Spunky?"

"I remember a lot, actually," William said, stifling a grin as he sipped his coffee.

"Well, I don't." She turned for the kitchen. If she didn't know better, she'd think he was flirting with her. She slapped the bell at the pass-through window and rattled off an order for Miles.

"Cluck and grunt and a dry stack! Times two!"

Mia bustled in behind her. "Scrape two, burn the British, Miles!" Miles nodded, cracking eggs in a fury. "Karrin and I are going out tonight if you want to join, Annie?"

"Thanks, sweetie, but I can't."

"You need some fun, girl. I know you've got your troubles, but if you don't blow off a little steam, you're gonna lose it."

"I can't afford to lose it, Mia. I have Betsy and James to think about."

"*I know*, I know. You're a good mama, but an hour of gossiping can't hurt."

Annie knew she was right, but when she got off work all she wanted to do was get home to James and Betsy. Perhaps she just wasn't as *spunky* as she used to be.

As she faced the dining room, she noticed Joyce and realized she wasn't the only one who'd spotted her boss.

"Mornin', Joyce," Earl said gruffly, tucking away his newspaper and tipping his Kromer hat. Joyce fluttered her fingers in a delicate wave. "Beautiful day, isn't it?" Earl asked.

"Yes, it certainly is. How's your coffee today, Earl?"

"Very good, very good," he said as Danny and Joe nodded in agreement. "Yous have the best coffee in town, Joyce."

"Do we now?"

"Didn't ya know that, Joyce?"

Her peachy cheeks rounded with amusement. "Yes, Earl, you tell me all the time."

After seating new customers, Annie slipped

behind the counter to collect the coffeepot and William's sour disapproval.

"Who's that?" William said, motioning with a thumb toward Earl.

"He's been coming in for a while."

"All of them?"

"Yep."

"Anything to do with my mom?"

"Probably. She's a good-looking woman, you know."

"Annie, that's my mom you're talking about." William eyed Earl.

"So?"

"She's too old to flirt like that."

"She's talking to her friends."

"Hmm? I'm not sure that's…"

Annie scowled. "You're impossible. What are you doing here anyway?"

William leaned back on his stool. "Aren't I allowed to visit my mom?"

"It's been twelve years, so *yeah*, I'd say she was due a visit."

"What's the matter with you, Annie? You've been on my case since I showed up."

Annie grumbled something under her breath as she reached for the coffeepot. William jostled his cup on the counter toward her with a playful tinkering.

"I'll take a refill while you've got it."

She paused in front of him as his eyes scanned hers.

"You're not in my section," she said before strutting away.

WILLIAM STEPPED OUT onto the curb in front of Pop's Place and raised his arms above his head in a deep stretch. As he released a breath, he imagined what life would be like locked away from the simple pleasures nature had to offer: the late-morning sun warming his face, the cool lake air filling his lungs, a tasty sausage casserole expanding his gut. He knew the lumberjack special wasn't one of nature's finest breakfast offerings, but it satisfied him all the same.

The forecast called for sunny, mild days ahead, which was perfect weather for the first leg of a long road trip. If he wanted to be gone by then, he needed to get the bike running by the end of the day and tell his mother he was leaving.

As he was about to cross the street, he noticed a little boy sitting alone on a bench alongside Pop's Place. A sweet, timid-looking child with sandy-brown hair and gray eyes slumped his shoulders heavily as he stared at dangling feet. William scanned the area, but without an adult in sight, he strolled over to the little guy and eased down beside him.

"Hey, buddy. Are you okay?"

The little boy hugged himself tightly and shook his head in a resounding no.

"Are you waiting for someone?"

"I got sick in the car."

"Where's your mom?"

"Inside."

"Do you want me to take you in there?"

The little boy nodded, still clutching his side.

"What's wrong with your stomach?"

"It hurts really bad," he peeped.

William gently held his hand to the little boy's side. "Right here?" he asked, inspecting the boy intently. Just as the child's face screwed up in a hearty cry, William scooped the boy up into the crook of his arm and carried him into Pop's Place.

He knew it was generally a bad idea to have a stranger pick up a child, but leaving the boy seemed like a worse idea. William searched the diner for any woman fitting the mother description. As it turned out, he didn't have to search for long.

"James!" Annie called, racing from around

the counter. She stroked James's hair back from his face with frantic concern. "How on earth did you get here?"

"I found him outside," William explained. "I think he has appendicitis, Annie. We need to get him to the hospital immediately."

"Does it hurt, sweetie? This is all my fault." Her voice trembled as she gingerly put her hands on James. "I didn't think he was really that sick."

"James!" a voice boomed. Sean was on the threshold, the sleeves of his dress shirt rolled to his elbows, tie loosened around his neck. "I told you to sit your butt on that bench!"

"We have to get him to a hospital, Sean," Annie explained as Joyce brought her her purse. She tore off her apron before accepting James from William's arms, struggling with all her might to hold the clinging child.

"Hospital?" Sean scoffed. "He just yakked in my luxury sedan. If you had answered your cell phone, the school wouldn't have had to call me. I had to leave a deposition early. Do you know how that makes me look?"

"He's sick, Sean," she said in a quavering voice.

"I'll drive you," William offered, shuffling Annie and James past Sean and out the front door. "My truck is right here. We can put James in the middle. Hang in there, buddy."

Out on the sidewalk, Annie's eyes pleaded with him in a way that made him ready to charge into battle. "He's so hot, William. He's so hot."

"We'll get you fixed up in no time, James. It'll be okay, Annie. We'll get him there in no time. Do you think—"

"Who the heck do you think you are?" Sean said, racing up behind them and shoving William aside. Sean steered Annie and James toward his BMW that was parked on the curb. William straightened his shoulders and aligned his jaw at the sight.

He knew it wasn't the time or place to remind Sean of proper etiquette. All that mattered was getting James to the hospital as quickly as possible. But he certainly wouldn't be forgetting Sean's shove anytime soon. "Get in the car, Annie," Sean directed, beeping the doors unlocked.

Annie carefully eased James into the back seat and snuggled in beside him, guiding his head to rest against her chest. William kept watch from the sidewalk, a twinge of helplessness tightening in his gut. As Sean flipped his sunglasses on, threw the car into gear and peeled away, Annie mouthed something through the window to him. He couldn't be sure, as the late-morning sun had cleared the rooftops, making him squint to see. But as the car disappeared in a flash, he would have sworn it was thank you.

CHAPTER FOUR

WILLIAM SQUATTED BESIDE Old Red, meticulously polishing the chrome.

"It's really coming along," Brandon offered, kicking his feet up onto an old bench.

"I took it for a spin earlier."

"Then, you got it running?"

"Before you got here."

"I snuck out of work just in time."

"You only come over to drink my beer…"

"*My* beer."

"…and drool over Old Red," William supplied.

"That, too." Brandon flicked his pop tab into a trash bucket and heaved a sigh. "So, how's the little guy?"

"I haven't heard. I'm sure my mom will have an update soon."

"Is that it?" Brandon asked.

William glowered. "Well, his dad is a first-rate jerk."

"Is he ever."

"I don't know what Annie saw in him."

"Money," Brandon said, taking a swig of beer.

"Really? That doesn't seem like her...unless she changed a lot since I knew her."

"Well," Brandon said, "more like...security."

"Security?"

"She and Betsy were practically destitute when Sean made his move. Didn't you know that?"

William squatted next to Old Red, his back to Brandon. "Why would I know that?"

"Right, I guess no one would have called to tell you."

"I wouldn't have answered anyway." It pained him to imagine Annie so desperate that her best option was to marry Sean. If only William had been there to help her...

He shook his head at the thought. He'd had his own problems back then and wouldn't have been able to offer much assistance. In fact, he would have probably caused her more harm. It was no use wondering what might have been, since she certainly didn't have feelings for him anymore.

"How is Annie?"

William scoffed at the question. "She's a piece of work, man."

"Really?"

"She has it out for me—*bad*."

Brandon chuckled in disbelief. "What?"

"Oh, yeah. She can't stand the sight of me."

"Annie? She's the sweetest person I've ever met."

"I have yet to meet this amazing Annie Curtis you gush about so often. The last time I saw *her*, I was eighteen years old." He neglected to add *and in love*.

Brandon laughed. "Let's start with what you did to her."

"I've been nothing but nice to her since I got back," William said.

"What about before that?" Brandon asked. "I'm not judging," he quickly added when William shot him a glare. "You had to do what you had to do back then, but…"

"*Yeah?*"

"Some folks have a *long* memory."

AFTER BRANDON LEFT, William retrieved his cell phone from the workbench and stared at it for a few minutes, pressing the button to illuminate the screen every few seconds after it had gone dark.

One new voice mail.

"Will?" his mother called from the back porch. William tucked the phone in his pocket and locked the shed for the night. With the bike finally running, he could be ready to leave by morning if absolutely necessary, though he'd be out the money for his truck.

"Yes, ma'am?" he asked, shuffling up the back porch steps.

"Would you lend a hand tomorrow? Annie's taking the day with James."

"I...guess. Is that really necessary?"

"It would help me out so much," Joyce insisted. "I'm too old to pull another double shift."

"Don't you have anyone else to wait tables?"

"Karrin and Mia are both coming in, and Bobby agreed to pull a double shift busing. I've been meaning to hire on more staff, but..."

"What?"

"Coulda, shoulda, woulda, you know? That'll teach me for putting it off."

"Wait," William said before Joyce could retreat inside the house. "What happened with James?"

"It was a virus. Annie's pushing fluids and popsicles. He'll be shipshape in a few days."

"That was it?"

"Fevers come on quickly with little ones."

"I guess so."

Joyce paused and smiled. "I remember one time when we were living in Duluth, you were supposed to go out with your father to…what was that place called? Oh, yes, Mr. Twister's. He'd promised you a frozen yogurt after dinner, and you were jumping all over the house with excitement until you left. But by the time you two had returned, you had a fever of 102 and were sicker than a dog. You spent most of the night in between us in bed." Her gaze drifted off as she recalled the bit of nostalgia. "You were a cute kid back then, even when you were sick." She sighed. "Good night, love."

William strained to remember a time when his stepfather hadn't been front and center. Once Dennis and his mother had married, she had stopped telling stories of his father, and as a result the memories had faded. She had shushed him away at first when he'd asked to hear a story, and over time he'd stopped trying.

With his mom out of earshot, he plucked his cell phone from his pocket to finally retrieve the voice mail.

"Mr. Kauffman, this is Special Agent Denver Corrigan again. I'd like to remind you that the Miller case has been reassigned to me and you are required to meet with me or risk us issuing a warrant for your arrest. You can reach me day or night at this number. Thank you."

William deleted the voice mail on Denver's final breath. He had no intention of ever going back, regardless of what the consequences might be. He and Old Red were rocketing west as soon as he could sell his truck and secure a little cash. If he could manage to leave Chinoodin Falls on good terms, even better.

ANNIE MET MARJORIE on the front stoop of her house.

"Thanks for coming, Margie. I need to run a few errands."

"Is he sleepin'?"

"Watching cartoons."

"Of course. Take your time, honey. We'll be fine."

"Keep the doors locked in case—"

"I know the drill, sweetie."

There were few people in the world Annie trusted her children with, and Marjorie was one of them. "I'll be back in a half hour," she said.

After two days of bone broth and popsicles, James had finally developed an appetite. She intended to get him anything he wished, which at the moment was a special request for peanut butter pie and french fries.

Arriving at Pop's Place, she hesitated when she spotted William's truck parked in the back lot. She slipped through the door and bypassed the office, but not before catching a glimpse of William at her desk. He was pouring over papers again.

Annie kept moving.

"How's the little guy?" Karrin asked, sidling up beside her as she fixed a take-home container. A lifelong waitress in her early forties, with silver-streaked black hair, Karrin reeked of coffee and old-time diner as she crushed Annie in a sideways hug.

"He'll be better with some peanut butter pie. Please tell me we have some."

"I think we have a piece left." Karrin followed Annie to the dessert case and hung close by as she hunched over and delicately jostled the last slice of pie into a Styrofoam box. "So… have you talked to William?"

Annie jerked her head. *"Why?"*

"He was asking about James."

"So."

"Joyce mentioned something about you two… You know…"

Annie straightened, her eyes darting around for eavesdroppers. "No?"

"You two...used to be an item?"

"What did she say?" Annie wafted her hand in the air as Karrin drew a breath to explain. "No. Never mind. I don't want to talk about this right now. I have to get home to James."

She pecked Karrin on the cheek and hurried to the back door, relieved she was about to duck out without anyone else spotting her. But before she did so, she hesitated and listened to William shuffling papers a few yards away. Before her brain knew what her feet were doing, she found herself creeping closer until she was loitering in the office doorway. She was just as surprised as William was when he noticed her.

"What are you doing here? How's James?" he blurted, jumping to his feet.

"He's fine. It was a virus. He'll be better with rest...and french fries." She jostled her take-home container.

"Good." William nodded, clutching the back of his neck. "He was holding his stomach... If I overreacted about it, Annie, I was only—"

"*No.* Actually I came back here to tell you..." She paused, admiring a sweetness behind his eyes that she hadn't seen since before he'd returned to Chinoodin Falls. He had looked at her like that when they'd snuck out to Little Foot Mountain so many years ago, and she'd been in the topsy-turvy early stages of falling in love for the first time. She had been wearing a yellow sundress she'd bought specifically for their date, and he'd told her she had brightened his day. Lying beside him on an old afghan he'd had in his truck, he had run his fingers playfully down the front of that dress, delicately plucking at each tiny button in between peppering her lips with soft kisses. For years afterward, though it had fallen out of style, she'd hidden the dress at the back of her closet, unable to part with it or perhaps unable to part with him.

"What?" he asked, taking a step closer.

Annie bit her lip, trying to jar herself free of the memory. "Thank you for intervening with James."

"It was my pleasure."

"He shouldn't have been sitting out there alone."

"No."

"He's only a little boy, you know?" she whispered.

William's eyes squinted in seriousness. "Yes, I know."

Annie swallowed a lump in her throat. "When I think about it... I can't stop thinking about it..."

"It wasn't your fault, Annie. He's okay now."

"Sean just doesn't..." She vigorously shook her head and squeezed her eyes shut. "I don't know what to do sometimes."

"You mean with Sean?"

Annie opened her eyes to a dark look falling over William's face. "He's difficult."

"Difficult?" William's eyebrows shot up, and she knew it was no use dancing around her troubles with Sean.

"Well...you saw."

He nodded. "I have a feeling I haven't seen the half of it."

"You want to know why I married him, don't you?"

"Well..."

"I know you do."

"The thought *had* crossed my mind."

"And what have you come up with so far?"

"From what I know about you—"

"What on earth do you know about me?" Annie sighed. "You've only been back a few days."

"I knew you once," he replied, his voice a low drawl like the morning sun warming over her. She lifted her face, searching his for any explanation as to why he didn't know her that way now.

"And?" she mustered.

"I know you wouldn't marry him for his money."

Annie feigned a smile. "Is that what you've heard? And how do you know that? Women marry for money all the time."

"Not you."

"How can you be sure?"

"I've seen you with Betsy. You're such a good mom, I know you wouldn't put her in a situation like that unless…"

"What?" Her eyes glistened with hot tears she refused to shed. Not now and never in front of William. "Tell me."

He brushed her on the arm, his weathered skin gentle as her nerves rose. She teetered on her feet, and he seemed to sense her light-headedness, steadying her. "I didn't mean to upset you, Annie."

She didn't know if he meant by his words or his touch, and as her eyes fell to his perfect lips, slightly parted, she could only assume he wasn't sure, either.

"You didn't," she said. She knew as his furrowed brow softened, he didn't believe her lie.

"Annie, dear." Joyce smiled, scooting past her into the office. "What are you doing here? Joe, Danny and Earl were asking about you. Apparently you are really goofin' up their routine. How dare you miss two days in a row! The way they were talkin', they were going to send a search party for you."

Annie slipped from William's grasp, but she couldn't draw her gaze from him and the spell he'd cast over her. Her arm cooled from where he'd touched it, eliciting yearnings she'd thought she'd buried long ago with that yellow sundress. "I should be back tomorrow. I wanted to say thank-you for the other day, William."

"You're welcome, Annie," he replied, straightening his stance as she edged farther from him.

"Kiss the kiddos for me," Joyce called, but Annie had already escaped to the safety of the parking lot, uncertain from what she was running or why.

WILLIAM PINCHED TWO hot dinner plates between his fingers and gave Miles a pleading look.

"Table six," the cook answered, sending William on his way.

He had never served the public a day in his life, and it was with good reason: he hated it. Busing tables and working in the kitchen as a kid couldn't be considered serving the public, because he'd been serving only one person back then—Dennis.

William had tried to keep his head down as much as possible, toiling away the hours with the occasional insult from the old man. But as he worked the dining room now, he realized Dennis had done him a favor by banishing him to the kitchen. Only two hours on the job serving and it had felt like twenty. The rest of the afternoon stretched before him.

He was a person who had always believed he knew what he was doing. Right or wrong, he was confident in his decisions and steamed straight ahead. But as he hustled between tables, scratching out orders and juggling plates, he hoped he could skate by for the day pretending he knew what he was doing.

"How are you doing, Will?" Mia asked, zipping up beside him at the order window. "Miles! Give me a full house, whistle berries, burn one with yellow paint, frog sticks and a bowl of fire!"

"What was all that nonsense?"

Mia giggled with amusement. "I thought you used to work here, Will."

"The culture has changed dramatically," he grumbled.

Mia reached for the coffeepot. "That was a grilled cheese with bacon and tomato, baked beans, a burger with mustard, fries and a bowl of chili."

William slapped his ticket down. "Give me two hot dogs with fries and onion rings."

"Two bow-wows, frog sticks—"

"Whatever!" William howled.

Mia dissolved into giggles as he lumbered back to tables. Mia and Miles could keep their shoptalk to themselves. He had no desire to learn the lingo or work any longer in this place. He had to get out of here.

"Someone to see you, Will," Karrin called, motioning to the front. "Something about your truck?"

"Perfect," Will breathed, meeting a lanky kid at the entrance.

"Is that your truck out there?" he asked, smoothing too-long hair out of his eyes.

"Interested?"

"Maybe. Does it run?"

"Of course."

"Can we take it for a spin?" the kid asked, his eyes glued on the truck.

"Yes," William replied, eager to leave the diner and make some fast cash.

Unfortunately, there was nothing fast about it.

Carter turned out to be a college student, hoping to upgrade his Mazda for something with traction and haul. But after pining over William's truck for a half hour, he admitted to not having his finances completely in line to make the purchase.

"Let me know if you come up with the cash," William muttered. He returned to the diner in a huff only to be confronted by Karrin and Mia. They nearly had smoke billowing from their ears, and he squared his shoulders at the sight of them.

"What?"

"Excuse me?" Karrin fired back. "You can't walk out midshift, Will."

"I don't work here," he said through gritted teeth.

"News to us. You were serving those tables and then disappeared."

"I don't answer to you, Karrin. Now step aside."

"We took flack for you while busting our

butts double time, Will. The least you can do when you duck out is tell someone."

"You knew that kid was asking for me."

"I didn't know you were going to disappear for half an hour!"

"That's because it's none of your business!"

"Office," Joyce interrupted, yanking William by the elbow and pulling him into the back.

"William, Karrin is right. You can't walk out in the middle of a shift."

"I had someone interested in my truck."

"You have *customers*."

William pinched the bridge of his nose. "I'm trying to help you out, but I have to sell that truck."

"What's the big hurry? Are you short on cash?" Joyce asked.

"Listen, I don't mind pitching in a little today, but I didn't come back to Chinoodin to work here. You of all people should know how I feel about this place for heaven's sake."

Joyce's eyes welled with tears. "I thought you came back to…" She shook her head, pressing her hands to her lips, composing herself.

"What do you want from me?" William asked.

"If you don't want to be here, I don't want to guilt you, but…"

"But?"

Joyce dotted the corners of her eyes with her fingertips and returned to the dining room, passing Mia on the way.

"You've missed a lot, you know." Mia didn't look at him. "The last few years have been hard on her."

"News flash, Mia. They were hard on everybody." William sent the back door banging open and gulped the early-evening breeze.

CHAPTER FIVE

ANNIE STARTLED AWAKE, the glow of the television casting shadows and adding to the fear she was all too familiar with. She silently eased up off the couch, tucking her blanket over James, who was snoring beside her. Straining to hear a repeat of whatever had woken her, she tiptoed to the front window to catch a sliver of who or what was lurking on her front walk. She didn't need to check the locks. She meticulously bolted the doors whenever she entered the house, a habit she could rely on in moments like this.

A shadow moved past the window. But as her heart lurched, each quickened heartbeat thudding progressively harder against her chest, the light rap on the door puzzled her. Hesitantly, she glided up against the frame, pressing her cheek to the wood to peer out the peephole.

"Annie?" William called. "It's me."

Annie flipped on the porch light and paused

to study William through the tiny bit of glass. There had been a time when she had anticipated his visits, watching from her bedroom window with her hair done and lipstick at the ready.

The first time he'd appeared in her bedroom window, she hadn't been prepared to see him. He had crouched on the windowsill, a proud grin stretched over his boyish lips. For her, he had always been a mix of fear and excitement as he had quietly entered and then wrapped her in his arms, kissing her wildly while her mother moved about the house a floor below them.

Annie cracked open the door, meeting his gaze.

"May I come in?" he asked. His voice sounded as disheveled as his appearance. Sporting a hooded sweatshirt that was smeared with grease stains and dirt; his blue jeans looked as if they had spent the week crumpled in a ball on the floor.

She shook her head. Slipping outside onto the porch, she shivered, her T-shirt and pajama pants a thin barrier between her and the night chill. His eyes fell over her body, and she clasped her arms around herself firmly.

After a moment he unzipped his hoodie and offered it to her.

"I'm okay," she said, although her skin prickled with goose bumps. William disregarded her words and swung the hoodie over her shoulders, apparently oblivious to how dirty it might seem to anyone else. But she couldn't balk at the stained garment as his familiar scent enveloped her in a warm hug.

"I can't talk to you if you're shivering like that."

"Why are you here, William? Is something wrong?"

William folded his arms across his chest and shifted his weight to the back of his heels. "Will you be back at work tomorrow?"

"What?"

"Your shift? Will you be there?"

"I told Joyce I would be," she replied, eyeing him. "Is that why you came here tonight? You couldn't text me that question?" Her eyes narrowed.

"What's the big deal?"

"I don't like people coming to my house in the middle of the night. That's the big deal."

William pulled his cell phone from his pocket and chuckled at the sight. "It's only nine o'clock."

"So? It's dark."

"And?"

"I thought you were... I don't know...an intruder."

William glanced from side to side. "Do intruders usually knock on the door and announce themselves first?"

"Don't you laugh at me." Annie scowled, peeling his sweatshirt off in a frenzy. "Take this back and get off my porch."

"Hey, hey, hey," William replied, gently coaxing her to stop. "Wait a minute here." He slowly eased the sweatshirt back up and over her shoulders, cinching it under her chin. She stared up at him, her pulse racing. "What did I do wrong? Did I scare you?"

"No."

"But you don't like me coming here at night?"

It wasn't *him* coming here at night that bothered her. Annie retreated to the end of the porch. "Why are you here, William?"

"I can't cover another shift at the diner."

"No. What are you doing *back*? *In Chinoodin.*"

William tucked his fists into his front pockets. "Why?"

"I need to know."

"Why?"

"William," she snapped. "Can't you answer a question straight, just once?"

"This is my hometown, Annie. I didn't know I had to register with you when returning."

"You know that's not what I meant."

"Isn't it? You've been giving me the third degree since I arrived."

"Can you blame me?" she cried. "I haven't seen you in more than a decade and when I do, you act as if…" She searched his eyes for any understanding of what she yearned to say. She needed to know if she had meant anything to him. Had he thought about her over the years? Did he miss her? Did he want her the way she had wanted him? "Forget it. Take this back," she said, shoving his sweatshirt into his hands on her way to the front door.

"A lot of time has passed, Annie. I'm not the same person I once was."

"Neither am I. You apparently don't think about what it was like twelve years ago, so forget I mentioned it."

"Do you?"

"What?"

"Think about life back then?"

"Why would I?"

"Come on, Annie."

"I'll be at work tomorrow. That's what you came to ask, isn't it?"

William twisted his sweatshirt in his hands. "I've got someone interested in my truck. Once I sell it, I'm heading out of town."

Annie felt a chill crawl down her spine as his words hung over her. "What about your mother?"

"What about her?"

"Didn't you come back to help her?"

"Help her do *what*?"

"Run Pop's Place."

"Jeez. Everyone has a lot of plans for me."

"Well?"

"I never said that."

"She did."

"When?"

"Well, maybe she assumed that's what you were going to do."

"Yeah, there's been a lot of that going on lately."

"You can't take off again, William. Not yet."

"Annie," he said on a sigh. "There's nothing for me here anymore."

"Why did you come here tonight?"

"I didn't want mom stuck in the lurch tomorrow if you didn't show."

Annie scoffed at his words, shaking her head in disgust. "Well, at least you said something this time instead of running off into the night without a word." William worked his jaw as Annie stepped inside her house. "You've made me hate front porches, you know that?" she loud-whispered before shutting the door on him.

WILLIAM ROLLED OLD RED out of the shed and down the driveway to the street before firing it up. He thought he had heard his mother up as he'd crept out the back door, the early-morning cold a reminder that the hot days of summer were still a ways off. Chinoodin Falls typically only had two seasons, winter and July, so for early June it was still quite cool by early afternoon and brisk in the morning.

After watching the hours tick by all night, tossing and turning in fitful sleep, the promise of dawn lurking over the horizon was bait enough to get him up and out for the day. A cup of coffee and the cold lake breeze pelting his face would perk his senses and snap him out of the funk Annie Curtis had sent him tailspinning into the night before.

Tugging his knit hat over his ears and wrapping a bandana over his nose and mouth, the only sliver of unexposed face, subject to the wind whipping off Lake Superior, were his eyes, which he covered with the clear goggles he'd picked up the day before. Once the sun had risen, he'd switch them out for sunglasses. Right now he needed a ride around town to confirm Old Red was ready for the long haul with him. Then he'd pick up some chaps and new boots at Miner's Leather Goods and be on his way before dinner. That is, if he could sell his truck. Luckily he had lined up a new buyer.

Over the rumble of the engine, he felt his cell phone vibrate in his pocket. He stopped and dug it out, knowing he'd regret even glancing at it.

William held the phone away from him as if it were a rattlesnake gearing to lunge and sink its fangs. His eyes immediately registered the phone number.

Denver Corrigan.

He gripped the phone, willing it to silence itself. The seconds ticked by with each vibration… Three…four…five…

He released a breath when it finally fell silent and waited for the inevitable vibration to signal a new voice mail.

"Mr. Kauffman, this is Special Agent Corrigan. I trust you have received my prior voice mails and understand the consequences of your actions…and inactions. I take your failure to return my calls as your intended response. Let me remind you that it is still in your best interest to contact me immediately, however, an arrest warrant for you will be processed. Thank you."

William shoved his cell phone back into his pocket, tugged on his gloves and adjusted his goggles. He shifted the bike into first gear, eased off the clutch and applied the throttle, thundering down the neighborhood streets with an eye on Lakeshore Boulevard. Today was the day to kiss Chinoodin Falls goodbye forever.

ANNIE POURED COFFEE for the Old Timers with one eye on their table and the other one sneaking a peek out the window. William's truck had been parked on the street outside Pop's Place for a couple of days and was drawing interest that morning. A fellow had been loitering around it for at least ten minutes, but William was nowhere in sight.

"'Bout time you were back, dear," Danny said, raising a coffee cup to Annie's honor. "The place don't feel right without yous."

"Did you have fun giving Mia and Karrin a hard time?" she asked.

"They don't have the right sense of humor, dontcha know?"

"They're not gluttons for punishment the way I am, Danny."

"You dish it just as much, though. Dat's what makes it fun."

Annie took the few seconds of quiet to jet out the front door. A middle-aged man in overalls and haggard work boots moseyed next to William's truck.

"Can I help you?" she asked.

"I'm supposed to meet a guy about this truck in a bit."

"Oh, no. That's what I was afraid of."

"How's that now?" the man asked, rasping his hand over a bristling jaw.

"I hate to be the one to tell you this…"

"What?"

"He stood you up."

"Eh?" The guy tipped his ear toward her.

"Yeah. He decided to keep the truck. He didn't want to call and tell you, so he sent me to keep an eye out for you."

"That dirty son of a—"

"*I know,*" Annie said, her face twisted in sympathy. "He's left people out on a limb before, I'm afraid. Twisting in the breeze. I'm so sorry to be the messenger of bad news."

"I got off the night shift almost an hour ago, and I've been putsin' about all this time for nothin'?"

"He says he's really sorry, but—"

"Tell him to stick his apologies." The man stomped off. Annie checked over her shoulder for any sign of William before zipping back into the diner.

"Is everything okay?" Joyce asked.

Annie smiled. "Yep. Just peachy."

WILLIAM TORE INTO the parking lot of Pop's Place. A nasty voice mail from a prospective buyer for his truck had sent him speeding all the way from Miner's Leather Goods, blowing through two yellow traffic lights and nearly skidding onto Main Street. He'd barely hurtled through the back door of the diner when he spotted Annie. Her eyes flashed with alarm when she spotted him moving toward her.

"You!" he hollered.

"Take it easy, kid," Karrin called after him, but he didn't slow as he followed Annie into the kitchen.

"What's wrong?" Miles asked, leaning away from the grill.

"Outta my way, Miles," William cautioned.

Annie, feigning innocence, was all wide-eyed and smirking.

"What's your problem, William?"

"*You*, Curtis, have got some serious explaining to do."

"I don't know what you're talking about," Annie protested, backing out of the kitchen and into the storage room. William wasn't letting her out of his sight.

"Mike said he talked to a waitress with sad brown hair and paintbrush eyelashes. Sound like anyone you might know?"

"Is he still going to buy your truck?"

"Come on, Annie."

"What?" she scowled, frantically eyeing the doorway.

"You're not getting off that easy."

She defiantly thrust out her chin and blew wisps of hair from her face.

William leaned closer, the scent of her strawberry lip gloss that stained her pout clouding his senses. Scrambling to focus on his anger instead of her rosebud lips tilted up toward him, he pushed on with his interrogation. "What are you tryin' to pull?"

"Nothing," she sputtered.

"Something."

"Let me pass, William."

"Or what?"

But as soon as the words left his mouth, he sensed her defiance turn to panic. The whites of her eyes flashed with more than a fear of being confronted for her foolish trick.

"I mean it, William," she shrieked. "Get out of my way."

"I'd never hurt you, Annie," he declared, putting several feet between the two of them.

"Are you sure about that?" she snapped.

"I'd *never* hurt you," he said again, his words slow and deliberate.

She smoothed her hair off her forehead, her nerves noticeably frazzled. "I… I… Don't do that again."

"I won't."

She focused on him then, as if searching for an authenticity he hoped he projected. If she had genuinely been worried that he could… what?

"Are you okay?" Miles asked, standing in the open doorway. William's eyes still latched on Annie.

"Sure," Annie said, nodding. "We're fine, Miles."

William waited for Miles to leave before beginning again. "Why'd you sabotage my sale?"

"You can't leave yet."

"Because?"

"Joyce needs you."

"Nobody needs me, Annie."

"She won't tell you because she doesn't want to guilt you into helping."

"Guilt me? All my mother has ever done since I was a kid was guilt me. Every time Dennis got revved up into one of his dark moods and took it out on me—"

"*I know.*" Annie sighed. "I know, William, but you can't leave right now."

"Why do you care?"

"I care about Joyce."

"Is that all?"

"Isn't that enough?"

William shook his head. "I can't stay here, Annie, regardless of what you think I can do."

"*Fine.* Do what you want," Annie huffed, storming away. "You always did anyway!"

William ran his hands through his hair and released a long breath. There had been a time when he would have walked to the moon and back for Annie Curtis, not that she had been the kind of girl who would have ever asked him to. Seeing her was stirring up old feelings he had long forgotten. But if he indulged himself for even a minute, he might not be able to leave her again, and he had to leave—while he still could.

ANNIE HURRIED TO the front door as soon as she heard Sean's car pull into the driveway.

"Hi, pumpkin," she greeted James, her mood dancing with merriment as soon as she spotted her son running up the sidewalk. But her relief of having him home turned to concern when he pushed past her and fled up the stairs. She lingered as Sean strode toward the house.

"You'd better get back here and show your father some respect!" he shouted loudly enough for Mr. Mosely from across the street to peer up from his gardening and gawk.

"He's probably tired, Sean. I'll get him to bed early tonight." Her placating voice an unwavering calm meant to soothe his temper.

"You baby him," Sean mocked. "And when I try to toughen him up, he can't handle it. Then I'm the bad guy."

"He's just a little boy."

"Don't start with that 'he's just a little boy' hooey," he said, protesting. "He's my son, Annie, and no son of mine is going to grow up to be a weakling."

"Then love him like a son. Talk to him, listen to him—"

"What do you think I've been doing all this time?" Sean yelled.

Annie faced off in front of him, her gentle facade dissipating. "I don't know, Sean. *He's* the one crying."

"Listen, I'll…ah…never mind."

"Good night," Annie said, hastening to close the door, but Sean stuck his foot over the threshold at the last second. She firmly pressed on the door to prevent him from opening it any wider. "It's late, Sean."

"Late? What do you mean *late*? The sun is still out."

"I have to get the children ready for bed, and I've had a long day."

"I had a long day, too, but I still took the kid out for a slice of pizza, didn't I? You don't seem too grateful about that."

Annie clenched her jaw. She didn't want Sean to come anywhere near James, but she appeased him with these mini outings to keep him from taking her to court for custody. He really was dense. It pained her whenever he took James for a visit, and she certainly didn't feel gratitude. "I could come in for a while," he offered. "After you put the kids to bed, I could put *you* to bed."

"I really can't, Sean."

"You're a little flushed, baby." He smiled. Annie's heart thudded hard, her fingertips whitening against the door. She wondered if Mr. Mosely was still paying attention.

"I have to get to the children."

"I could make you forget about your long day, you know. We could make each other feel better tonight."

"I don't need anyone else to make me feel better."

"That's not what I heard. Rumor has it Joyce's son has been hanging around here."

"That's not true."

"Are you calling me a liar?" Sean grinned, though his eyes narrowed on her.

"Where did you hear that?"

"You can't keep secrets from me, baby. I know everything happening in this town."

"William hasn't been hanging around, not that it's any of your business."

"It's *all* my business," Sean whispered. "You'd be wise to remember that."

"Good night, Sean," Annie stated forcefully. After what seemed like an eternity, he reluctantly eased off the door.

"I want a rain check, baby," he said, puckering an air kiss. "Don't forget it."

Annie didn't wait for Sean to step down off the stoop before bolting the door and racing upstairs to find James. She could only assume Sean felt threatened by William and was tossing out suspicions to gauge her reaction. The other possibility, which she shuddered to entertain, was that he had been watching her house the night William had turned up on her front porch. But she didn't have time to think about that now.

Hidden in his bedroom, in a tent he'd strung out of bedsheets, James was nestled beside Betsy. She cradled an arm protectively around him. Annie dropped to her belly and crawled into the tent so the top half of her body could fit snugly beside them. James stared at her, his big brown eyes pleading with her to make him feel better, safe. She didn't need to know what had happened with his father. Sean was always in the wrong. And the longer she subjected James to his mean-spiritedness, she was in the wrong, too.

CHAPTER SIX

WILLIAM POKED HIS head out of Dennis's office, straining to hear if anyone was approaching. When he was sure the noise had been something other than his mother arriving home, he returned to the filing cabinet jammed full of paperwork.

Dennis would blow a gasket if he could see his office now in complete disarray. When William had snuck in here to check out his stepfather's baseball card collection—the lure of the antique cards too much for his thirteen-year-old self—he'd taken several mental pictures before placing a finger on anything. He'd exercised the stealth moves of a ninja to prevent leaving even a speck out of place. The old man had had a few things that set off his temper, and when he'd somehow discovered William had snooped around his office, William sure heard about it.

He heaved a stack of disheveled papers from the filing cabinet to thumb through, still wondering how Dennis had known he'd been in his baseball collection. He'd probably only guessed and then read the guilt on William's face.

It was nearly impossible to find anything in the office today. Every surface, from the desk to the chair to the filing cabinet, was covered with old bills, junk mail and magazines. He'd have to think like his mother, not Dennis, if he were going to place his hands on the title for Old Red. He assumed only Dennis's name was listed on it, and he wanted to get a look at it before his mother arrived home with a dozen questions.

Fumbling through a bunch of tax returns and old bills, he figured he was getting closer. He paused, running his fingers over a hefty red folder that read KEEP at the top and flipped it open. Inside were medical bills, all for his mother, with the top one dated two weeks prior to his arrival. As he scanned the billing codes for treatments and procedures she'd had over the last couple of years, his gut seized as particular words and phrases jumped off the page, practically nipping him on the nose: *oncology, radiation therapy, chemotherapy, exploratory surgery.* He poured over the pages, double-checking and then triple-checking that the bills were in her name, but each page showed procedures for Joyce Green.

After a few minutes, William's head was spinning, so he couldn't concentrate anymore. The words and numbers had blurred together in a muddled collection, mocking him from the page. William carefully slipped the bills back into the folder and tucked it into the filing cabinet. His mother would never know he had been in here. She probably couldn't find the title to the bike any faster than he could because of the clutter.

He just stood there, taking in the piles of disorganized junk that had accumulated since the last time he'd been home. Tidying would easily be ignored when a person was in the throes of fighting for their life.

Cancer.

Was that possible? He couldn't fathom how self-absorbed he must have been the last few days to not see the signs that his own mother was undergoing cancer treatments. Had there been signs? Had he even paused to notice?

"Will? Are you here?" Joyce called from the back door.

William turned, unable to shift one foot in front of the other. "Yeah," he said. The word barely uttered from his throat.

"There you are," she said in a breathy voice as she pushed the office door fully open and greeted him with a grin. "What are you doing in here?"

William stared, mouth agape, at his mother. She had seemed more tired and out of breath than when he'd left home, but he'd chalked that up to her aging. Everyone was a decade older since he'd last seen them, including his own reflection in the mirror each morning. The weariness in her walk hadn't alarmed him, either. Her hair, which had been a wavy chestnut brown falling below her chin, was now a short, cropped auburn and gray. He tried to picture her soft, beautiful hair falling out in clumps and growing back into the straight, wiry texture it was now. He puzzled at how he hadn't realized it before. He'd been too consumed in his own worries to give her more than a second thought. She'd been so thrilled to see him, it hadn't even occurred to him…

"Things have changed since I've been back."

She sighed, glancing past him to the filing cabinet.

"I suppose. The diner keeps me too busy to mind after the house. I really do need to hire more help. I'm too old to put in overtime."

"You seem tired, Mom."

"We're all tired." She chuckled, leaning against him and taking his arm. "I defrosted some meatballs last night if you want to make yourself a sandwich for dinner. I haven't gotten to the supermarket this week, so there isn't much selection."

"Are *you* hungry, Mom?"

"Oh, no. I think I'll go lie down for a spell. You go ahead and eat when you're ready, honey."

William nodded as she gave his arm another squeeze and shuffled to the stairs, climbing each one with a labored effort. He needed answers but couldn't bear to ask his mother. After all, if she had wanted him to know about the cancer, she would have told him when he'd first arrived. Someone had to fill in the blanks, and as much as he didn't want to admit it, there was only one person who could tell him exactly what he needed to know.

WILLIAM SQUINTED, STRAINING to find Annie walking among the rocks of Peninsula Bay. He coasted along, finally bringing the bike to a crawl once he'd spotted her lounging on a park bench, her black sunglasses facing a kids' play structure as the lake lapped in the background.

"Hey," he said, sliding onto the bench beside her. She hesitated, pushing her sunglasses up over her forehead to pin back wisps of hair blowing in a lyrical dance on the late-afternoon breeze.

"William, what are you doing here?"

"William!" Betsy yelled, waving furiously from the top of the wooden structure that resembled the tower of a castle. He tipped his chin up to acknowledge her before continuing.

"Why didn't you tell me about my mom?"

Annie's face fell before turning her attention back to the children who darted across a swaying rope bridge.

"I'm surprised she told you."

"She didn't."

"Then how did you find out?"

"I have my ways," he said. "How bad is it?"

Annie sighed. "She was diagnosed after Dennis died."

"Good timing," William grumbled. "He didn't have much of a bedside manner."

"She underwent chemo. The children and I moved in with her temporarily when I separated from Sean."

"Why?"

"Well…she was so sick."

William gaped. Her eyes, which were soft, flooded with empathy for him. "I didn't realize…"

"I know. Of course you didn't." The assurance in her words threw him. He managed not to wince at the thought that his mother had been ill and hadn't called him, hadn't wanted to bother him, and *why*? Had she been *that* certain that he wouldn't come to lend her a hand? And here all this time it had been Annie who'd stepped in.

"And now?" he asked.

"She's been in remission for over a year. Her hair is growing back, her skin has better color, but she's tired and her immune system is weak. The medication is expensive. If the diner closes, she won't be able to—"

"Closes?" William's eyes snapped wide open.

Annie brushed absently at her forehead before settling her hands in her lap.

"Pop's Place has been limping along for years, William. I honestly don't know how we made it through the winter."

"Mom!" Betsy called, barreling across the wood chips. "Did you see me jump off the railing?"

Annie's lips parted in a reply to her daughter, but William couldn't register if she had spoken. A heavy fog had settled over him, clouding his mind into a dense sea of dismal grays and blues. Annie didn't know how they had made it through the winter? No wonder his mother had dissolved into tears when she learned he had plans to ditch Chinoodin Falls. She was pinning her future, her security, on *him*, but the last thing he was capable of being to anyone was a savior. He had his own miserable mess to sort out.

"William." Suddenly alert, he found Annie's hand rested lightly on his arm. "You're ringing."

"What?" he croaked, fumbling for his cell phone.

It was Mike. He had cash.

William pulled himself to his feet and started toward his motorcycle, throwing one foot in front of the other.

"William," Annie asserted again. He stopped, raising his eyebrows to expedite whatever she still felt inclined to say. "What are you going to do?"

"What would you have me do, Annie?"

She rose, her eyes pleading.

"Stay."

He managed a shrug. "I gotta make a sale right now."

He'd been in Chinoodin Falls only a few days, but already it seemed everyone was demanding something of him. If he stayed for much longer, he might have an armored escort to assist him out of town. But if Annie learned that, she'd have to learn…all of it, and that was something he couldn't bear to let happen.

MIKE HAD THE truck hood popped open and was leaning over the engine with an inspector's scowl.

William needed this sale. He needed the cash. He needed to cut ties and be on his way. No one could blame him for leaving if they knew the whole story. If he stuck around, he was only bringing more trouble for his mom… and Annie.

"How's it runnin'?" Mike asked as William stared off into the distance before fishing the keys out of his pocket and tossing them to Mike.

"Take her for a spin."

"Thanks. I'll do a couple laps."

William settled on the curb, hands in his front pockets as Mike eased out onto Main Street and disappeared around the corner. He needed the couple thousand bucks in the worst way so he could afford to put enough distance between him and his past. He had to stick to the plan.

Annie wanted him to stay and help his mother, because she thought he was good. She thought he was the same person she had loved when they were kids, but if she really knew what kind of life he had lived since he'd last taken her in his arms...

"Hey, swabbie."

William recognized Sean out of the corner of his eye but refused to engage him.

"Swabbie," Sean persisted, a cell phone pressed to his ear. "I'll call you back, Diane," he said before hanging up and lumbering toward William. "I thought that was you. Got nowhere special to go to, eh?"

William swallowed a response, staring out over the street.

"Yeah, I thought you came back to swab the deck of this old place, but then I heard you're selling your truck. Something wrong with it?"

"Nope."

"No, eh? It's a decent enough truck."

"It has a few miles left in it."

"Interesting."

"You got something to say?"

"I'm just wondering what your new ride will be."

"You're looking at my ride."

"This old Indian?" Sean chuckled, circling the motorcycle. "She's a classic—that's for sure. I thought about gettin' one myself."

"It's a free country."

"True…" Sean nodded, running a hand over his stubbly chin. "See…this one is a beauty. One of a kind. Those curves…mmm-hmm. They don't make 'em like that anymore."

"They call that vintage."

"Vintage. Ain't she, though?" Sean admitted, straddling a leg up over Old Red and adjusting himself on the seat.

William's jaw tightened at the sight of it. He was about two seconds away from dragging Sean off his motorcycle and teaching him a lesson in manners, so to speak, but he had to make the sale with Mike.

"What I wouldn't give to take her for a spin. What'dya say?" Sean asked.

"It's not a good time," William answered once he saw his Chevy approaching.

"Of course. I didn't mean to step on your toes. I can read between the lines here. She's *yours*."

William kept his eyes fixed on his truck

crawling up to a red traffic light, two blocks away. He willed himself to not be baited into an altercation Sean seemed so desperately to want.

"I do mean," Sean continued, "If someone else tried to get near her, tried to lull her away from you, you'd do whatever it took to protect her, wouldn't cha?"

William shifted his eyes toward Sean.

"She's *yours*, and you wouldn't want anybody else touching her." Sean glared at William from under hooded eyes.

"I don't get what you're saying," William mustered.

"Oh, I think you do," Sean replied, his voice an acidic whisper. "We're alike, you and I. You don't take too kindly to another man moving in. Right now you're trying to decide if you should yank me off this bike or swallow your pride. I know what *I'd* do, but I'm itchin' to see what you'll do."

"We're different."

"I doubt it," Sean said, easing off the bike. He straightened his belt, sizing William up as Mike approached in the truck. "I don't respond too kindly to anyone touching anything of mine. And once something is mine, it's mine...*forever*."

"I gotta make a sale," William said through gritted teeth, the vein in his neck throbbing harder than the last time he'd gotten his knuckles bruised.

"Of course," Sean said. "Do whatcha gotta do, swabbie...and I'll do what I gotta do."

William's eyes were honed like beacons on Sean's smug grin. "What's that supposed to mean?"

Sean sucked his teeth. "I'm sure you'll figure it out."

He sauntered across the street to his BMW as Mike pulled onto the curb in front of William.

"This'll do fine," Mike hollered, climbing out of the truck, her engine still rumbling in idle. "Do you have the title?" William glowered as Sean peeled his tires in front of them, shooting down the street with an alarming squeal.

"Sorry?" William asked, aware Mike was nearly standing on top of him.

"The title? I'll take it. I've got cash in hand."

He studied Mike and knew he'd wake up the next morning, gripped by regret or a shiny new pair of handcuffs. Probably both. But as much as he wanted those two scenarios to scare him straight, he found himself muttering a response that was sure to tick off the buyer once again.

William groaned with an apologetic shrug. "Mike, I hate to do this to you, but it's not for sale."

CHAPTER SEVEN

ANNIE DARTED BETWEEN the kitchen and dining room as tables began to fill up for breakfast. She had woken up in a cheery mood and was determined to not let anyone—especially William Kauffman—bring her down today. The children had been excited about a visit down by the lake with Marjorie, the sun was shining with the promise of summer and Mia's enthusiasm about her upcoming wedding was contagious.

"Mrs. Mia Howards has such a nice ring to it, dontcha think?" Mia bubbled.

"Two dots and a dash, whiskey down, Miles," Annie called, slapping the order slip down at the window. Miles twirled his spatula in the air as acknowledgment while Bobby slipped around them to bus more tables.

"Hatton told me the other night he wants to wear his Kromer and swampers down the aisle. I about fell off my chair."

"He wasn't serious, was he?"

"If he had any inkling I thought it was funny, he would probably try it. Come to think of it, I've never seen him in a suit."

"Never? Your own fiancé?"

"Ha. Most of our dates all winter were scheduled around deer camp."

She giggled more as Annie spotted the Old Timers waving her over to their table.

"Now, Annie, darlin'," Danny began, "what has Mia so up in a tizzy dis mornin'?"

"She's young and in love."

"Is dat all?" Joe asked, accepting a refill of coffee.

"And she's counting down the days until her wedding."

Danny nodded. "I remember what it was like to be young and in love. Gracie and I will celebrate forty-nine years in September, dont-cha know."

"You'll have to plan something big for your fiftieth."

"Well, I been tinkin' about dat, and dere are tree tings she might like—jewelry, goin' out to eat in a fancy restaurant or goin' on a trip."

"You should definitely take her on a trip," Annie said.

"I could do dat. Maybe I'll surprise her and take her early. You know, as I was tellin' Earl here, you can't wait for the right time—you have to *seize* it."

"You were telling Earl that, eh?" Annie asked. Earl lowered his newspaper and grumbled something before flipping it up to cover his face again.

"Yes, and I'll tell yous, too," Danny continued. "You are too young and purty to not be with a good fella, Annie dear. There are some stand-up fellas out at deer camp who would woo you in a second. You just have to know how to skin a deer, shoot a bow and ride the grade."

Annie laughed. "I'm a trooper, Danny. Remember? I don't think I'd fit the bill."

"Well, even gals born south of the Mackinaw Bridge deserve a good man to love. There are some nice trooper fellas around here, too. Take William, for example."

"That's true," Joe agreed. "He's been off seeing da world for all these years, and I don't think he and Joyce moved to the Upper Peninsula until he was in grade school. He's a true trooper, and yous two would be perfect together."

"Why are you so determined to fix me up?" Annie asked, glancing at the other tables she needed to visit. "Why don't you find Earl a girlfriend already?"

Danny leaned forward and motioned for her to do the same. "He's a bit slow to warm up. We've been workin' on him for about tree years."

Through the front window, Annie spotted William, surprised to find him still driving his truck. Entering the diner, he nodded to the Old Timers before continuing to the counter. Annie tagged close behind him.

"Your truck," she sputtered.

"What about it?"

"You still have it."

"Haven't you sold that thing yet dare, William?" Joe called over the clanking of coffee cups and morning conversations.

"I might hang on to it a while longer, Joe."

"Aw, that's fine, that's fine." Joe nodded.

"Are you helping, then?" Annie asked as he moved behind the counter and plucked a pastry out of the display case. William looked away as he chewed a large bite of cheese Danish. "Well?" she persisted, pressing forward. William, apparently unconcerned about hurrying on her behalf, kept chomping. In fact, a grin spread over his face as if he were amused with her questions. *"William."*

"Listen, Annie," he finally began. "I don't need you breathing down my neck for the next couple of weeks."

"*Couple* of *weeks*? Is that all?"

"I need to get mom set up with a system that works around her before I move on."

"What's wrong with my system?" Annie scowled.

"Your system?" William huffed. "Well, for starters, you're not making any money, or isn't that what you told me the other day?"

Annie spun on her heels and scooted around the counter. "I don't have time to listen to you. I have tables to wait!"

If William thought he was going to loiter around for a few weeks and put a bandage on Pop's Place to solve his mother's problems and alleviate his guilt, he was in for a rude awakening. Joyce didn't need a few weeks; she needed a full-time son. Annie wouldn't let him leave town again without Joyce—

CRASH!

Annie's heart jolted as she tore around the counter.

"Good heavens!" Joyce screeched. Sprawled on the dining room floor, broken breakfast dishes scattered about her, Joyce flailed helplessly.

"I'm so sorry, Joyce," Bobby cried, his face white with horror. "I didn't see you there."

"It was my own fault," Joyce wailed, trying to clutch her foot. "I was hurrying and knocked into you."

"Ma, what happened?" William exclaimed, sprinting over to her.

"Your dear old mother is a certified klutz. *That's* what happened. Get me to a chair, would you?"

"Here," Earl immediately offered, hurrying to grab Joyce's other arm. "You can elevate your foot on this bench."

Annie did a double take as Earl pushed in front of her and hoisted Joyce gingerly into a booth.

"Oh, my. Thank you, Earl." Joyce beamed, patting him gently on the hand as soon as she was settled. "It's nice to know there are still good men around." Earl nodded curtly without tearing his eyes from Joyce.

William knelt down, gently taking his mother's foot into his hands. "Does it hurt, Mom?"

"Oh, my, yes," she moaned, wincing at his touch. "I can't go anywhere on it."

"I need to get you to the emergency room."

"Yes, but not right now, dear. Your appointment with Arnold is in ten minutes. That's why I was hurrying in the first place. Please let me just rest here for a while."

"That's not a big deal. Arnold will understand why we need to reschedule."

"We will do no such thing! You said yourself that time was of the absolute essence. You go on ahead and meet him, and please take Annie with you."

Annie's eyes widened in surprise. "Who's Arnold? I have tables to cover."

"It's really not necessary, Mom. I know what we're in the market for."

"Nonsense," Joyce insisted. "Annie knows the ins and outs of running this place the way I do, and she will have valuable insight. You two take a few tours and let me know what you find. I'll take it easy here and try to keep the swelling down. I wouldn't mind a morning off to sip coffee and catch up with old friends." She beamed at Earl again, making his ears flush red.

"Don't worry," Earl interjected, straightening his Kromer hat. "I'll personally care after Joyce."

William straightened and rubbed his jaw. He looked as though he were deep in thought. "Well… Annie, are you up for a drive?"

"Does somebody want to fill me in, please? *Who's* Arnold?"

"There's no time, dear," Joyce said, her voice laced with urgency. "Mia can cover your tables."

Annie eyed William. "I guess I can go if you really need me—"

"I don't think I need you to go, but if you want to tag along for the morning—"

"Oh, for goodness sakes!" Joyce cried. "Will you two get out of here? The appointment is in six minutes."

Annie removed her apron and grabbed her purse. In the blink of an eye she had been roped into spending the entire morning alone with William, and she didn't have the faintest idea why.

ARNOLD HARDY WAS dutifully waiting outside the first location, trying to end a phone call. A stout man in his late fifties with thick black hair and capped white teeth, he resembled a caricature of a person.

"How are we doing?" he greeted them, his eyes darting back and forth between him and Annie.

William clasped Arnold's hand in a firm shake. "Eager to get started."

"Come on in then!" Arnold led them inside a detached shop that years earlier had been Cappaletti's Italian restaurant. William gazed longingly around the spacious dining room, savoring love at first sight. The place had a gorgeous view of the lake and plenty of room to expand. All it needed was a coat of paint and new window treatments, and the place could be ready in a week. He couldn't believe their luck.

He didn't want to spit right out in front of Arnold how he'd fallen for the spot, so he came up next to Annie to get her read on it.

"What do you think?" he whispered as she picked up a buyer's sheet. He and Arnold both jumped in alarm when she burst out laughing.

"Not what you're looking for?" Arnold winced.

"We can always negotiate," William began, but Annie started laughing, turning to the real estate agent.

"Where's the next place, Arnold?" she asked.

"Don't you even want to check the kitchen?" he suggested, trying to lead her there.

"No need."

William cracked his neck and held out an arm toward the door. "After you," he managed to say, his voice straining. As they proceeded to the next possible location, he found himself royally irritated with Annie Curtis. If she didn't like the place, all she had to do was politely say so instead of embarrassing them both in front of Arnold.

Their next stop was a tiny shop squeezed between a sports store and post office. Farther uptown and away from the lake, it was the ugly stepsister of Cappaletti's. Dingy, dark and reeking of mildew, it would take a lot of elbow grease and time to fix up. But as William poked around, he determined it wasn't an impossible feat.

"It's a bit of a fixer-upper, eh?" William said.

"You could always remodel it to fit your needs." Arnold smoothed a hand over his hair and spun a large gold ring around his chubby finger.

Annie shook her head and led William into the kitchen. "It wouldn't fit our needs, William."

"This place used to be a sandwich shop," Arnold called, turning on all the overhead lights. William couldn't recall the sandwich shop, but as he scanned the buyer's sheet, he thought the price was in their range.

"It's not too bad."

Annie frowned. "It's a pass for me."

William clucked his tongue. "Why? What's wrong with this one?"

"For starters the kitchen isn't equipped for a diner. It was designed for a simple sandwich shop, so you're going to have to sink a fortune into it—grills, exhaust system, major appliances." William leaned back into the kitchen again to see what he had missed. "And I came in here once before when it was a sandwich shop. I couldn't get a parking space, so I never returned. No amount of money will enable us to build a parking lot when there isn't land for it. Plus there are two similar restaurants within walking distance of here. Why would we want to set ourselves across the street from the competition right out of the gate?"

William slapped the buyer's sheet back down on the table and signaled they should proceed to the next location. He hated to admit it, but Annie did know what she was talking about, even if she dampened the initial excitement of real-estate shopping.

By the time they'd visited and rejected the fourth location, William knew he wasn't the only person feeling defeated.

"Okay, kids," Arnold said on a sigh, locking the front door. "I have another appointment I need to race to, so let me sift through your feedback and see what else I can find." He handed them his business card with the motto It's not hard with Hardy, flashed his pearly white trademark smile and jetted off.

They loitered in the parking lot a minute, Annie clutching her purse against her side and studying him.

"You're disappointed, aren't you?" she finally asked.

"Me? No." It was a lie, and they both knew it.

"I didn't want to waste anyone's time, William, especially mine."

"You certainly didn't, Annie. We made record time."

They strode through the parking lot to his truck. After he walked ahead of her to open her car door, she paused, leaving him to stand awkwardly, waiting for her. Her brow twisted.

"What's the problem?" he asked after a few moments.

She shifted her weight to one foot and readjusted her purse strap on her shoulder. "Why do you always do that?" Her question was more of an accusation.

"Do what?"

"That."

"Standing? Breathing? Aging by the second? You're going to have to be more specific, Curtis."

"You've been holding the door open for me all morning."

"And?"

"You don't have to do that, you know."

It dawned on him that her furrowed brow was merely a guise. For the first time since he'd arrived back in Chinoodin Falls, she seemed self-conscious. Any annoyance he'd had with her while looking at properties melted away as he saw now that her tough exterior was a facade, most likely built and crusted over in the last few years she had spent wrangling through life with Sean.

Even though she had known him once, *loved* him once, she didn't trust him now. That much was apparent.

She expelled an exasperated sigh, and he yearned to assure her he was a good guy, like the Old Timers she trusted so much. But as his past flashed through his mind, he wasn't sure he could make a convincing appeal.

"I didn't mean to make you uncomfortable," he said softly. She straightened at his wise observation.

"I'm not uncomfortable," she protested, hurrying to slide into the car. "You just don't have to do that—that's all."

As they cruised back to the diner, he knew that if he were to make an ally of Annie, he would need a lighter touch. After all, if they were going to move Pop's Place to a new location, she had to be on board. She'd be the person to help Joyce run it. With any luck, he'd be gone, west, free...

"So what are the kids doing this summer?" he asked, breaking the silence.

Annie readjusted in her seat, seeming to relax a bit at the mention of her children. "Marjorie, my neighbor, babysits them when I work. They'll spend the entire summer at the lake if she lets them."

"And what about you?"

"I learned this morning I'll be watching you relocate Pop's Place."

"You'll be doing a lot more than watching, Annie—trust me."

"*Hmph*. Easier said than done. Tell me again why Pop's Place can't stay put?"

"Do you want Joyce to make money?"

Annie rolled her eyes. "I'll admit the place could use a bit of a facelift."

"More like a total reconstruction. You've

been working there so long, you don't notice how bad it is. I'm seeing it through fresh eyes."

"I suppose that's the silver lining of you being gone."

They arrived at the diner, so William drew his focus from the road to face her, but she refused to make eye contact. She had begun to climb out of the truck when he stopped her. "Annie. Wait." She leaned back against her seat, giving him a chance to continue. "You knew what you were talking about this morning, and you gave me a lot to think about before the next meeting with Arnold. Thank you."

She shrugged her shoulders. "Oh…you're welcome."

"Are you willing to visit more prospective locations with me?"

She drew a quick breath. "If Joyce can't do it, I'll go with you."

As she hustled ahead of him into the diner, her defensive wall was apparent to him. How had he not seen it before? Was the girl he loved still in there, still yearning to be near him again? There had been a time when she would have been excited to spend time with him, but these days…

Brandon was leaning against the counter,

talking with Annie as she cinched her apron over her dress. William stopped short when Annie threw her head back and laughed. He hadn't heard her laugh wholeheartedly since he'd been in town, and the lilting melody of it sailed through the crowded diner to him, tinkering with his heart. It reminded him of times gone by, of high school, of their youth. She had been so fun-loving. Her eyes flashed with joy whenever she saw him, and it had always made him catch his breath. Like now.

"There he is," Brandon called out when he saw him. "Annie and I were reminiscing about Mrs. Peebles's class."

"How are you doing, man?" William replied, slapping Brandon on the back. "She was a character, that's for sure. Do you remember how she used to stare at me for long stretches, trying to catch me doing something wrong?"

"That's because you usually were." Brandon grinned.

"Some things never change," muttered Annie.

Their morning had been civil enough that William pretended not to hear her. "Where's my mom?"

"How should I know?" Annie coughed.

Brandon rested his chin in his hand, his eyes

shifting back and forth between William and Annie. She took off to wait on a table, and Brandon broke out into chuckling once she was out of earshot. "Well, it's definitely not in your head, man."

"Right?" William agreed, sliding onto a stool.

"She went from hot to cold in five seconds flat." Brandon really began to laugh. "Wow, man, that was terrible. I thought you were exaggerating before because you still liked her."

"What? No, you didn't."

"Oh, yeah. *Annie Curtis?* I thought you'd make a move by now."

"Why would I?"

"Why *wouldn't* you? I mean, now I can clearly see she can't stand you, but other than that…"

William frowned. Anybody would have gone for Annie Curtis ten years ago, but now she was so guarded, he couldn't imagine what an actual date with her would be like. Although she hadn't been guarded at all with Brandon. She apparently thought *he* was hilarious.

"Maybe you're attracted to her. She was giggling like a schoolgirl for you a minute ago."

Brandon slapped the counter and beamed.

"Nope. I'm going to pop the question to Kim this weekend."

"Really? Congratulations."

"Congratulate me after she says yes."

"Any reason why she wouldn't?"

"Only if you start spreading rumors that I'm interested in Annie—*that* could stall things."

William chuckled. "Nah. I'd never do that."

"She's cute though, right?"

"Kim?"

"Annie."

William hesitated to respond. Annie was bustling around the bar to fill drinks at the soda fountain.

"Annie," Brandon began. "How do you like having William hanging around here again?"

Annie's mouth set in a hard line as she kept filling soda glasses.

"Did you know William back in the day, Annie?" Mia asked, emerging from the kitchen.

"We went to high school together."

"It was more than that," Brandon corrected.

"Annie was pretty hard to miss," William added without thinking. His comment caused her head to jerk, giving him a once-over. The fierceness of her gaze surprised him, and a thrill surged through his body at having gotten such a reaction.

"Were you a heartbreaker, A?" Mia giggled.

Annie rolled her eyes at the question and hid her face behind a tipped soda glass, but Brandon was eager to supply an answer. "A good-looking woman is always a heartbreaker. Right, William?"

Annie's eyes rose to William, whose face broke into a lopsided grin at having been put on the spot. "Uh...a good-looking woman is always a heartbreaker," he repeated matter-of-factly.

Mia smiled mischievously at him.

"What?" he immediately demanded.

"Oh, nothing," Mia replied. "I can just picture you and Annie in high school."

"What does that mean?"

"I would bet *you* were the heartbreaker, William."

William spotted Annie's grimace as she rushed off to seat new patrons.

"It's funny how things turn out, isn't it?" Brandon whispered.

"How so?"

"Of all the guys back then, did you ever think she'd marry Sean?"

William shook his head. The fact still amazed him. She wouldn't have ever given Sean a second glance, but a lot had obviously happened since he'd left Chinoodin Falls... To the both of them.

CHAPTER EIGHT

ANNIE DROPPED HER purse on the back porch, plopped down next to Marjorie on the steps and leaned on her elbows.

"Long day, honey?" Marjorie asked, patting a hand on her knee.

"You could say that. You three are a sight for sore eyes."

The children frolicked in the sprinkler, taking turns jumping over it and back again. The temperature was barely warm enough to allow bathing suits, but the sun was shining and Annie was ready to relax for the night. As long as the children's lips weren't turning blue, she was happy if they were happy.

"I think I did something wrong," Marjorie said, wincing. Annie sat up in concern. "Sean stopped by a little while ago to see if you were home from work yet. While we were talking, I mentioned that I was called for jury duty."

"When?"

"I received the notice this afternoon. It

was on my mind, and before I could think, it slipped right out of my mouth. It wouldn't have been so bad, but Sean then said he'd arrange to get off work so he could take James on a trip during that time. I was so shocked at his suggestion, I didn't know what to say. I tried to backtrack, but the more I talked—" her voice broke "—the more adamant he became that he was going to do it."

Annie's body straightened into a fighter's pose. "He can't take James for a trip. I won't let him."

"I know, dear. Goodness, I know that. I feel awful that it would cause a point of contention for you. I shouldn't have opened my big mouth. You know how flustered he makes me."

"It's okay, Margie. You didn't do anything wrong." Annie wrapped an arm around her friend. "I'll take care of it."

"James heard us talking and was really upset about it," she explained hurriedly. "After Sean left I could tell he was getting worked up, so I distracted the two of them with popsicles and scooted them outside to play in the sprinkler."

"You're so good to us, Margie. Don't worry

about anything. Sean can make anyone flustered."

Marjorie patted Annie's leg again. "I would bury him in my backyard for you, Annie. You know I would."

Annie chuckled. "He's so stubborn he probably wouldn't stay put."

"I'd make him stay put. That man makes my blood boil."

Betsy and James bounded over, throwing their sopping-wet bodies into Annie's arms.

"Mom, what's for dinner?" Betsy asked.

"Uh, I haven't gotten that far yet."

Betsy nodded at James. "Pizza? Puh-lease?"

"I'd go pick it up," Marjorie offered.

Annie laughed. "Are you in on this, too?"

Marjorie winced again. "I may have suggested pizza for tonight. As long as you don't mind the company."

Annie nodded her approval. She smiled as Betsy and James cheered and followed Marjorie into the house to place the order, but her stomach was churning. She imagined Sean whisking James away for a week. Her chest tightened as she clasped the flesh of her neck in a panic. Her only option was to flat-out refuse his plan and deal with whatever repercussions came her way.

WILLIAM PULLED INTO his mom's driveway and was surprised to find Annie's car parked along the curb. He sat for a moment before cutting the engine. He hadn't been able to shake a mental image of Annie all day. Something about the way her eyes had flashed at him when he'd admitted she was a beautiful woman had sent his heart racing. He couldn't stop replaying it in his mind, deciphering the moment when her eyes had sparked. Whatever it took, he wanted to elicit that kind of response from her again.

Curious, he stepped through the back door as quietly as a puma on the prowl. If she and his mother were talking, perhaps he could catch a glimpse of her before her guard went up again. The hum of the television drew him to the family room, where Joyce was camped out on the couch with a cup of something steaming hot nestled in her hands. Quickly glancing around, he spotted Annie's jacket slung over the back of a chair.

But no Annie.

Navigating his way to the foot of the stairs, he strained to listen and began to climb only after the creak of floorboards above clued him in on Annie's presence. From the upstairs hallway, he spotted her poking around his bedroom. One delicate step after another, he stalked the distracted visitor and watched in fascination from the doorway as she breezed around his room, flitting over his belongings.

The corner of his mouth curled in amusement at having caught her snooping. How relaxed she seemed as she picked through the assorted coins and receipt stubs he had scattered across his dresser. Carefully crossing his arms over his chest, he leaned against the wall and cleared his throat.

"Need change for a dollar?"

Annie yelped, clasping her throat as she jumped back in alarm. "You startled me," she blurted out, the blood from her face drained in an instant. "Don't you know you shouldn't sneak up on people?"

"In my bedroom?" William smirked, sauntering forward. "Didn't hear me coming? That was your *first* mistake. You'd never make a good cat burglar."

"I'm not stealing anything," she protested, but he wagged a finger at her.

"Tsk, tsk, tsk. You need to have a better poker face than that. Second mistake—you underestimated your target. You wasted a good thirty seconds rifling through the nightstand when the good stuff is actually hidden inside the dresser."

The blood began to surge back into Annie's cheeks. "Let me guess. You hide your valuables in your underwear drawer. A little predictable, William, don't you think?"

William playfully opened his underwear drawer and rummaged a hand inside. "Aha! There it is! Phew, that was a close one. I'm glad I caught you when I did."

"Very funny," Annie mocked. "I don't care about the few dollars you have hidden in your balled-up socks."

"Folded, not balled," William corrected. "You really didn't peek in here?"

"Disappointed?"

William shut the dresser drawer and rasped his hand over his chin. "You snuck up here while an old woman was distracted in front of *Jeopardy!* Now, that's appalling."

"I didn't—"

"That is really low, Annie Curtis. She trusts you like the daughter she never had."

"William—"

"Which brings me to your *third* mistake— no believable reason for being in here."

Annie rolled her eyes. "I just stopped by for a minute to check in on your mom and bring her some pizza. I figured she can't do much on her hurt foot. I had to use the bathroom."

"*Now* who's being predictable?"

"I was about to go downstairs when something caught my eye."

"Otherwise known as, 'I decided to snoop around William's room for a while—'"

"*No.* I noticed the pictures you have hanging on your bedroom door. A bedroom door that was already open, by the way."

"And you casually strolled over to take a peek? I said a 'believable' reason, Annie. *To me.* My mother will believe anything."

"It's not my fault you can't believe the truth."

William peered at the photographs he had taped on the door as a teenager. They were curled and yellowed from Dennis's smoking, but still clinging to the door by delicate pinches of tape. It was the picture of himself and Annie that had most likely intrigued her. He was lying on his back in the grass, hands resting under his head while Annie's head lay on his stomach. She laughed for the camera. Brandon had snapped the picture just as a gust of wind had caught the linen of her skirt and had begun to blow it up, much to her surprise. She had framed the picture in purple metallic paper with heart stickers and taped it to his door for him. And there it still hung. He'd been so single-minded ever since he'd arrived back in his mother's house, he hadn't taken a second to study the collage. Most of his memories in this house weren't worth reliving.

He faced Annie, the little wrinkle between her eyes pronounced as she waited for his response. Perhaps her eyes were pleading with him to believe her story. Perhaps she was worried he'd embarrass her in front of Joyce. As he relished making her squirm more, he asked himself why she was really in his room. Had she lingered in front of his door, admiring the picture? Did she muse about how young and in love they looked? Was she searching for some remembrance of their time together? Had she been missing him? What?

"Were you visiting Mom?" he finally asked, venturing back down the hallway with Annie close behind.

"I had to make sure you were taking good care of her."

"Is that right?" William replied drily. "And what did you decide?"

"She's in good spirits," Annie said softly as they descended the stairs. "I couldn't even tell she'd hurt her foot."

William nodded. The truth was, he had begun to suspect there wasn't anything wrong with his mother's foot. The doctor hadn't found anything sprained or broken, and though she insisted it was swollen, he couldn't see it. It didn't really matter, though. If she needed to cook up a reason for a few guilt-free days off work, she probably needed them.

After Annie called goodbye to Joyce and grabbed her jacket and purse, they cut an angled line through the grass to the curb, her stride matching in time with his.

"I have a few appointments lined up for us tomorrow. We'll start bright and early," he said.

"Can't wait," Annie retorted while fumbling for her keys.

"Really?"

She hesitated. "I'm being polite, William. The whole idea of moving…"

"I think you'll like these locations, Annie. There's one on the website that looks promising."

"Okay." Unlocking her car door, she paused, her hand caught at the handle. "Will?"

"Yes?"

"I—" her voice faltered. "Nothing."

"You don't want to go tomorrow?"

"That's not it."

"Then what is it?"

Annie gave him a weak smile. "I had a good talk with your mom before you accused me of pillaging your room. She's didn't seem to know you're leaving in a few weeks. Why haven't you discussed your plans with her yet?"

"I don't have any plans."

"Then why leave again?"

William was confused. "Why are you so eager that I should stay?"

"I think of Joyce as my own mother, William."

"Is that all?"

"I care about her very much."

"I mean…is she the only one you care about?"

"What do you mean?"

"You may not have been pillaging my room, Annie, but you were interested in something up there. What were you looking for?"

Annie shook her head. "I'll see you tomorrow, William."

"Is that it?"

"I'm going to go before you accuse me of anything else tonight."

"Wait," he blurted. "Before you go, I know you won't like me doing this, but with the way you're standing there like that, I really can't help myself." Leaning toward her, he noticed she drew a sharp breath and her cheeks flushed red. He hovered, drinking in the image of big brown eyes that stared at him like a startled yearling's. The urge to brush his mouth over her hot, supple cheeks and on to her slightly parted lips struck him with abandon. Her fidgety body fell instantly motionless, admitting more than her words could ever convince him. He gently clicked the handle and eased open her door as she bit back a smile.

"What did we discuss about holding doors?"

He grinned. "I'm a slow learner."

She nodded and slid into the driver's seat, but she couldn't pull away quickly enough for him to miss her blush. It wasn't the response he'd been musing over all afternoon, but as he strutted back into the house, he figured it'd do.

WILLIAM SAT AT the end of the counter, running through the menu's cost sheet as the usual suspects enjoyed their second cup of coffee. He had one ear on their conversation, as it sounded a bit scandalous for Chinoodin Falls standards.

"That land is untouchable. No one should be able to build on it," Danny spouted. "Not one lousy soul. Otherwise what's the point of preservation?"

Joe nodded vigorously. "It's dirty dealings, I tell ya. It'll come out in the wash soon enough if *The Chinoodin Chronicle* keeps pressing the politicians for answers."

"Derek is supposed to be writing an entire series about it. He's the best investigative reporter they've got."

"He's the *only* one they've got. Where's he getting his information?"

"I'm not sure," Danny replied, sipping his coffee. "But he's got a good head on his shoulders. He'll sniff the dirty dog out."

William looked up as Brandon breezed in the front doors and spotted him.

"Hey, man," he said, taking off his suit jacket and laying it on the stool beside him. "I thought I'd catch you."

"I'm eavesdropping on the daily gossip."

"Anything good?"

"A company acquired rights to build on some land preservation? There's apparently a big write-up about it in the paper this morning."

"Ugh," Brandon groaned, flipping over his coffee cup for Mia to fill. "Someone got bought off big-time, and it's about to blow up in the mayor's face."

"Anyone you know?"

"Probably." He smiled. "I know everyone."

"So what's the story? I'm out of touch."

Brandon loosened his tie. "Madelyn Helmswith—"

"The Heiress of Chinoodin. I remember all the stories."

"Yeah. In her will she left a thousand acres to the city of Chinoodin Falls on the condition that they never sell it or build on it. She feared the Upper Peninsula would become commercialized and wanted to do her part to preserve the beauty of the land."

"Where's the land?"

"Just west of here. Mostly lakefront."

"A gold mine, in other words."

"*The Chinoodin Chronicle* discovered someone managed to find a loophole in Helmswith's will—"

"Don't tell me. And is now buying up her property?"

"A land developer out west just acquired the rights to buy the property and the mayor quietly approved it."

"But it's not so quiet now. Madelyn is probably rolling over in her grave."

"It became public a lot sooner than the mayor expected. With all the money she had, you'd think her will would be airtight. I need that coffee."

"How are you doing today, Brandon?" Mia chirped, handing him a menu.

"I think the question is, how are *you* doing, Mia? How many days left as a bachelorette?"

Mia gushed. "I have a calendar countdown hanging in my apartment and a million things to do before then. I just submitted the final numbers to the caterer."

"It's going to be the wedding of the year," Annie added, scooting past her to refill sodas.

"You never submitted your RSVP, Miss Curtis, so you'll never know."

Annie feigned a pout. "I told you I was coming, of course. Don't tell me you didn't mark me down."

William was only half listening as he noticed his mother enter the dining room, limping slightly with each step. He couldn't recall her hobbling the same way when they were home. It was the first time in days he felt inclined to help her, and he puzzled at that.

Apparently he wasn't the only one who noticed her limping.

"Hey dare, Joyce, I've gotta seat right next

to me," Earl offered, guiding her to his booth. "You go ahead and take a load off, darlin'."

William's mouth twisted as Joyce gleefully accepted his arm and slid in tightly against him. After a minute spent pondering what the appropriate defense was against a man flirting with his sixty-year-old mother, he heard his name.

"What about William?" Mia declared, rapping the counter in front of him. William jerked, scrambling to piece together the conversation that had led up to Mia's mischievous grin. Annie stood behind the counter, her eyes as wide as sand dollars.

"What?" he asked.

"Now, that *is* a good idea," Brandon agreed, waggling his eyebrows at William.

"What is?" William asked again, searching Brandon and then Mia for an explanation. As his eyes finally shifted to Annie, she ducked into the kitchen.

Mia leaned across the counter, resting her chin on her fists.

"Will, we have a proposition for you."

"Who's *we*?"

"Annie needs a date to my wedding, and we think you two would have a fun time together."

"*Who* thinks that?" William huffed, staring at Brandon, but his friend only pressed his coffee cup to his lips, gleaming at him out of the corner of his eye.

"My wedding is 'adult only,' so she can't bring the children, and that girl needs a night out desperately."

William screwed up his face. He did think Annie needed a night out, but he certainly wasn't the man to show her a good time, as she could barely stand him. True, they had shared a moment after he'd caught her in his bedroom…

"Listen, Mia," he began. "I think I'm already taking my mom."

"Your mom? Really?" Brandon jested.

"You want me to send her off by herself on a bum foot while I take a date?" William countered. "Come on."

Brandon spun his stool around and called to Joyce.

"Is William taking you to Mia's wedding?"

Joyce's face turned up in thoughtfulness.

"Well, I don't know, dear. It doesn't bother me none if he can't get a date."

"Oh, get serious," William grumbled. "It's not that I can't get a date."

"You can always count on your mother, William. Don't you ever forget that," Joyce said as Earl leaned over and whispered something in her ear that made her beam.

"Aw," Brandon teased, spinning back around. "You can always count on your—"

"Shut up," William choked out. "I just got back to town, and I don't know anybody."

"Mmm-hmm," Brandon mocked.

"Jerk."

"I thought your mom was going with Earl," Mia said.

"What?" William asked. It was news to him.

Brandon muffled a laugh. "Your mom has a date and is letting you tag along as the third wheel? Wow, man, it's really gone downhill for you since high school." Mia giggled, egging Brandon on further. "I never thought I'd see the day when William Kauffman couldn't get a date."

"Again, it's not that I *can't*—"

"I know, I know. I'm only messing with ya, buddy. You and your mom will have a lovely time together. Hopefully she lets you lead on the dance floor."

"Shut it."

"Do you think she'll ask you to drive so ⸺ ᵈ Earl can make out in the back seat?"

"Fine. We'll go together if you stop your jabbering."

"You and Annie?" Mia squeaked, clasping her hands together in delight.

William reluctantly nodded. Annie shot out of the kitchen and headed straight to the front door to seat newly arrived patrons.

"Annie!" Mia called.

"Hmm?" she replied, her lips pursed.

"William will be your date for my wedding. It starts at four o'clock, William, so you'll need to pick her up about 3:15 p.m. Okay?" Annie's eyes bored into Mia. "It's a date!" Mia called, speeding off to one of her tables.

Annie slowly pivoted to face William. "When Mia gets her mind set on something..."

"I'm sure."

"What?"

"I mean... I'd be happy to take you, Annie."

"Oh."

"If you want."

"I... That's fine with me."

"Good."

"Good."

Brandon's eyes gleamed.

"I'm glad everybody's good," he teased some more. "I'm good, too. Mia? You

She can't hear me, but I think she's probably good."

Annie rolled her eyes, smacking the swinging door on her way into the kitchen. Once she was out of sight, William slugged his friend hard on the arm.

"The fix was in, huh?"

"What?" Brandon chuckled. "Hey, man… it's all *good*."

ANNIE WAS RELIEVED to be alone. She smoothed the front of her apron several times and studied the plaster on the ceiling in her office, feeling as gawky as a thirteen-year-old. Even though her friend was happily engaged and bubbling with hearts and roses and tiny cupids, it didn't mean she had to play matchmaker and meddle in *her* love life…or lack thereof.

Annie paused at a mirror, tucking wispy stray hair behind her ears. As if she didn't have enough on her mind, now she had to anticipate an arranged date with William. But as she double-checked her reflection, she reminded herself that it wasn't a *real* date. They each needed to attend Mia's wedding, so they were driving together. He was a warm body, if not a handsome one, to sit next to in the church pew and eat dinner with. There would be light drinks, light conversation, light dancing…

Annie shook out her hands at the thought of slow dancing with William, his broad shoulders and strong arms… The other night when he'd leaned over to open her car door, she thought he was going to kiss her, and what would she have done?

She grazed her fingers delicately down her neck and again imagined him leaning in for a kiss. The daydream only delighted if he was kissing her because he wanted to and had been wanting to since the day he'd left Chinoodin Falls.

"Are you okay?" Mia asked, coming up behind her, her friend's voice dissolving her reverie.

"You," Annie said, spinning around.

Mia feigned an innocent, doe-eyed stare before a grin burst across her face. *"What?"*

"What was all of that back there? I don't need a date for your wedding."

"Girl, *yes* you do, and you're welcome."

"Since when have you and Brandon been in cahoots?"

"It was a team effort—I'll grant you that."

"I hope William doesn't think this is a real date."

"Uh, girl, I hope he *does*." Annie arched an eyebrow as Mia launched into a fit of giggles. "Loosen up, A. You need to have some fun." She pinned her hands behind her head and jostled her bosom toward Annie.

"Stop that," Annie whispered emphatically. "Somebody's going to see you."

"Who? William!" Mia called through laughter.

"You're ten years old. Did you know that?"

"Relax. He's talking to Brandon, although probably about you."

"Ugh."

Mia grabbed Annie by the shoulders and shook her gently.

"I want my wedding to be a giant party, and parties mean you come to have a *good time*. That's all this is, Annie. You can admit you need a good time and a good man by your side for a few hours."

Annie made a sour face and pulled away from Mia. She had forgotten what good times felt like. Somehow she would have to trick herself into thinking this wasn't a big deal, and that she wasn't on a forced date with the man who'd broken her heart twelve years ago.

"Annie," Mia continued. "Don't make too much out of it, okay?"

"I'm not," Annie protested, strolling past Mia. "You're the one making it a big deal." Suddenly Annie stopped short. "Except..." Her voice trailed off as her eyes widened with panic. "I don't have anything to wear."

CHAPTER NINE

ANNIE CASHED OUT her last customer of the afternoon, anxious to finish her shift and get out into the sunshine. She waved at Marjorie and the children as they passed in front of the diner, Betsy stopping to press her forehead against the window before puckering the glass. Annie didn't know what she'd do without Marjorie and never wanted to risk finding out.

"Mommy!" Betsy called, sprinting for her mother as soon as Marjorie opened the front door. She bounded into Annie's arms as James flung himself onto the heap and followed her declaration of excitement with, "I'm hungry."

"You came to the right place." Annie laughed, landing a kiss on top of Betsy's head.

James tugged on Annie's apron, pulling her focus to him.

"Can we go to the art fair?"

"Please, Mom?" Betsy begged, joining the cause. "I really have a taste for an elephant ear."

"When have you ever had an elephant ear?"

"You and Sean took me before."

Annie thought for a moment before recalling they had taken Betsy years ago, when she'd been expecting James. Sean had also punched his fist through the sliding glass door later that night. She'd all but repressed it.

"I can't believe you remember that."

"We saw the art fair on the way here, and the children spotted the elephant ear stand," Marjorie explained.

"Do you want to come with us?" Annie asked.

Marjorie shook her head. "Thanks, child, but I have too many errands to run."

"So we're going?" Betsy pressed.

"Please, Mom?" James chimed in, wrapping his arms around Annie's waist and peering up at her. She had to check her tips, but she could probably squeeze together a few loose dollars for an elephant ear. His innocent little face could always sway her.

"Okay, I suppose elephant ears win the day."

"I love elephant ears," William added, his voice light and cheerful.

"Me, too," Betsy sang, skipping around the counter to greet him. "Do you want to come with us?"

"No," Annie quickly interjected. "William has to work."

William shrugged. "I'm done for now. Gosh, I can't remember the last time I saw The Peninsula art fair."

"Come with us!" Betsy squealed. "*Please*, William."

James smiled up at William as he considered the invitation.

"How's your tummy, buddy?" he asked, squatting down to be eye level with the little boy. "The last time I saw you, you were nearly green."

"It's okay," he said, his voice small but his eyes glistening. William poked James lightly at the belly button, making him giggle and stick his belly out farther for another go.

"Children, go use the restroom before we leave. I have to…uh…check something in the office." She went to the back, hoping William would get distracted, and she could quickly wrangle the children out the door.

"Are you leaving?" Mia asked, picking up an order from the kitchen.

"Yep. See you tomorrow."

"Is William going with you?"

"What? No."

"You should invite him along. Break the ice a bit before the wedding."

"Break the…? Goodbye, Mia."

Annie grabbed her purse and returned to the dining room only to find William and the children waiting for her outside on the sidewalk.

"Ready?" William asked, putting on his sunglasses. Annie squinted at him, surprised he had enough nerve to tag along on her outing with the children. "You might want your sunglasses, you know."

"I have sunglasses," she quipped, fumbling through her purse for them as she located her keys. "I'm parked over here."

"There won't be any parking available this time of day. We can walk. Come on." And with the jerk of his head, he and the children were on their way. William cruised down the sidewalk like the Pied Piper of Hamelin as the children paraded behind him.

"Traitors," she mumbled as they giggled and bounced along. But as she hurried to match her strides with his, an inkling in her heart told her his company wasn't the worst thing that could happen to her children—or her— that day.

WILLIAM STROLLED BESIDE Annie as Betsy and James bounded all over the walk in front of them. The artists were tightly lined up in their designated spots, most of them in tented booths and all of them eager to make a sale. Clay sculptures, oil paintings, quilts, textiles, pottery, woodwork and metals adorned the rocky stretch of Lakeview Boulevard, with Lake Superior as the backdrop. Cobalt blue and generously peppered with white waves cresting, Lake Superior was the ideal backdrop to inspire the collection of creativity that had congregated that afternoon. While the breeze whipping off the lake kept the black fly swarms at bay, it also caused the artists to tamp down their tents and anything else that could be lifted from a sudden gust.

"Have you kept up your artwork since high school?" William asked, a booth of sketches triggering a memory.

"Not really," she replied. "I'm surprised you remember that."

"You drew something about Halloween, wasn't it? For one of the art shows?"

"It was for *El Dia de los Muertos*, the Day of the Dead. It's a Mexican holiday."

"I was close."

"Yes, that's pretty good." Annie chuckled. "Do you still sketch?"

"I haven't in a long time. I should, but life seems to get in the way."

"You were good, as I remember."

Annie smiled at him. "Thanks."

"Is that something you want for yourself?" he asked. "Time to sketch?"

"Sure. Time to sketch or paint or...create. Walking around down here reminds me of how much I miss it, but it'll be a while before I ever have the time again."

"We'll need a new sign for the diner. You could start there."

"What's wrong with the old sign?"

"Just that. It's *old*."

Annie meandered a ways, contemplating his suggestion. "I suppose I could paint something."

"I want to change the name, too."

"Why would you change the name? Pop's Place has been a fixture in this town for decades."

William stopped at a booth of photographs. "Pop's Place was Dennis's place. The new diner belongs to Joyce. New diner, new name."

"Does she have anything in mind?"

"She told me to pick it, so I have to come up with something good. No pressure, huh?"

Annie flipped through a stack of photographs of Lake Superior, as William thumbed through a stack of his own. The artist was a local and each picture of the Upper Peninsula was more majestic than the next. After a few moments, Annie plucked out a small print, holding it tenderly in her hands.

"That's a good one," he said, noticing. The full moon shining over the bay at night gave off an aura even he could recognize. "Do you like the moon?"

"Who doesn't?" Annie sighed. "My problems always seem so much smaller and insignificant when I stare up at a full moon, you know? Sometimes late at night when I can't sleep and my mind is reeling with thoughts, I load the children into the car and drive down to the lake to stare up at the moon."

"Why?"

"To marvel at it."

"Do you do that often?"

"More often than I'd care to confess. I'm lucky the children are deep sleepers."

"Even in the winter?"

Annie shut her eyes tightly. "Don't judge me," she winced with a grin. "I don't really do it anymore now that they're bigger. But…" She trailed off, biting her lip in hesitation. He grinned and raised his eyebrows.

"Let's hear it, Curtis."

"Well, sometimes even if it's really cold, I climb out onto the roof."

"In the snow and ice?" William asked. "You'll break your neck!"

"I know! I know. It's not one of my brightest ideas, but sometimes I can't help it. I'm drawn to it. Maybe somewhere else in the world there's another Annie who's staring up at the moon, too, and she doesn't have the problems I do. Maybe if I stare at the moon long enough, we'll trade places."

"An alternate life?"

She heaved a heavy sigh. "Have you ever wanted to trade places with a different version of yourself? A version who chose differently."

William felt something stir inside him as he studied her. In all his life he hadn't ever been drawn to another woman the way he had been to Annie. She'd hung her heart around his neck a long time ago, and as he admired her long black eyelashes batting like butterfly wings, something surged within the depths of his soul. A longing to be near her again gripped him; he wanted to hold her. She'd been wounded—that much was evident—and he ached at the realization that it had been his fault. His voice rose slowly as he carefully chose his words. He had to get this right.

"I never wanted to leave you, Annie," he began, his voice paced with caution. While she showed little reaction to his admission, her fingers halted over the print. He continued. "That night, when I was supposed to come to you, Dennis and I got into it…*again*…and this time… I couldn't take any more from him—I snapped."

"Why did it have to be that night?" she whispered. "If you had to run away, why didn't you run to me?"

"If I had a logical reason, I'd tell you, Annie, but something inside me needed to fight back and win."

"And did you win?"

"I'm not sure, but it was a relief to get out from under Dennis's thumb. But you…" He gently brushed a tear off her cheek as she met his gaze. "You were the only good thing I had in my life back then, Annie. If all your troubles now are because of me…"

"I waited on the porch for five hours."

"Five hours," he repeated softly, studying the supple curve of her cheek. The image of her there, crying when he didn't show, made his gut twist.

"I did. But you never called or wrote or *anything*. You vanished into thin air, leaving me to wonder if I had imagined your feelings for me."

Annie turned back to the photograph as William gently touched her hand.

"I was in a bad place."

"How bad?" she asked, pleading for an explanation he could never give her. He shook his head.

"Is it too late to apologize?"

"No, it's never too late. I guess it's no use wondering what might have been."

"Do you still?"

She wiped another tear off her cheek and shook her head. His gut twinged as he found himself hoping it was a lie. He'd thought of her over the years, but only as the pretty girl who had loved the person he had been. As he had trudged through his twenties and a pattern of bad decisions, pining for her had been too painful. He'd learned to shut her memory out of his heart early on. But now, since arriving back in Chinoodin Falls, something deep in his soul had begun stirring. It was a yearning to connect again. How many years had he cut his own tracks across the globe, looking out for only himself and his best interests? He'd done it to escape the past, to protect himself and protect his heart. He had needed to feel free, to cast all others aside while he convinced himself he didn't care. He couldn't care. He could face the whole world all on his own. And now…

He fished his wallet from his back pocket.

"I'd like to buy that for you," he said, counting through his cash.

She quickly tucked the print into the stack. "You don't have to do that," she muttered, but William leaned over her and retrieved it.

"How much for the small print?" he called to the artist.

"Forty-five for the lady."

"See? It's meant to be," William said, handing over exact change. Annie reached again to stop him.

"William, I don't need anything from you…" But before she could finish her protest, he clasped her outstretched hand tightly in his and closed the gap between them. Her eyes widened in surprise, her breath catching under the sharpness of his stare.

"Anyone who loves the moon as much as you do deserves to have this at her fingertips. This way you'll always have the moon with you."

Even if I can't be with you, too, he thought, a sinking melancholy banking against the inside of his chest. He placed the print in her hands as her eyes searched his.

"Are you in a bad place now, William?"

"What do you mean?"

"Breezing back into town and then readying to leave again... What haven't you told me?"

He paused, his hands grazing over hers before pulling away. "Nothing."

Her wide eyes slowly narrowed. "*Something.*"

"You and I haven't gotten off on the right foot, Annie, and I'd like to make a fresh start with you."

"A fresh start?"

"If it's possible."

"I don't really know what to say."

"Consider this gift a peace offering for all the times I should have been with you, staring up at the moon. I really wish you would."

"You missed a lot, William."

"I know..."

"And to suddenly start a friendship now..."

"I'm sorry. I should have been here."

"No. You should have called me instead of dropping off the face of the earth. I didn't know what happened to you. I assumed you didn't care about me anymore."

"I always cared," William whispered. "I *care.*"

Annie clutched the photograph to her chest.

He wanted her to believe him. *Needed* her to. Even if they couldn't continue a friendship initiated years ago, he needed to calm the squalls of regret in his heart. If he left Chinoodin Falls as no more than her acquaintance, he needed to know she believed his words. He needed to know she still saw something of the man he once was and still believed in him. If she could acknowledge *that man*, then perhaps he was still in there, even if somewhere very hidden and buried with mistakes.

"Then let me ask you one more thing, William."

"Shoot."

She drew a deep breath as the sun emerged and caught each fleck of gold scattered throughout her brown eyes. "Can I trust you?"

His throat cinched. Images from his past flooded over him as he recalled nights of binge drinking and blackouts. He couldn't tell her everything without risking the small gains they'd made over the last couple of days. For now he just wanted her in his corner. He needed her there. Her presence left him aching for more, like nourishment for his soul.

"Always," he whispered.

"We found the elephant ears!" Betsy called

as she and James scampered up, their little faces pink and dewy.

"Lead the way." William winked as the children each took one of his hands. But it was Annie who glided to the front of the pack, setting the pace through the crowd to the elephant ear stand. When she peeked back over her shoulder at him, a glisten in her eyes took his breath away and for the first time in a long time, he felt like he was walking on air.

ANNIE SETTLED THE children at the kitchen table with snacks and crafts before leading Mia up to her bedroom. She wanted to talk to someone about what had happened at the art fair, but the embarrassment of exposing her feelings about it made her stay tight-lipped in front of Betsy and James. After all, she wasn't exactly sure how she felt about things. William had apologized for leaving her when they were teens and genuinely seemed remorseful. As much as she'd desperately craved to hear it, she struggled with where they could go from here. Mentally batting around the prospect of a friendship with William, she'd spent the night staring at her new moon picture and imagining...

It was ridiculous. She was a mother of two.

William was leaving Chinoodin Falls. She'd had her heart broken enough times to know when to quit when she was ahead. Stay focused. Be responsible. Hold her cards close.

She sprawled out on the edge of her bed as Mia dropped two bags on the floor and began pulling out the contents.

"You're a little smaller than me, so you can have your pick of the lot," Mia said, holding out a black strapless cocktail dress and a red halter that fell above her knee.

Annie scrunched up her face, holding the two dresses as if they were about to bite her.

"Do you have anything a little less…"

"Amazing?" Mia laughed.

"That wasn't exactly what I was going for."

"You have a dainty little figure under there, A, and you need to show it off once in a while."

Annie dropped to the floor to rummage through Mia's bags herself, but every dress was short or formfitting. Mia was a young twenty-four, and Annie felt much older than her thirty years.

"Do you have anything in here someone my *age* could wear?" Annie asked, shaking her head.

"Whatever self-deprecating inner monologue you have running away in your head, girl, you need to give it up *now*. I'm not leaving until I get you into one of these fabulous dresses."

"Ans? Are you up here?" Karrin peeked around the corner before proudly handing over a purple gift bag.

"Did you get it all?" Mia chirped.

Karrin snickered. "And then some."

"What is this?" Annie asked, peering into the bag.

"Goodies." Karrin popped open a bottle of wine. "Hair color, makeup, nail polish, strapless bra—"

"Are these falsies?" Annie gasped, extracting two pads resembling raw chicken cutlets and wiggling them in the air.

"I didn't know what you might need for the dress," Karrin howled, dodging a chicken cutlet.

"It's a wedding, you guys. It's not *my* wedding."

"That doesn't mean you can't look your best. As a woman nearing my forties—"

"Nearing?" Mia coughed. Karrin raised an eyebrow and sipped her wine before beginning again.

"Fine. As a woman *dipping a toe* into my early forties, I can personally attest to the miracle of hair color and under-eye concealer. They are a girl's best friends."

"And falsies." Mia giggled.

"I'm *not* wearing those," Annie protested, throwing the other cutlet at Mia. "I'm not sure I can even wear these dresses."

"Yes you can, A!" Mia assured her, holding out the red dress. "This is the one I really want to see you try on. Puh-lease?" Annie scowled before reluctantly yanking the dress out of Mia's hands. Karrin poured Annie a glass of wine while she slipped into the dress and cautiously stepped in front of the full-length mirror hanging on her closet door.

"Shoes!" Mia shrieked, flinging Annie her nude open-toed high heels. Annie wrangled the shoes on and stood awkwardly in front of the mirror, scrutinizing her reflection.

"It's too much," she whimpered, simultaneously trying to pull up the front of her dress while tugging down the bottom.

"It's supposed to hang like that," Mia assured her. "You're allowed to wear a hemline above your calf, you know."

"I'm too old to wear this. I'm a mom."

"You're not *his* mom," Karrin snickered, taking a sip of wine. Annie stuck out her tongue before considering herself in the mirror. After spending time with William at the art fair, she had been feeling… Well, that was part of the problem. She didn't know. He'd touched her hand and bought her a present and told her he'd wished he could have been with her to stare at the moon. For her entire adult life as she'd given her heart away to Julian and then Sean, secretly she'd always desperately missed William. Her heart had flown to him years ago and when he'd promised she could always trust him, she realized she had never ever gotten it back.

"Mom, you look hot." Betsy giggled. Annie spun around to discover her daughter gawking at her from the hallway.

She gasped. "*Hot?* Where did you learn that word?"

"It's true, A," Karrin agreed. "Don't try on any more dresses. That is the winner."

"No. I'd rather wear this one," Annie whined, pulling the only formal dress she owned out of her closet: a peach-colored floral sundress that fell midcalf.

"*No,*" Mia moaned, prying it from Annie's fingers.

"It's a pretty dress," Annie objected, hoping to rally Betsy for moral support.

"I like the red one much better, Mom."

"Everything else is coming with me so you can't chicken out later," Mia ordered, frantically gathering the peach sundress, along with the rest of the dresses and shoes.

Karrin retrieved a falsie from the floor and held it out for Annie. "Speaking of chicken…"

"What is that?" Betsy asked, carefully reaching for the strange flabby pad Karrin wiggled in the air.

"No!" Annie laughed, snatching both pads and tucking them in her sock drawer. "You got me in a halter dress, and that's as much as I'll do!"

"Now take it off so I can color your hair," Karrin ordered. "Betsy, would you grab us an old towel?"

Annie stood in front of the mirror for a moment and took a dainty sip of wine, wondering what William would think of her. With the dress and heels and coloring her grays away, she was doing a running leap outside her comfort zone. But as she gazed at herself in the mirror, even she had to admit she didn't look half bad.

CHAPTER TEN

WILLIAM HUNG UP with Arnold in time to wave goodbye to Mia. She wafted her engagement finger in the air while making a grandiose exit out of the diner.

"When next you see me, I'll be Mrs. Mia Howards!" she sang before letting out an excited whoop and holler.

"*She's* excited," William uttered with an exaggerated eye roll. Annie sighed as Mia disappeared around the corner.

"I hope she knows what she's doing."

"Do you have any reason to think she doesn't?"

"I meant," Annie quickly continued, "I hope it's what she wants."

"Maybe it will be."

"Maybe."

William slid the buyer's sheet he'd picked up earlier that day across the table.

"Speaking of getting everything we want,

check out this place. Arnold says the sellers are highly motivated."

Annie scanned the sheet before offering a half shrug.

"Maybe."

"Maybe," William said, sliding back the sheet. "You're a difficult woman to impress, Annie Curtis. Did you know that?"

"I've grown more discerning with age."

"Discerning or scared?" he teased. Annie's eyes narrowed, making him instantly regret his words.

"Scared? *Of what?*" she demanded.

"Take it easy, Annie. Jeez. I was only kidding."

"I'm not scared, William Kauffman. You're the one pushing things along faster than they should go."

"With the diner?"

Annie's throat went dry, his question catching her off guard. The discernment in his eyes read as much into his question as in how she fumbled to answer.

"Of course with the diner. What else would I have meant?"

"You're oscillating with such a fury over there, I wasn't sure we were still talking about real-estate hunting."

Annie willed her cheeks to not flush under his scrutiny. He planned to make all the changes to Joyce's restaurant and her life, and then abandon her to navigate a new normal on her own. It wasn't a ridiculous reaction for her to be a little upset about it. But as she sputtered to answer him, she knew the person she was most concerned with was herself.

"And just what is it you think I'm scared of?"

William contemplated her question for a moment before playfully continuing. "Taking a risk?"

"I've taken plenty of risks," she spat on her way to the end of the counter. "And don't you laugh at me."

William ran his hand down his face. "I wouldn't dare," he called after her.

Annie cashed out a few customers as she noticed Earl stumble into the diner while fumbling with his hat. Taking it off and tugging it on again, he nodded briskly when he spotted Annie watching him.

"Earl?" Annie called. "Did you forget something?"

"No," he replied, his stance and voice equally stiff.

"Can I get you something to drink?"

"Uh…no."

"How about a piece of pie?"

"Well," he replied. "I was tinkin' about dat."

"What did you decide?"

"I'll let you know."

Before Annie could press him further, his face broke into a grizzly grin. Joyce had hobbled out into the dining room and stopped short in front of him.

"Fancy seeing you here, Earl." She smiled warmly.

"I'm trying to decide on pie," he said, strumming his calloused fingers on the counter. "Whatdya like?"

"Apple is my favorite."

"Ah, yes. Dare's nothing more American than a slice of ol'-fashioned apple pie."

"With a slice of melted cheese on top."

"Is dat right?" he said as Joyce continued to the front door. "Now where are ya off to dare, Joyce?"

"I need a little fresh air to lift my spirits. Would you care to join me?"

"I could do with some fresh air myself," he said, moving ahead of her to hold open the door.

"Earl had better not end up as my new dad," William said with a groan once they were out of earshot, but Annie's face had softened at the sight of them.

"Don't say that. They're sweet together."

"I guess."

"She could do worse, you know."

William nodded. He had to agree with her. Joyce could do a lot worse—and she had.

WILLIAM PARKED IN the rear and followed a crowd of college-aged students through the back door of The Grove. A Chinoodin staple since William's youth, The Grove offered more than food and drinks on Thursday nights. By ten o'clock the place was crowded with folks ready to sing along with Snips and Polly, a husband and wife duo who covered classic rock songs armed with a couple of guitars, a harmonica and a mental repertoire long enough to impress any musical aficionado. He entered the room, spotted Brandon at the bar and jogged through the crowd to meet him.

"Another round?" William asked, signaling to the bartender while easing onto a barstool.

"I'm ahead by two," Brandon said, his eyes glassy from drinking.

"Then I need to catch up."

"Making any headway?"

"With Annie?"

Brandon chuckled. "I meant Pop's Place, but we can talk about her instead if you'd like."

William gave a half shrug. "We put in an offer on a new location. Hopefully it'll pass inspection. Long day?"

Brandon forced out a deep breath, swirling the last swigs of beer in his glass. "You could say that."

"Politics are slimy, man."

"That's especially true when you work with worms. I'm half inclined to go to *The Chinoodin Chronicle* myself."

"What's wrong?" William turned to study his friend and strained to hear him amid the boisterous crowd.

"I think the mayor is taking kickbacks."

"Is that news?"

"It is if it's as bad as I suspect it is. Someone in the office is working both sides."

"Anything to do with the land preservation?"

A microphone powered on, a brief static cutting through the crowd's excitement as Snips strummed a few notes while tuning his guitar.

"Speaking of worms." Brandon nodded to Sean, who had moseyed in through the back entrance. He squinted when he noticed them and lumbered over, much to William's disappointment. Calmly sipping his beer, William stared straight ahead, but Sean wasn't the type to be ignored.

"What are you doing here?" he challenged, towering over William; his breath reeked of whiskey. William slowly cocked his head.

"Excuse me?"

Sean sneered a few vulgarities under his breath before slamming his palms on the bar, making the bartender and nearby patrons snap their heads in alarm.

"Hey, sweetie," he bellowed. "Take your time over there. I don't need a drink anytime tonight."

The bartender gave Sean the once-over. "You've had enough. I think you'd better move along."

"No, thanks." Sean cackled. "How about you stick to your business and pour me a Jack and Coke?"

"Bouncing you is my business," she replied. She had more weather on her face than the three of them combined and had the easy saunter of someone who knew how to handle things.

"You want me to come over this bar and fix it myself?"

"Five hundred dollars bail, and a criminal record says you won't," Brandon jested.

Sean gnashed his teeth for a moment, pondering his options.

"Give me something for the road, sweetie."

"My liquor license ain't worth you."

Sean scoffed at her dismissal and turned around to face the stage, leaning back heavily against the bar and uncomfortably close to William.

"'Free Bird'!" he yelled over the murmur of the audience. William took a swig of his beer and jabbed his elbow into Sean's side.

"Are you trying to start somethin'?" Sean growled.

"You're the one standing so close, sweetie."

"Like hell I am. Brandon, you'd better keep an eye on your buddy here or he'll hate the day he ever met me."

Brandon hurried a few gulps of his beer. "Sean, old pal—" he wiped his mouth on the back of his hand "—everyone hates the day they met you."

Sean lurched after Brandon, but William anticipated him, spinning on his stool and shoving Sean to the ground, thanks to his own momentum.

"Timber!" Brandon called as Sean sprawled

out on the floor for several seconds before hustling to get up. William pointed to the bartender to call the police, but the phone was already pressed to her ear. He and Brandon scrambled to their feet, knowing full well that Sean was going to come up off the floor swinging.

Sean stood hunched over, trying to catch his breath as the crowd anxiously scattered.

"I called the cops!" the bartender yelled, his voice forceful, but it did little to squelch Sean's aggression. The slits of his eyes rose to meet William's gaze and he charged like a linebacker into William's gut, toppling him to the ground. It wasn't his smartest decision of the day, but William knew this was one fight he had to win.

ANNIE PARKED HER car at Sean's apartment complex and eyed the front doors, which loomed like the gateway to her next nightmare. James slunk silently in the back seat, staring down at the toy steamliner clasped in his little hands.

"Your dad wants to see you for a couple hours, and then I'll come right over and pick you up."

"You won't be late?" he asked, his voice no louder than a mouse's squeak.

"I would never be late. *Never.* Maybe he'll order a pizza and let you watch cartoons the whole time."

James caught his lip between his teeth, carefully holding his toy boat. Her eyes fell over his mop of wavy hair and how delicate his profile was, still that of a little boy. Her nerves tinged with concern, an ache only a mother could suffer.

After Sean buzzed them up, they found his apartment door swung open with him sprawled on the couch, his back to them. James peered up at her and she slipped her hand around his shoulder reassuringly and led him along. They rounded the corner of the couch to face Sean, and James broke free and crept to the far side of the kitchen table.

"What's your plan for today?" she asked.

Sean didn't break his gaze from the television.

"I'm not a cruise director," he said.

"Are you staying here?"

"Probably."

"James hasn't had lunch yet. Do you have anything in the fridge?"

"It's only ten thirty, Annie. I know how to take care of the kid."

"I didn't know if you had groceries or not."

"I'll order a pizza if it comes to it," he grumbled.

Annie eyed his profile carefully. His hair was disheveled and his cheek reddish. The button-down shirt he normally wore to work was wrinkled and untucked, and his dress trousers were all scuffed up. She quickly scanned the apartment. Aside from the fact he'd apparently slept in his clothes, the place was spotless.

"Are you okay, Sean?"

"Never better."

"You don't seem…"

"James! Tell your mother to quit her worrying," he burst out, never taking his eyes off the television as he reached for a large plastic tumbler and took a sip. "She's giving me a pounding headache."

James flashed his doe eyes at her from under the table.

"Are you drinking?" she whispered.

"What does it look like?" Sean replied, tipping the tumbler to his lips.

"You know what I mean."

Sean readjusted on the couch rather than

answer. As he turned his head slightly, she noticed his profile wasn't right.

"What happened to your nose?"

"You dropped the kid off, Annie, so *see ya.*"

Annie hesitated before walking to the door and quietly motioning to James to join her. As he scooted out from under the table and inched toward her, Sean turned and spotted them out of the corner of his eye.

"Why don't you take the day for yourself, Sean," Annie began as he leered over the back of the couch. "Get in the car, James."

"You'd better stay right where you are," Sean ordered, stumbling to his feet, but Annie guided James out, sending him on his way down the stairs. As she turned back to face Sean, she spotted that his right eyebrow was bandaged, and his lip tattered and swollen.

"Sean, what happened?"

"None of your business."

"It is my business if I'm going to leave my child with you."

"*Our* child. You seem to need frequent reminders of that." As he stumbled closer, Annie caught a whiff of the whiskey sweating from his pores.

"You're drunk." She cringed, unable to mask her disgust. "I'm not doing this today."

"Hungover," he tried to correct. "You can't keep me away from my son, Annie."

"Drunk…hungover… I don't care, Sean. You can't take care of James when you're like this."

"Quit babying him for crying out loud. I'm his father, and I have to do my job."

Annie scoffed as she turned toward the hallway. "Which is what exactly?"

"Toughening him up."

"That's not what fathers do, Sean."

"How would you know? Your own dad bailed on you when you were, *what*? Ten? Or did you forget that?"

"Sleep it off," she called. Her throat stung with emotion as she hurried down the stairs.

"Then your boyfriend knocked you up and *bailed*," Sean jested, thundering down the stairs behind her. "I'm the best thing that ever happened to you, baby, and you know it."

Annie was relieved to find James already in the car as she reached the driver's side. But before she could crack open the door, Sean threw his weight at it and slammed it closed again.

"He's trying to turn you against me, you know."

"Who?" Annie gasped, surprised at how brittle she sounded.

"I don't want you seeing that swabbie anymore. I've seen how he stares at you. Don't deny it."

"I'm not leaving James with you when you're like this," she repeated. Panic scrambled through her as she heard the fear in her voice and tried to smooth it over. "Take today for yourself, and I'll talk to you later, Sean."

"Do you think I'm going to let you waltz away from here with your nose in the air?"

"Sean…"

"This is *my* family. I won't let him move in on you."

"Whatever you think has happened…"

"I know him!" Sean's voice reverberated off the walls of the building. Her eyes darted in a frenzy, searching for anyone who could come to her aid. "He can't fool me, and neither can you." Her only thought was of James, cowering in the back seat, likely burying his face in his hands to will the scene away. This madness has to end, she said to herself. How much more could one little boy take?

"Stop it, Sean." She raised her chin.

"You think you're better than me?"

"I think you're drunk, so everything makes you angry."

"Hungover!"

Annie steeled herself. "Stop, Sean. You're frightening him."

"Hey!" Sean yelled, pounding on the car window. "Get back up there, James!"

"Can we help you, ma'am?"

Annie shouted a silent thank-you to the sky as two men pulled up in a black sedan.

"I'm trying to get in my car," she called out, the quiver in her voice skimming out past Sean and onto the wind.

"Do you need help with that?" one of the men asked, a dead stare set on Sean.

Sean's stance softened as he eased back off the car door, raising his hands in mock surrender. Annie slipped inside her car, whispering thanksgiving under her breath. As she locked the doors and started the engine, Sean gave a finger waggle to her and James before setting his jaw and staggering back to his apartment.

ANNIE FIDDLED WITH the frayed edges of her napkin when she heard a gentle rap at the screen door.

"Honey, are you okay?"

Annie bit her lip as Marjorie let herself in and eased into a kitchen chair next to her. She gently rested her aged hand on top of hers.

"You tellin' that napkin who's boss?" she

asked with a wink, but Annie's face scrunched as the tears fell hard and heavily. "What's wrong, sweet pea?"

Annie glanced over her shoulder at the children, who were hypnotized in front of the television, before turning to her friend.

"James," she managed to say between sobs that wouldn't dissipate fast enough for her to speak the words she needed to.

"James?" Marjorie whispered, surrounding her in a hug of faint lavender and facial powder. Marjorie smelled of all things feminine, all things comforting. Annie longed for the mother who couldn't be with her, but soothed the wounded child within herself, thanks to Marjorie's tender embrace.

"I can't do this anymore."

"Sean?" Marjorie supplied. Annie accepted a wad of napkins and buried her nose in them. "What happened, child?"

"It doesn't matter," she whimpered. "It's always the same. It's always hardest on James."

"Is there anywhere you could go? Do you have family in another part of the country?"

Annie shook her head, covering her face with her hands.

"It's just us."

"And *me*," Marjorie replied, wrapping an

arm around her shoulder. "I'm always here for you, no matter what you need."

"I know. It's one of the reasons we've stayed."

Marjorie sat back in contemplation. "Do you want me to take the children out of the house while you're at the wedding later?"

The wedding. She hadn't thought about it since arriving at Sean's apartment.

"*No.* I can't tonight."

"Of course you can. Don't let him rob you of this, too."

"I need to stay home with James tonight."

"Even if I take the children swimming for the afternoon?"

"Swimming!" Betsy called from the family room.

"How on earth did you hear me from all the way over there?" Marjorie laughed as Betsy hurried into her arms. James quietly followed, hesitating at Annie's side as she wiped her eyes.

"Are we going swimming, Mom?" he asked.

"Do you want me to take you?" She wrapped her arms around his little body as he shook a reply into her shoulder.

"Marjorie can take us."

"Your mother has to take a shower and get dressed now. You two go find your swimsuits and towels."

"I can't tonight, Marjorie," Annie sighed. "I really can't."

"You go get in the shower, child, and hurry up. He'll be here in less than an hour."

"Are you going to wear that pretty dress you showed us?" Betsy asked, pivoting from one foot to the other.

Annie groaned. "Don't you want me to go swimming instead?"

"No." James smiled. "I want to see you in your dress."

"Really?"

"Dress!" Betsy squealed.

"Majority rules," Marjorie declared, pulling Annie to her feet and swatting her on the backside. "Get your tuckus in the shower and wash the day off you."

Annie trudged upstairs and locked herself in the bathroom. She sat on the edge of the bathtub and started the hot water, listening to it pelt the side of the shower. As her face warmed to the steamy mist, she contemplated how difficult it would be to take the night off from worrying. Perhaps she could hit the pause button on her problems and celebrate with her friend on her wedding day. With James and Betsy safely cared for by Marjorie, she could have a drink and talk and dance…

With William.

Her mind lifted from the fog Sean had settled over her as she pictured William's face. She'd felt loved once. Safe once. How she'd wished to return to those days again when William had been the only person, the only thing, the only future she could see.

Annie tested the water. It scorched her skin. Just what she needed. She yearned to spend an evening enjoying herself, but as she slipped into the shower and dipped her head under the water, she worried attending this wedding with William was just another mistake she would make with a man.

WILLIAM PEERED INTO the rearview mirror and inspected the damage. His cut lip wasn't too obvious. He poked a finger on the purple bruise donning his cheekbone, still quite tender and pronounced. There was no camouflaging that beauty.

He didn't want to lie to Annie about how he'd enjoyed brawling with her ex-husband, but in order for the two of them to make it through the evening, he'd have to practice some serious misdirection. He'd already had a close call the night before, cracking Sean in the nose and hightailing it out of the bar before the police had arrived. Luckily Sean was smart enough to recognize it was in his best interest to flee, too. After all, he'd started the fight. But as William gave the bruise one last poke in the mirror, he knew the outcome the night before could have been much worse for him if he'd been arrested. It wouldn't have taken long for him to show up on Denver's radar and for Denver to then show up in Chinoodin Falls. He couldn't afford to press his luck again, even if the temptation to sock Sean in the jowl presented itself.

Before he could climb the steps to the front porch, he heard giggles from the other side of the screen door.

"Mom's not ready yet!" Betsy informed him. With the cheeriness of a puppy dog, she swung the screen door open as James ran down the walk to him, stopping short with a meek grin.

William rocked back on his heels. "Are you my welcoming committee?"

Betsy giggled, wafting her beach towel to lead the way into the house. "Come in! Come in, William!"

"You have to move out of his way first," a petite woman with smiling eyes directed. After introducing himself to Marjorie, William settled on the edge of the couch with Betsy and James perched attentively at his knee.

"Do you like boats?" James asked, tugging at William's pant leg.

"He was in the Navy, James," Marjorie reminded him.

"James *loves* boats," Betsy explained with an eye roll as James proudly presented a battleship replica. William turned the toy over in his hands, aware of its value to the little guy.

"Do you ever watch the steamliners dock?" William asked.

"He loves that, too!" Betsy exclaimed. "He could sit there for hours and hours."

"That's enough, Bets," Marjorie scolded. "Let James speak for himself."

William winked at Betsy before shifting his attention back to James. Instead of answering, James sprinted off and returned with three more ship replicas.

"He has hundreds," Betsy said, before slapping a hand over her mouth and shrugging apologetically at Marjorie.

"More like a dozen," Annie corrected, descending the stairs.

William's eyes fell down the length of Annie's body. He kicked himself for not bringing her flowers. With the dress she was wearing, this was a date. It was a red-hot, hugging-her-in-all-the-right-places, making-him-catch-his-breath *date*. She needed flowers—a bouquet. He ran his hand through his hair while trying not to gawk.

"You're beautiful," he said.

Annie brought her fingers to her collarbone, a delicate modesty coming over her. "So are you."

"I haven't seen your hair down before."

She hesitantly flipped the curtain of chocolate-brown curls off her shoulder. He'd only ever seen her hair tied in a messy knot with sad wisps framing her face. She grinned sheepishly.

"No?"

"Not since high school."

"Oh."

"It's pretty."

"Yeah?"

William grinned. He generally didn't care for surprises, but knowing he'd be cozied up all night with Annie Curtis, who was model-ling that dress, he eagerly anticipated the evening stretched out before them. As she kissed her children goodbye, he couldn't tear his eyes from her, even at the risk of making a fool of himself in front of Marjorie.

"What happened to your cheek?" Annie asked as he opened the passenger-side door for her. He scrambled for a reply.

"Clumsy" was all he could manage before climbing in and speeding them on their way.

"Did you fall?"

"Kind of," he said, considering the sliver of truth in his reply.

"There must have been a full moon out last night, because…"

"Hmm?" he asked as Annie gently smoothed the hem of her dress over the top of her thigh.

"I had to talk to Sean this morning, and he…"

William plastered on the most innocent expression he could manage. He clutched the top of the steering wheel and stared at the road.

Annie studied him carefully. He could feel her scrutinizing the side of his face, but just as he was about to fess up about the brawl, she giggled. He jerked his head, puzzled, and when he did she tossed her head back in a laugh.

"What's so funny?"

"I can't help it," she admitted with another peal of laughter. Her eyes twinkled as tears glistened in the corners.

He basked in her delight, having finally

gotten this reaction from her. It had been a long time. As her curls caught all colors of the sun and her laugh crashed over his senses— jubilant, melodious. He wished he could bottle the sound. The few seconds that he basked in the warm intensity of her amusement could last a man a thousand years.

"I've had a long day and that struck me in the right spot. You have no idea how much I needed that." Her laughter subsided with a heavy sigh, her mocha-colored eyes suddenly molten with mischievousness. She covered her lips with the tips of her fingers as she paused to explain. "I think Betsy did a number on you."

"What?"

She reached out and plucked a daisy from his hair, holding it out for him to see.

"Was that from Betsy?"

Annie nodded and rolled down her window a few inches, flicking the flower to the breeze.

"She marks people."

"She what?"

"No, it's actually a compliment. If she likes something or someone, she marks them with a feather or flower or something."

"Where did she come up with that?"

"Oh, she's done it for a while."

William stole a glance at Annie grinning at him, her eyes seemingly unwilling to fall away.

"So she likes me, huh?"

"Yes, I assume so."

William nodded with satisfaction and hoped Betsy wasn't the only one.

CHAPTER ELEVEN

ANNIE DUCKED INTO the bathroom at the reception hall to check her mascara.

"Did you tear up, too, dear?" Joyce asked, following her inside.

Annie met her boss's gaze in the mirror. "Weddings always get me. Mia was a vision."

"And so excited. Have you ever seen a happier bride?"

Annie hadn't. "I wish the best for them. I really do."

Joyce traced the edge of Annie's shoulder as her eyes crinkled.

"It's nice to see you out with my William."

"We only came together to keep from going stag," Annie explained, an excuse she had repeated to herself ever since the fix up.

"Not in that dress, dear. You really are a beauty."

Annie turned in surprise. It had been such a long time since she'd felt worthy of such a compliment.

"Really?"

"Oh, honey." Joyce snickered. "Please go easy on him. He couldn't take his eyes off you during the entire ceremony."

Annie blushed, but inside her stomach turned somersaults. If William was looking at her with any type of longing, she had to resist any urge that might lead him on. She had two little children to think about, and she didn't know what Sean would do if he learned she was on a date with another man. She'd made so many bad decisions in the past, she had to keep a clear head when it came to men…particularly William.

"Was it something I said, dear?"

Annie snapped her attention back to Joyce.

"Did Earl give you that corsage?"

Joyce held up her wrist to display the pink and white flowers, her face glowing in happiness. "Even I know how old-fashioned this is, but I still love it. Bless his heart." She clasped Annie's hands in her own and pressed her forehead to Annie's. "Now, don't think about anything else tonight. I'm ordering you to dance and drink champagne and enjoy yourself. You deserve it, my dear. Goodness me, we both do!"

Maneuvering through the crowd toward

her table, her breath caught. A tinge of excitement shot through her when she spotted William waiting for her. Hands dipped casually in his pockets, the tan suit he'd most likely borrowed nonetheless looked like it had been cut for him. His tall frame stood impressive, broad shoulders supporting muscles firm and taut. Against his white-collared shirt, his skin glowed golden, bronze and smooth. His eyes were piercing, zeroing in on her from across the room, anticipating her every step. Her skin prickled. *Honey, please go easy on him*, Joyce had told her, her words echoing over and over again. As Annie snagged a glass of champagne from a waiter, she knew the person in the most trouble was herself.

"Are you okay?" he asked as the disc jockey announced the wedding party.

Annie slugged back half the glass and beamed at him.

"Never better."

He moved gently, taking her champagne glass and setting it on a nearby table. "Yes, I see." Eyes watchful, he brushed his hand on the small of her back and guided the way to their table. "When was the last time you had a drink?"

Annie twisted her mouth in thought. "Depends. What year is it again?"

"That's what I figured," he said with a chuckle, pulling out her chair. She slid onto it and readjusted as he gathered a plate of cheese and crackers. After she had had a few bites, he continued. "So, what did you think of the wedding?"

Annie nibbled on a piece of cheese, as the champagne had already gone straight to her head. "I hope they look at each other the same way fifty years from now."

"Who says they won't?" Annie let out a grumble and William laughed. "Annie Curtis, the cynic."

"I am not," she protested. "At least I don't think so."

"You don't think Mia's found true love?" he asked, dipping his head low with discretion.

"It's not that…"

"Were you thinking about your own wedding?"

Annie paused and let her eyes meet William's. "Unfortunately."

He nodded. "It's impossible to not think about yourself at a wedding."

"You?"

"The usual stuff."

"There is no usual stuff." He shrugged, denying her implied question. "No," she pressed. "You're not getting off that easy. Were you seeing someone before you came home?"

"No."

"No one?"

"Is that so hard to believe?"

Annie cocked her head to scrutinize his answer. "I guess I assumed…"

"Stereotyping sailors, are we? Keeping a lady in every port, am I?"

"That's not it," she said, fumbling to redirect. "What were you thinking about during the wedding?"

"You first."

"*You* brought it up."

William chuckled. His eyes slowly traced a cursive line over the contours of her face as if cementing her features into his memory. Her heart raced under his unwavering focus. She wanted to know what he was thinking, what he saw in her. From where she sat, he was handsome, still handsome after all these years. The old photographs she had of him as a young man didn't do him justice now, each line he'd acquired in his travels adding character and depth to the face she'd once pressed to hers. She flushed at the memory, but it was fleeting.

"Why didn't you marry Betsy's father?"

Annie sucked a breath to launch a defense of her character, but instead closed her mouth with a nearly audible snap. Her track record in her twenties left plenty to be desired and in this small town, plenty to be ashamed of, but she wasn't inviting any of that shame tonight. *No*, she hadn't married Julian. He was halfway to San Francisco before Betsy's first ultrasound picture was taped to the refrigerator. And *no*, she didn't want to think about it, because the old biddies around town had often reminded her of that fact.

Annie shot William one seething look and looked transfixed, his hand tight on her arm as she struggled with whether she wanted to leave or not. There they stayed for several moments, Annie staring at William's hand as he stared at her. It was William who finally broke the standoff.

"Forget I asked," he whispered, cautiously releasing his grip to steal a cracker off her plate. "And what I was thinking during the ceremony," William slowly began as Annie settled back onto her chair, "is how time slips by far too quickly."

"Is that what you were thinking?"

"Among other things."

"Such as?"

"I was thinking about how stunning you are tonight." The soft timbre of his voice had her wavering on her earlier promise to herself. She couldn't be responsible for her own actions when a man's voice took such care.

Annie lowered her eyes to her lap before taking a deep breath and raising her head up with resolve.

"Julian was gone before the subject of marriage even came up."

"He left you?"

"With nothing. We had nothing."

"And your mom had already passed away by then…"

She nodded. "It was just Betsy and me for a long time."

"What a fool," William said on his breath as other couples joined them at their table. "He missed out on a really great kid."

"She sure is," she said with a wistful smile, the champagne making her feel sappier than usual.

"And that's because of you, you know. You're a wonderful mother."

"Not some days…" Annie began, but William touched her hand, letting it linger there for longer than was needed to convey the point.

"You are, Annie. It's obvious."

"Thank you," she managed to tell him as their table bustled with excited guests. "It's kind of you to say so."

"It wasn't something really kind. It's true. A fact."

She waited for him to take his hand away and when he didn't, her heart warmed. She felt safe, understood and for the first time in as long as she could remember, right where she wanted to be.

WILLIAM HAD BARELY finished his dinner, taking bites in between making eyes at Annie. She had transformed into the woman he remembered. This was the Annie Curtis whom Brandon had talked about. This was the Annie he had first fallen in love with. With every toss of her head and playful lilt in her voice, she had dropped her guarded exterior and taken up who she'd once been. Confident, feminine, open. After the first wedding dance, the disc jockey had welcomed all the guests to join the happy couple on the floor, drawing the crowd to its feet with a fast-tempo song and Annie along with it. William's brows lifted as Annie flew off her chair.

"I love this song!" she exclaimed.

"Are you ready to dance?" he asked, but Annie's lips had already curled into a sly smile. She reached out for his hand, beckoning him to follow her. Navigating in between fellow guests who had been enjoying the open bar, she led him to the center of the dance floor, where his heart thumped along to the bass line. He had wisely stopped Annie after half a glass of champagne, but as he watched her in front of him, he couldn't contain his surprise. She moved without reservation as the new Annie. Or was it the old version come alive again? Whatever her metamorphosis, she made him feel like he was eighteen again as he hastened toward her. He yearned to be close to her, to touch her and to be touched by her.

He slid his hands around her waist, stepping in time to the music as she playfully toyed at his necktie. Pulling him within inches of her pouty mouth before pushing him away again, she sashayed her hips with a playful ease he couldn't tear his gaze from. Every time he thought she wanted him, he'd reach for her waist only for her to take a half step away again, her eyes flashing as if daring him to try harder.

When she cast him a smoldering look, he couldn't resist any longer. As she lifted thick curls off her hot, dew-stained neck, exposing the perfect curvature of her back from nape to tailbone, he swooped toward her and wrapped his arms around her waist. She startled, but this time, with hands holding her to him, he dipped his lips to the base of her neck, her curls curtaining the side of his cheek. Her body stiffened for only a moment before her hands rested on top of his own.

As the music faded to a slow number and the neon lights transformed to faux starlight, the dance floor cleared except for paired silhouettes. William swayed methodically, his mind cleared to nearly nothing except the sensation of Annie spooned against him. Her dainty figure fit effortlessly against his own like the missing puzzle piece he'd been hunting for for so many years. Her delicate scent mesmerized him, a fragrance as if she'd slipped out of the bath and into a lush garden. It didn't overwhelm; it invited.

He softly nipped at her earlobe. But before he could whisper, she inched around to face him. She pressed her hands to his chest, her eyes never lifting higher than his parted lips. As their faces hovered only inches apart, his pulse surged, making him lean in for more.

He slowly tasted the flush of her lips, but as if dragged by doubts, she pulled away. Before he could catch her hands, she slipped like sand through his fingers and fled from the dance floor.

As she pushed open the exit door, warm sunlight blinded him, his starlight reverie completely dissolving. Shielding his eyes as he followed her outside onto the second-story deck overlooking the lake and beach below, he blinked frantically to find her. The heavy fire door clicked closed behind him, cutting off the music with an abrupt snap. Guests straggled along the railing as the breeze coming off the lake cooled to late evening. Once his eyes finally adjusted, he spotted Annie farther down the beach, her high heels clasped in hand. After descending the steep deck stairs and finding his footing in the sand, he sprinted after her.

"Annie," he called, pulling on her hand to stop her as she gasped to catch her breath. The breeze whisked locks of hair wildly around her face. "It's all right."

Annie dropped her heels in the sand with an exasperated cry.

"Is it?" she asked, gazing up at him. Her pecan-brown eyes gleamed as the evening sun caught them, exploiting every flicker of gold hidden within. She was everything to him that she had once been, swaying in front of him with the abandon of a child. When the wind shifted at her back, it was all he could do to muffle a chuckle of amusement in how helpless she appeared trying to keep her hair off her face.

"Don't you laugh at me, William Kauffman," she warned, threatening him at finger point before storming down the beach.

"I wouldn't dare. I've learned my lesson," he called, plucking her shoes from the sand before quickly sidling up beside her and leading her to a bench. "Annie, sit with me."

"It's not a good idea," she replied.

"It's a terrible idea," he mocked. "But do it anyway."

She hesitated but reluctantly followed. The sun sank closer to the horizon, it's warm glow fusing broad paintbrush strokes across the sky in burnt orange, coral and fuchsia. Aside from the distant murmur of voices on the deck and a straggling seagull gliding effortlessly past, they were alone.

"You're in for a treat," he said, relaxing his arm on the back of the bench.

"I've seen a sunset before."

"Not like this."

"No?"

"Nope."

"What's so special about it?"

"You."

"Me?" Annie huffed. "You need a better line than that."

"That's not what I mean," William replied, becoming serious. "We're approaching something special. At this very moment, before the sun is swallowed below the horizon, it's light has to travel the greatest distance through the atmosphere." He drew closer toward her before continuing. "More blue light is scattered about so the sun makes the light in the sky appear more reddish. You and I are basking in the golden rays known as magic hour."

"Really."

"You seem unimpressed."

"I always thought it was called golden hour."

"You've heard of it?" Annie tried to muffle a smile. "What?" he asked, before the realization dawned on him. "Did I tell you this before?"

"How can you not remember?" Annie burst, a hearty laugh resonating up from within her until it pulsed over him. It was contagious.

"Did I call it golden hour back then?" He chuckled.

"Yes. It was after Jerry Renaldo's birthday party—"

"Over by the lake—"

"And you suggested we go out to the boat-house—"

"Before Ashley and Miranda snuck up on us. *That's right.*" He laughed. "Getting pelted with water balloons while I was trying to get to second base kind of overshadowed the golden hour memory for me."

Their laughs subsided as the memory misted over them. First love, innocent love, unexplored territory. William recalled how eager they'd been to kiss that night.

"So you're going with magic hour now?"

"I like magic hour better for tonight."

Annie smirked. "Okay, I'll bite. Why magic hour?"

"Well…I have an idea."

"I'm not kissing you."

"That couldn't be further from my mind."

At this, Annie chuckled again, snuggling closer. "I'll answer one question for you... anything you want to know," he said.

"That could be interesting."

"There's a catch."

A wry smile thinned her lips. "Of course there is."

"Then you have to answer one question for me."

"About?"

"Anything I want."

"I don't know if I really want—"

"*And,*" he inserted, "because it's the magic hour and all the beauty of the cosmos is peacefully settling down for the night, you and I can *relax.* Here on the beach with all this beauty wrapped around us, nothing bad can happen to you, no matter what you say."

Annie studied him carefully, tucking a strand of hair behind her ear. "Who goes first?"

"Lady's choice."

A soft murmur tickled within her throat as he waited for her to contemplate her options. "Why did you really come back?" she finally managed.

"I told you already. I—"

"No," Annie whispered. "It's magic hour. You have to tell me the whole truth."

William hummed a beat before replying. "I wanted the bike."

"Dennis's motorcycle?"

He nodded.

"And?"

"I was coming to say a final goodbye."

"Final? To whom?"

"Everything, everyone. To mom. *Dennis*."

"Dennis?"

"I need to take his bike to end it once and for all."

"End what?"

"The turmoil I have in my head because of him. He's dead, I'm alive, and I have to move on and let go of my old demons if I ever want to be happy."

"And have you? Let your demons go?"

William hesitated. "I don't know yet. Almost. Are you disappointed?"

"No, I guess not."

"I'm not so sure. I'm surprised that was your question." He shifted even closer, causing her to offer a half smile. "My turn," he said in a hushed tone.

"What if I don't want to answer?"

William was instantly concerned. "You don't have to do anything you don't want to do, Annie. You should know me better than that by now."

"You're right. I do," she murmured. "What do you want to ask?"

"Do you feel something for me?"

"What?" Annie's eyes fell to his lips before meeting his gaze. "I don't know what you mean."

"No?"

Her forehead wrinkled in defense. "I can only imagine how many other women you've spouted this line to."

"No other women. Only you."

"I… I don't know."

"Your quickened breath says otherwise."

"Are you telling me or asking me, then?"

"I'm telling you." He paused, his breath grazed over her ear. "I'm telling you, Annie, that I have feelings for you. You've entranced me tonight."

"William…"

"You don't have to say anything."

Parting his mouth slightly to brush his lips along her cheek, he tenderly grazed her neck. He recalled how he had delighted her with each caress when they were younger. He had wanted no other woman but her and only her then. No other companion for his life, his adventures. He had assumed she'd be by his side through it all, but their courtship had come skidding to an abrupt halt. Unfairly. Unjustly. And she'd been wounded so heavily since then, the emotional scars written on her like a blueprint of how *not* to proceed. The coulda, shoulda, wouldas were impossible to ignore. The lost time urged him to hold her now.

Under the warmth of his touch, she tipped her head back, asking him to take her sweet, delicate mouth with his own. He kissed her tenderly as he had once done so many years before.

CHAPTER TWELVE

ANNIE SWEPT INTO Pop's Place early. Oscillating about the empty dining room, she tried to calm her nerves and funnel her energy into work before they opened the doors. She hadn't had a moment's rest since the wedding, including the two sleepless nights since she last saw William. He had bid her goodbye on her doorstep, and she'd swooned with equal parts anxiety and excitement.

He had said the sunset on the beach was magic hour, and he'd been right. Between his bronze skin pressed against her, his soulful eyes following her every move and those delicious lips tracing a path across her collarbone, she'd arrived home later that night feeling as if she were coming up for air. His presence had had a simple hint of warm familiarity, although he was no longer the smitten boy she'd fallen in love with over a decade ago. As a fully grown man, his stature was stronger, his hands steadier and his kisses hinted at a practiced skill that had developed during their time apart. She'd melted more quickly than she could have ever anticipated, the fast tempo of her heart racing as eagerly as the tide lapping up on the beach only yards away from them.

When the sun had sunk and the last pin-pricks of light in the distant horizon had calmed to purple hues of darkness, his kisses had accelerated. When he'd gingerly placed his hand on her thigh, she'd frozen. She'd been here before, the mistakes of her youth all too pungent on her tongue. As she primed her rejection, she prepared herself for his groan of dissatisfaction, or an irritated grimace at her attempt to thwart a hunger he obviously had for her.

William had smoothed his fingers farther up her leg, his lips dipping to kiss her shoulder, and she'd squeezed his hand with such a sudden force, he'd blinked his eyes open in surprise. She'd tensed, expecting him to complain.

What she hadn't been prepared for was him giving her space. He'd pulled back slightly to study her, and then he took his arms away.

"It's all right," he'd breathed as she'd shifted beside him, uncertain if she should apologize, pick a fight or just walk off down the beach.

Instead, she'd crossed her arms over her chest in a shivery hug.

She looked away, but knew his eyes were on her, most likely mocking, or maybe he was preparing a jest. She couldn't deny her feelings for him, but as the cool night air settled over them, and the magic they'd been cloaked in now evaporated, she cringed from foolishness.

When she'd finally glanced at him, his expression revealed a kindness she hadn't experienced in a long time. His lips flinched in understanding as he cast his eyes over her chilled skin. He slipped off his suit jacket and draped it around her shoulders effortlessly, as if he had been doing it for her every Saturday night for the last twelve years.

"My sweet Annie," he'd hummed, each deep note as unforgettable as the one before it. His eyes had crinkled in a smile, and she wanted to ease into his arms again, but he'd guided her to her feet.

"Let's get you back," he'd said, leading her up the beach with her hand secured in his left hand and her shoes dangling in his right.

As she moved through the diner, trying to focus on her morning tasks, all she replayed in her mind was how protected she'd felt. His assurance, his respect, had her swimming in dreamy pools of attraction, filling her senses as fully as his musky sycamore scent. Was this what real love felt like? Was this flip-flop, bubblegum-tinged whirlwind she'd been blissfully tumbling in for the last two days what all the Romantic poets had been professing for centuries? Could she even risk considering it so? She'd had her share of stormy days, when loving hurt and needing was squelched. It had been a long time since anyone had stretched a banner of love over her, and on the beach with William, she'd so easily embraced it. She'd relived his touches, his whispers and his self-control unceasingly in the nights since his hand had clasped hers and led her home.

Through it all a nagging voice in the back of her mind hissed at her. A jagged splinter of self-doubt had taunted: *this bubble will eventually burst.*

Sooner than later William would realize she had too much baggage. He'd move on like most men did. In fact, he'd already made it clear he had one foot out the door, biding his time until the diner was doing better. She was a fling, an old itch he wanted to scratch again. She'd be sorry. She'd be the fool soon enough.

Perhaps that was why she hadn't returned his call the day after the wedding, choosing instead to replay his voice mail a dozen times and fawn over his velvety voice whispering in her ear. It was as close to William as she should ever get again. She'd wondered over the years how it would feel to kiss him again, and now that she knew, it was imperative that she distance herself. She needed to be wiser than her seventeen-year-old self, or the inevitable would happen. He'd break her heart all over again.

"Mornin', honey," Karrin crooned, cinching her apron around her waist. "How are you faring after your walk at sunset?"

"How do you know about that?" she demanded.

"Easy, Annie. What are you so worked up about?" Annie finished refilling a canister with creamer and rocketed to the other side of the dining room. Karrin raced to keep up. "Everyone knows," Karrin continued, pressing up beside her. "Joyce saw you run out of the reception."

"I needed fresh air."

"I'll bet," Karrin snickered, her eyes wide with curiosity. "Is he a good kisser? I bet he's a really good—"

"No."

"Seriously?"

"I don't know."

"Ooh, yes, you do. It was either good or it wasn't."

"He's fine."

"Fine?"

"It doesn't matter because it was a onetime thing, okay?"

Karrin stuck out her lower lip. "Why?"

"Nothing is going to happen," Annie replied matter-of-factly. She'd make sure of it, even if it took her a long time to forget how good it felt to be entwined in William's arms.

"Mornin', William!"

Annie's body jolted at Karrin's singsong greeting, her heart flooding with enough adrenaline to propel her on a half marathon. She scooped up the remaining creamer canisters from nearby tables and dashed off around the counter and into the supply closet. She'd barely dropped the canisters with a clank when she noticed William waiting patiently behind her.

"Hey," she managed, pretending to search for something, anything, on the storage shelves to avoid being drawn into conversation.

"What are you doing?"

"Hmm?"

"What are you *doing*?"

"I'm grabbing a few things before doors open."

"I think you're avoiding me."

"What?" She laughed, scoffing at his implied question.

"You're cute when you're nervous."

"I'm not— What do you want?" she asked, busying herself among the salt packets and ketchup bottles.

"You forgot this."

Annie snuck a peek over her shoulder. There he stood, boldly, with an outstretched fist. He shook his hand playfully, piquing her curiosity.

"Well...what is it?"

"What do you think?"

"I didn't forget anything, William."

"No?"

Annie crossed her arms. "No."

"Then you won't miss it," he replied with a dismissive shrug, pivoting to leave. He had barely taken a few steps when she let out an exasperated gasp.

"*Okay*. What did I forget?"

"Nope. You didn't think you forgot anything."

"*William.*"

He balked teasingly, strolling over to her. "You didn't call me back."

"I knew I'd see you eventually."

"You didn't want to see me sooner?"

Annie shifted her weight to one leg. "Was that why you called?"

"You know it is." He closed the gap between them in an easy stride, his eyes ever fastened on hers. He presented his loosely clasped fist again. After several moments, she nervously tapped on it and he slowly peeled his fingers open to reveal the blossom of a white daisy.

"I don't understand..." she began.

He pinched the daisy's short stem gently between his fingers and brought it to her ear, softly tucking it within the wisps of her hair. After it was secure, he leaned back to admire it, his lips curling in clear satisfaction. Annie's cheeks fell, any tightness in her face now emollient from his gesture.

"When are you going to let me take you out on a real date?"

Annie bit down on her lip. Distancing herself was going to be harder than she'd thought.

"Oops. I didn't know anyone was in here," Bobby said, backing out of the doorway.

"It's okay," Annie called, desperate to evade William's question and risk fawning like a lovestruck fool. "We were on our way out." She slipped around William as he brushed his fingers against hers, trying for her hand. But she was too fast and pushed out into the dining room as he followed behind. She thought to pour herself a cup of coffee before the Old Timers ambled in, which signaled the unofficial ceremonial start of her shift.

"Did you have fun Saturday night?" Karrin called after unlocking the doors.

William paused in front of Annie as she peered at him from over the top of her coffee mug. "It was a night to remember."

"Is that right?" Karrin replied, hip checking Annie on her way past. Annie shot her a scowl, but Karrin ignored it and continued her line of questioning. "So, what are your plans for *this* weekend, William?"

"I'd like to take Annie out to the breakwater. We haven't been there since we were kids."

"Oh, that sounds like a great idea."

"We could grab some dinner, walk the beach," he continued as Karrin encouraged him with a knowing nod.

"I have the children," Annie protested.

William's eyes danced as she squirmed. She knew he could see right through her, and that fact made her even more uneasy. She yearned to be near him, but a real date meant resolving issues she wasn't ready to face.

"We can go whenever you want," he offered.

Annie shook her head. "I can't."

"Girl, why not?" Karrin whispered.

"I just can't," she said, backing away. She was a single mother with two children to think about, and she couldn't afford to let her emotions carry her away. She wasn't sure she could recover this time.

Earl, Danny and Joe had settled into their usual seats by the time Annie went over to them. Seeing them, she breathed a sigh of relief.

"Did you have fun at the wedding, Earl?" she asked, happily focusing on someone else's life.

Earl's scruffy chin puckered. "Sure," he mumbled.

"Joyce loved her corsage."

"Got her a corsage, did ya?" Joe winked.

Earl ignored them and held up his newspaper for protective cover.

Joe wafted his hand at Earl with a resounding "Bah!"

"How'd little Mia get on, then?" Danny asked, flipping his coffee cup for a fill up.

"She was a beautiful bride."

Danny grinned. "When do yous think you'll be a bride again, Annie?"

"Ha!" Annie bellowed. "Never."

"Never say never, honey." Joe chuckled, pointing at Earl. "If this old sack of potatoes can find a sweetheart, you certainly can."

Finding someone she wanted as a sweetheart wasn't the difficult part. Deciding whether or not to trust her future to him again was what had her jittery and edging for the door.

WILLIAM HADN'T GOTTEN the image of Annie out of his head all weekend. She had consumed his thoughts with such a ferocity, he had tried to sleep just to find some peace. The details of their evening together were etched into his memory, allowing him to draw on them effortlessly like dipping a hand into a cool fountain for a drink on a hot day. He wanted to bury his face into her wavy curls; lose track of time in her caring brown eyes; and bask in the gregarious laugh she had apparently been rationing in recent years. There was one thing their kiss at magic hour had taught him: he needed to hold her again.

"Okay, Annie," he whispered to himself. "We're gonna do this at your pace." If attempting to spend time with her only spurred her to retreat into the shadows, he'd slow the pace even if he didn't have much time left in Chinoodin Falls.

"I'm taking mom to that property again," he said, approaching Annie in the office after the lunch rush.

"Oh?" Annie asked. "Is it serious?"

"I'd say so. We put an offer in."

"That was fast."

"There's no use in waiting around."

Annie nodded, her face solemn. "Sooner than later is better, I suppose."

"We have to do something to spark some business. The new place is near the water and has room to grow."

"Of course."

"Thank you for all your help looking at properties."

Annie fumbled through her purse for a few moments to the point he wasn't sure she'd heard him. He was about to leave when her head popped up.

"I had a good time the other night. You were nice."

"*Nice?* I haven't been called *nice* a day in my life, Annie Curtis. But I enjoyed myself, too."

She went back to searching her purse. "Anyway, it isn't that I didn't enjoy spending time with you—I just can't continue it."

"Can't?"

"It's not a good idea for us to…"

"See each other?"

"Right."

"Why?"

Annie dropped her purse into the desk drawer and slammed it shut with her knee.

"It just isn't," she huffed. "There doesn't have to be a reason."

"But you do have a reason?" William said softly, waiting for her to stop fidgeting. "Annie, I want to spend some time with you. You can pick the place, and you can pick the time. I don't care if we sit up at the counter of this old dive and share a piece of pie. So if you have any desire to spend some time with me, let me know."

Annie paused long enough for him to finish and for her to spin on her heels. He delighted at the sight of her as she strode down the hall-way, and he only tore his eyes away when the phone rang.

Miles peeked his head out of the kitchen. "Grab it, would you?"

"Pop's Place," William spoke into the phone receiver.

"Joyce Green, please," a familiar voice replied on the other end.

"She's out for the day."

"May I have her home number?"

William hesitated and tried to place the masculine voice. "What is this regarding?"

"A mutual acquaintance."

William's stomach lurched as he recognized the raspiness on the other end. He moved to the window, pried open the blinds to peek outside.

"I don't have that handy. Is it something I can help you with?" he asked, trying to sound as casual as before.

"What is your name, sir?" the voice inquired with an air of authority.

"Miles Dent," William responded, his sweaty palm clamping the phone in a death grip. "And you are?"

"I'll try Ms. Green again at another time. Thank you, Mr. Dent."

The line went dead, but William couldn't move. Had his tone given anything away? Was Denver in town? Would he try calling again?

"William?"

William finally dropped the receiver into the cradle and drew a sharp breath. Annie stood in the doorway, her lips parted with concern.

"Yeah?" he croaked.

"Miles asked if there was an order?"

"No…no order."

Annie came in and leaned against the desk. "How about tomorrow night?" she asked.

"Tomorrow night?"

"Marjorie's going to babysit the children at her place."

"Oh?"

"I want to see the breakwater after all…if you still want to take me."

William reached out and brushed the back of his hand down her temple to her jaw. Such beauty could leave a man like putty in her hands. Or at the very least, too distracted for his own good.

"William?" she whispered, her eyebrows knitted in what looked like worry as she took his hand in hers and pressed it to cup her cheek. "What's wrong?"

"Nothing," he said softly. "I'll pick you up at six."

CHAPTER THIRTEEN

ANNIE DIPPED HER fingers into the ice-cold water, admiring the ripples slicing their way across the glassy lake. Except for the two of them nestled in the rowboat and a freighter loading far off at the railroad ore docks, the lake was still without even a breeze to disturb them. The shrieks of children chasing each other on the beach and motorists zipping along Lakeshore Drive grew softer as William rowed farther from shore.

"It's frigid," she stated, pulling her hand from the water and shaking the blood back into her fingertips.

"It'll be this cold in July."

It was true. Lake Superior was the largest of the Great Lakes, its volume deep enough to easily hold the other four lakes within it. So even on the hottest day of the summer, the water was still cool.

Annie pushed back masses of untamed hair while admiring William, his navy polo shirt straining over broad shoulders as he rowed. She was thankful for sunglasses to hide her stolen glances and wondered if he could be doing the same, shielded behind black Oakleys.

"What are the children doing?"

"When I dropped them off, Marjorie was eager to make dream catchers. It's a craft where you weave string around sticks to look like a web."

"Dream catchers? Does anyone suffer from nightmares?"

"Why?" Annie asked, her head jerking at the question.

"Native American legend says they catch all your bad dreams and let only the pleasant ones slip through. You hang dream catchers over your bed."

Annie nodded. "I already know about that."

"So?"

"Yes?"

"Are you troubled?"

It was an almost laughable question, but Annie couldn't muster a chuckle. Ever since Sean had come into her life, she hadn't slept well. *Troubled* sounded like such a polite word for it.

"James has night terrors." She thought she

had only said it to herself until William halted his paddling. His expression grave.

"Often?"

She moved her shoulders. "Not exactly first-date conversation, huh?"

"Sean?"

"What else would he be frightened of?"

William craned his neck to the side and released a heavy sigh. "What can I do, Annie?"

Her eyes misted as she offered him a tender smile. "Keep rowing."

The freighter, which had been stationed at the railroad ore dock, now crawled away from shore. It jutted out to begin its voyage to Sault Ste. Marie, Ontario. It was a massive vessel, stormy gray and imposing against the delicate horizon. Annie could only watch in awe.

"She easily has 70,000 tons of ore onboard," William mused. "It never gets old watching that mammoth pull away from shore, does it?"

Annie nodded before turning her attention to the beacon at the end of the rugged stone breakwater. The octagonal base, topped by a white cylindrical tower and banded with a bright red stripe, still guided ships day and night as the breakwater protected the harbor from northerly storms. Lake Superior behaved as unpredictably and violently as the ocean at her cruelest, but on the early June day, which still carried the mild temperatures of spring, the lake was as peaceful as a sleeping bear, her power dormant and hibernating—for the time being.

"Care to climb out?" William asked, pulling the boat up to a narrow landing nestled between the jagged rocks that made up the breakwater's protective armor.

Annie peered over the edge. "I don't know if we can make it up there without getting wet or worse."

"I won't let anything happen to you," William replied in an even tone. He tied the boat to a cast-iron stake jutting out of a concrete slab and carefully navigated the side against the rocks before extending a guiding hand to Annie. She searched for a place to step. "Here," he directed, grasping her firmly on the back of her biceps as she found her foothold on the nearest, driest rock. Stepping from rock to rock, they finally reached a ladder that ascended up to a concrete crib, the base of the breakwater lighthouse.

"Oh, it's beautiful," Annie sang, catching her breath once she'd made it to the top. She steadied her balance at the aged steel railing and found William's hand already there.

Fighting an instinct to draw her hand away, she found herself lovingly grazing it over his knuckles where a scab gave a clue about his former life. Given how much healing still had to be done to it, he'd acquired the gash shortly before he had walked into Pop's Place and set her world off-kilter.

"Do you remember the last time we climbed all the way out here?" he asked. She giggled at the memory. It had taken them an hour to carefully climb from shore over all the rocks of the breakwater, knowing a simple skidding foot could lead to serious injury.

"I can't believe I talked you into that. I really didn't know what I was getting us into. The boat is a much better idea."

At their backs, the sun slipped closer toward the treetops of the forested park on Peninsula. Before them the sky and lake dueled in hues of blues and grays, horizontal bookends to the freighter quickly shrinking to toy size before their eyes. An angry storm cloud loomed far off in the distance, the only inkling the day would not end as peacefully as it had dawned.

Annie yearned to be as tranquil as what was spread out before them. As she listened to the water's edge lapping hypnotically at the shore, she mused at how safe she felt beside a man and was yet so uncertain of what it meant for her…and for him. She had plenty of questions for William. Why did he need to leave town? How did he get the scabbed gash on his hand? Had he missed her over the years as much as she had missed him?

She felt a rush of joy at his touch. His rugged hand covered hers with a strength and tenderness unique to him, to them. As much as she wanted to vanquish her questions for the time being, she knew they would loom over her as heavily as the darkness blowing across the sky.

William tugged her hand toward him. She knew he wanted to kiss her. Wasn't that why he had brought her up here again? A place where they had once stolen kisses against a hot, balmy backdrop. Wasn't that why she had agreed to come? The stirring in her heart couldn't be muffled forever, and drunk in the moment, she didn't want it to.

When she lifted her face to his, he pushed her sunglasses back, crowning her head, and then removed his own. His eyes twinkled as if he truly saw her. Saw into her heart and silently promised to mend together the parts of it he'd broken. Annie released a breath she hadn't known she was holding and without thinking, swayed into his arms and kissed him. Her lips molded to his and she prayed that the dreamland they had effortlessly drifted into was one from which they would never awaken.

"READY?" WILLIAM ASKED, cutting the engine and grabbing sodas. "Let's make a break for it."

Annie snatched the bag of sandwiches and barreled out of his truck, running up the walk to her front door in a peal of laughter. Rain pelted her body so hard, she didn't know from which direction it was attacking. She could only shield her eyes with an arm in a poor defense. Her keys, already in hand, jingled as she clumsily fumbled with the lock.

"Come on, Curtis!" he jested. "I'm getting soaked out here!"

Annie squealed until she felt the lock click, then thrust her body against the door and pushed her way into the house with William practically on top of her to escape the storm. As he slammed the door shut behind them, sheets of rain pounded violently against the house, their acoustic rendition transforming the tiny Cape Cod into a sanctuary rather than a home.

William shook himself in a rotten attempt

to dry off. Droplets still hung from his eyelashes like glistening morning dew as a hearty laugh bellowed up from his gut. Annie leaned against the kitchen counter and took in the sight.

"You look like a drowned rat!" she said and then burst out laughing.

He laughed, dropping the sodas on the counter. "You don't look so great yourself, you know." When his gaze locked on hers again, his wide-set eyes seemed to be willing her to reveal something. She relaxed on her feet, transfixed by his penetrating gaze. She yearned for a sign that falling in love with him all over again wasn't a mistake, and silently she pleaded to the heavens to grant her this prayer.

"I'll get you a towel," she said weakly, teetering back on her heels. She could feel his eyes still on her as he began to navigate his way around her living room, quietly assessing the family photographs strung along the far wall.

"There's no doubt you adore your children." He chuckled.

"Whose pictures would I hang instead? After all, it's only us."

She didn't want a pity party, but it was the truth. Aside from the occasional friend passing in and out of their lives, it had mostly been her and the children clinging together for dear life. And sweet Marjorie. And the diner.

"This is a good one." He had paused in front of a sepia-toned photograph of James and Betsy frolicking on the beach. "Betsy's a little ham."

"Isn't she?" Annie beamed, handing him a towel. "She's so much like my mom."

"She was a great lady," he said, sounding genuine. What little her mother had known of William she had liked, but she'd died so shortly after he'd left, there hadn't been time to talk to her about her heartbreak. There were days she was sure she would suffocate from the grief and sorrow. She had been all alone then. Desperately, tragically alone. Recalling those days made her shiver and yearn for any assurance she would be okay. Her subtle wince wasn't lost on William.

"Are you all right?" His stance had shifted toward her.

"I want to show you something," she whispered, hugging a towel around her shoulders. With William following, she went up the stairs, past framed pictures before pausing at a midway landing. A cushioned bench framed a windowsill overlooking the roaring rainstorm flooding the backyard. Annie carefully unfastened a frame from the wall. He pressed up behind her to view the photo, his quiet presence rapidly stirring in her an ache to be held.

"Betsy?" he guessed, eyeing the picture.

"Me," she said, grinning. "When I was a little older than she is now."

"She's the spitting image of you."

A clap of thunder shook the house while a bolt of lightning struck nearby. The surprise sent Annie into William's waiting arms. As instantly as the thunder and lightning had struck, the noise and brilliant flash dulled to total darkness inside as the two clutched one another. Her chilled body warmed against his.

"The power in the whole neighborhood is probably out," she babbled. Her eyes adjusted as her other senses heightened. She was thankful her blush was undetectable in the dark, as she couldn't tear her eyes from the outline of William's lips. "Maybe the breaker box…" she continued, barely audible. William whispered her name while coaxing her to sit on the bench. Her body quivered as he stroked back her hair and circled the nape of her neck with a hand. She pressed into him, and he pressed a kiss to her lips.

Annie squeezed her eyes shut, delving

into the embrace. Soft, salty, warm kisses. She relaxed and realized she missed how he touched, how he moved. She missed the calm strength of his voice as he whispered how he had longed to hold her again. She had longed for him, too, though, she suspected, for much longer.

Rain drummed against the windowpane, reverberating with such intensity, Annie couldn't differentiate where it stopped and her pounding heart began. Each time the thunder cracked, she eased closer to William. His arms flexed, his body strong and taut. And she instantly recalled a time when she hadn't been so scarred and alone. When they had been carefree and had fun all over town, and he had pursued her single-mindedly. She had reveled in his attention and returned his affection in varying degrees—from playful to sensual— her own naivete preventing her from knowing where she hoped those touches would lead.

William breathed her name again, his lips rasping over her throat, tickling each nerve along the way. She relished each delicious caress, each kiss. She savored the gentleness of his touch while fully aware he was holding himself back from asking for more.

For a minute she could hardly believe this

was happening. She was wrapped in William's arms and savoring each moment for fear the lights would power on and interrupt the fantasy. William enveloped her. She felt young again. Foolish, innocent, needing. But her desire was still outweighed by a fear she was about to tumble back down a rabbit hole that had nearly broken her once before.

"William," she whispered. "I can't."

All these years she'd imagined him returning home to sweep her back up into his arms and erase all the hurts she'd endured since the last time he'd said I-love-yous against her cheek. But no matter how she'd tried to drown those hurts with new dreams, they were there when she'd surfaced. Reality always sunk in. She wasn't a lovestruck teenager anymore, and they couldn't rewrite the past. She was a mother who needed to keep her senses. She couldn't afford to get her heart broken. Not by him. Not again.

"I can't," she told him, putting her hands on his chest, shoving herself away.

His face scrunched in confusion.

"What's wrong, Annie?" he asked in the same tone that had lulled her to kiss him at magic hour. "Did I misread something?"

She folded her arms across her chest, frightfully aware she had exposed her still vulnerable heart to the only man she had ever loved. "You should go." She scrambled to piece together an excuse.

"If I moved too fast…"

"The children might come home…because of the dark…and…the storm."

"You don't want me here?"

She willed herself to agree with his statement. It was all she had left.

"It's best." Another lie. Until she could get her wits about her again, she needed him gone, his smoldering gaze and all. She watched his shadowed profile as he seemed to consider her words.

"Are you going to send me out in this monsoon?"

"It's letting up," she replied, grimacing at her own coldness. He drew a breath and released it before rising. His stance was hesitant, arms hanging lifelessly at his sides as he looked at her. Words tumbled in her mind, so many words. But none of them would align into a logical explanation. None of them could suffice for all that cried out in her heart. "I can't."

When he attempted a goodbye kiss, she pulled away from sheer fear she'd be drawn to him all over again, his tender masculinity clouding her rational mind. One brief touch could lead her astray.

When she heard him slip out the front door, latching it behind him, she squeezed herself in a desperate hug and pressed her forehead to the chilly pane-glass window. Outside, the storm was ceasing while the one in her heart was still gearing up to rage.

CHAPTER FOURTEEN

WILLIAM GROANED. HE'D returned home to discover Earl's car parked in his mother's driveway. As if being tossed from the intoxicating haven of Annie's arms wasn't disappointing enough, he now had to make niceties with the man wooing his mother.

He sat in the parked truck for a few moments as the windshield wipers methodically dealt with the light rainfall. He replayed the date over again in his mind, recalling Annie's gaze, her touch. What had he gotten wrong? Didn't she want him the way he wanted her? When he held her in his arms, he felt as if they were picking up right where they had left off so many years ago. All the mistakes he'd made had been forgiven and washed clean.

Slogging through the wet grass to the back door, he didn't bother to outrun the rain.

"There he is," his mother called. She and Earl were canoodling on the porch swing, sipping tea and seemingly unaware of the irritating creak the swing made with each pass. "How was your date, dear?" she asked as the swing swayed with a mincing *waaaah*.

William shrugged, unable to politely shift his narrowed eyes from Earl's pleasantly relaxed face. "It is what it is."

Joyce tilted her head, her eyes filled with concern. *Waaaah*. "That doesn't sound good."

"We called it an early evening." He continued to the back door to escape further questioning and the assault on his ears.

Waaaah. "Your friend called the diner looking for you."

William halted at the threshold, his hand hesitating on the door handle.

"Who?" Joyce slowly took a sip of tea, testing his patience almost as much as the high-pitched wail of the swing. *Waaaah*.

"Your friend from the Navy."

Waaaah.

"Did he leave a name?"

Waaaah.

"Um...oh, dear." *Waaaah*. "Yes, perhaps he did...he left a message with Bobby, but I can't remember now."

Waaaah.

"Danny, didn't he say, Joyce?"

Waaaah.

"Like from the diner?" *Waaaah.* "No, Earl, I think I would've remembered that."

William's eyes darted between his mother floundering to recall the name and the chain link grating against the hinge. *Waaaah. Waaaah. Waaaah.*

"Don't you have any oil?" he finally snapped. Joyce and Earl slowed the swing to a stop, the silence between the three of them only broken by the light pitter-patter of rain on the porch roof. "Never mind."

"I'll ask Bobby tomorrow!" Joyce called after him as he retreated into the house. He tore into the kitchen, suddenly aware he was hungry, but before he could fix a sandwich, something caught his eye.

The counter was clear of all clutter, wiped pristine clean, except for a single piece of paper. Stark white, trifold crease, waiting to be read. He leaned over it, and a raindrop slipped from his hair, marking his presence with a re-sounding *plop*. He knew his mother had intentionally left it out for him to see, to read, to learn. The medical jargon, so blunt and barely decipherable on her bills he'd read days earlier, was missing. This, *this*, was easy to understand. It was an appointment schedule for a full-body scan.

Her appointment was on Friday, and to William, it loomed like impending doom. He slunk away from the note, breathing easier as he put more distance between himself and it. She hadn't mentioned the cancer. He hadn't admitted he knew. He preferred they kept to that arrangement. It was one thing to know she was fighting cancer; it was another to have to acknowledge it to her out loud.

As he heard shuffling on the porch, he stole away upstairs, quickly assessing what he needed to pack. Aside from a couple duffel bags, he could be ready in a few minutes if needed. Leaving was the easy part. Outrunning his past, and the women in his life, would be much harder.

ANNIE MUSCLED TOGETHER her pride and approached her shift with a fierce determination to proceed as normally as possible. Pop's Place had been her home away from home in recent years, and she wasn't going to tiptoe around the diner for anyone, let alone William Kauffman. She had reminded herself over and over again that while she might have been developing feelings for William, they weren't anything she couldn't control. Responsible, steady, wise. She was going to consult only her logical, rational frontal lobe. Yes, her head was going to prevail over her heart…or so she told herself in the bathroom mirror before leaving for work.

But no sooner had she finished her pep talk, she shuddered with goose bumps at the thought of him. He had pulled her close and brushed his lips to hers as if that was where he was meant to stay. He stirred an ache within her that yearned to be his forever. If her desire wasn't terrifying enough, the memories of having been hurt or abandoned in the past certainly were. The memories were difficult but were balanced by the joy she found in her children. For as much as she felt sad, she would double down to love them that much harder. And as much as she wanted to believe things with William would be different—*could* be different—she'd experienced enough to know that playing it safe was what she had to do. For her own protection. And theirs.

She'd barely made it into the office when she realized she wasn't alone.

"Morning."

Annie's skin flushed at the mere sound of his voice, like a lover's hand tracing the small of her back, confident yet gentle.

"Good morning, William."

"Were you okay last night?"

"I guess I should be the one asking you that question, considering I kicked you out in the pouring rain."

"You have to treat me a lot worse than that, Annie Curtis, if you want to get rid of me."

"Is that a challenge?"

William's eyes sparked with amusement. "I wouldn't put it past you."

This game they were playing had to end. "I don't want to hurt you, William," she began, though she was more terrified it would be her heart broken first and hardest.

"Then don't."

"I don't know what we're doing," she breathed.

William closed the distance between them. "I know what I *wish* we were doing."

Annie pulled away. "You're still leaving, right?"

"Eventually."

"Eventually *when*?"

"Soon."

"See? You can't even be honest with me about that small but very important detail. Why the big secret?"

"It's not a secret, Annie. I don't know the answer." He moved to her again, but she wouldn't be pulled back into his warmth without some answers.

"Tell me something real. Something I can hold on to, William."

"Annie Curtis needs something real? And I suppose the magnetic pull we feel towards each other isn't concrete enough for you?"

Annie tipped her head in the air. She had lived enough to know not to mistake infatuation for something she could count on. "Not for me it ain't. Let me know when you've got something."

She strode out of the office, sure of herself, but the feeling quickly crumbled away when she found Sean waiting for her at the counter.

"Look who decided to finally show up for work. Tsk, tsk. It's five after."

"What do you want, Sean?"

"We've got some things to discuss."

"Not now. I have to start my shift." Sean's eyes darted behind her, making her stomach drop. She knew what he would think when he saw William following her from the office. And this time his suspicions would be accurate.

"Well, well," Sean muttered. "Look who we have here."

"Sean." William's voice had downshifted

gears to deep and barely audible. Even the shuffling of the Old Timers and other patrons into the restaurant didn't detract from the tension mounting between the two men.

"*Now* I see why you were late," Sean jested, but a darkness had shadowed his eyes, proving there was nothing cute about it. The tightness in his shoulders made his arms billow to his sides awkwardly, puffing up his already stout frame.

"What can we do for you, Sean?" Karrin asked, the slightest crack in her voice the only indication she was anxious.

Annie braced herself. She could read his tells better than a professional poker player.

"I'm taking the kid on a little trip."

Annie's face fell as she tried to maintain her composure. "What?"

"I have vacation time coming up, and I'm taking James with me to check out California."

"No, you're not," Annie sputtered. She didn't care enough to ask when or where exactly. She couldn't part with James for more than two hours, let alone send him on a plane or train with the man she hated most in this world. The word *trip* made her want to cry nasty, ugly tears...or swing nasty, ugly punches.

"Are you sayin' no?" Sean snarled.

"James is too little to go away on a trip."

"I'm takin' him for a week, and if you want to argue about it, we can get a judge involved."

"There's no reason for that," William said, stepping between him and Annie. "And the diner isn't the place to discuss this."

Sean turned to William. "Are you telling me my business?"

"I can't talk about this now, Sean. I've got customers." Annie grabbed a pot of coffee and scooted around the both of them. "Just go."

"I know what's going on here," Sean warned. "You can't fool me."

"Nothing is going on, Sean. Please *go*."

"Big mistake, swabbie," he said to William before stealing out of the diner. Annie hurried to the Old Timers' table, coffeepot in hand, but she shook so badly while trying to pour, some of the liquid splashed on the table and splattered onto Danny's lap.

"Oh, Danny, I'm so sorry," she cried, hot tears stinging the backs of her eyelids.

"Give me that, honey," Danny told her calmly, taking the coffeepot from her hand. "Easy goes it."

She found Earl's face plastered with concern. The sight of his droopy gray eyes pitying her were more than she could bear. She had to flee faster than her legs could possibly take her or risk spiraling into a blubbering mess in front of everyone. Rushing out the back door and across the parking lot, the cars, the trees, the sky blurred into smears of color. Why couldn't she run quicker? Why couldn't she sprout wings and transcend this place? She was nearly to Veterans' Park, a block and a half away, when she noted she'd been followed.

Ducking behind a slide, freshly moistened with morning dew, she waited for William to catch up with her. She heard his pace slow once he hit the wood chips, the crunch beneath his feet crisper as he drew closer. When she sensed he'd stopped behind her, she spun and slung her arms around his neck. There was no doubt it was him coming for her, no possibility she could be wrong. He lifted her up, her feet almost leaving the ground as she buried her face in his chest and sobbed as though at any moment he might be torn from her embrace. He seemed to anticipate it and held her tightly as her body sank against his.

"Take me away from here," she whispered. "I can't breathe anymore." He stroked her head, pressing his lips to her temple. She didn't care if her eyes and face swelled, and he saw her at her worst. She needed something from him just then that could make her forget everything else. Her heart was calling to him to protect her, even if it was only for that one moment. She needed to draw from his courage until the disappointment wasn't so massive anymore. Until she could pick up her life and manage it again like she did every day. "If Sean gets a new job, he'll try to take James with him. He's plotting something. And I can't, William. I can't let him."

"It's all right," he soothed, cradling her head in the crook of his shoulder. "Shh, love. It'll be all right."

Annie released a hearty sigh as she squeezed him close and wished all he promised was true.

ANNIE STOOD AT Marjorie's screen door, a silent observer to her friend and children fixing dinner and chattering as though no one else were listening. When she cleared her throat, Betsy flew to unlatch the lock and sped straight into her arms. Annie groaned as she tried to support her daughter's weight.

"Pick me up, Mama!"

"I'm not sure I can anymore," Annie said,

laughing and then smooching Betsy on both cheeks, swinging her around.

"We're making you dinner," she declared, leading Annie by the hand to the stove. "James is snapping the beans, and I'm making the cornbread."

Annie planted a kiss on James's temple and hesitated a moment to savor his dewy brow, which smelled of all things boy—her boy.

Marjorie patted her hands dry on her apron. "You've quite the helpers, Annie. These two little 'uns have been fixin' us a feast. I hope you're hungry."

"I don't have an appetite, but I'd still like to try it."

"What's wrong, Mama?" Betsy asked. Marjorie raised an eyebrow, but Annie waved away her concern.

"Go ahead and pour the batter in the pan, Betsy. Then you two get washed up for dinner."

Annie sank her hands into the sink of dirty dishwater and began washing to keep herself from breaking down in front of the children. Once they had scampered into the next room, she could sense Marjorie hovering behind her.

"Sean is keeping up with his promise to take James on a trip."

"This is all my fault."

"No," Annie replied, spinning around to face her friend. "He would have pushed for a trip no matter what. He suspects there's something going on between William and me, and it's making him more agitated than usual."

"Is that possible?"

"You know it is."

"What is going on between you and William?"

Annie struggled to find the words because she didn't know the answer. She had fallen in love with him again, but what did it mean in the day to day? He had told her he was leaving town, so there couldn't be any type of future for the two of them. As far as she was concerned, he was using her to relive the good ol' days. To reminiscence about their times together while getting a little love and attention along the way.

She shook her head and plunged her hands back into the water. "Nothing. He's going soon so that's the end of it."

"Why not go with him? Anywhere else would be better for you and the children."

"And risk Sean ending our informal agreement that I have sole custody? Never."

"Maybe you could change William's mind,

then. He can build a life here." Marjorie fell in line beside Annie, snagging a towel to dry.

"Impossible."

"Goodness… Why?"

"He can't wait to leave. He was ready to go as soon as he arrived."

"But he's still in town?"

"Yes."

"What's keeping him here?"

"His mother."

Marjorie nodded, knowingly. "And?" she prompted.

Annie let her mind wander to William's smile. Had he begun to fall back in love with her again? She'd once thought they were soul mates. Ha. The thought now seemed like a naive fantasy. She'd believed in soul mates and fairy tales a long time ago, but she'd also grown up a long time ago and much faster than she'd wanted to. It was silly to place all of her hope in William. Not when he could distract her from bigger problems on the horizon. No matter how much she wanted to wish that he loved her, too.

Annie's heart leaped in excitement when she heard the rumble of a motorcycle pulling into her driveway. But as she peered through the kitchen sheers, her heart sank. *Sean*.

"Children, stay here with Marjorie," she said as they raced to the screen door.

"Do I have to go with Dad?" James asked, his voice raised an octave higher than usual.

"Not tonight. I'll be back in a few minutes."

Annie marched across the yard to meet Sean as he shut off the engine. She stopped in front of him, eyeing the motorcycle before raising her eyes to his smug face.

"What is this, Sean?"

The corners of his mouth turned up in a mischievous curl. "Like it?"

"Not really."

"This is the newest edition Harley-Davidson Street Glide, baby. Want to go for a ride?"

Annie crossed her arms over her chest. "Your newest edition must have cost a fortune."

"Not for me."

"You bought your BMW only a couple of months ago."

Sean scoffed at her comment, his chin protruding as punctuation. "Counting my money for me, eh?"

"No, but it does make me wonder."

"I'm being wooed."

"Wooed?"

"You shoulda stuck with me, baby. You could have been a California girl."

"I don't understand. Are you job hunting?"

"Send the kid out." Sean reached for the ignition. Annie took a breath to calm her nerves and widened her stance.

"James isn't going anywhere on that thing, Sean, not that it makes a difference tonight. He's staying home." Sean dropped his hand from the key and relaxed back on his seat. He eyed her for long enough that Annie felt goose bumps prickle her skin. "And what you said at the diner about going on a trip—"

"You don't want to do this." His eyes still fixated on her.

"Do what?"

"Make me cross."

Annie had never known a time when Sean hadn't been cross with her, with the children or with life in general. If life up until this point had been Sean on a good day, she knew things were heading south quickly.

"Why do you want to take him? Don't you want to go on vacation alone?"

"Who says I'll be alone?"

Annie bit her tongue to prevent a nasty quip. "He wants to stay here all summer with Betsy."

"He does, does he? And what about you and the company you've been keeping lately?"

"Excuse me?"

Sean paused and then licked his bottom lip. "I suppose I could forget about the trip for now...seeing as our custody arrangement needs to be reviewed anyway."

"What's that supposed to mean?"

Sean shook his head and tsked. "You need to pay better attention to the company *you* keep, baby."

"Is this about William?" Annie scowled. "We're not married anymore, Sean. You can't punish me because you're jealous."

"Jealous?" Sean replied. "How can I be jealous of an ex-convict who tried to bash my brains in at The Grove the other night?" Annie couldn't school her reaction. It must have played out on her face. "That's right. I think a judge will be interested to learn that. Maybe James would be in better hands with me."

"How can you say that? I'm his mother."

"It's not up to what *I* say. It's about what a judge thinks. Do you smell that?" Sean craned his neck, angling his nose in the air. "Winds of change, baby."

As he fired up the engine and thundered back down the street, Annie swayed with the breeze, unable to feel her legs beneath her.

How could she be standing upright when the world had begun to swirl around her. She squeezed her eyes to shut out the dizziness and prayed when she opened them again, everything would be as it should.

CHAPTER FIFTEEN

MANILA FOLDER IN HAND, William helped Joyce to his truck before climbing into the driver's seat. This was what satisfaction felt like, he thought, and slid the folder onto the dashboard.

"This is all moving so quickly," Joyce said enthusiastically while tightening her seat belt. "Do you think we could move in there before the end of summer?"

"Possibly." William nodded, firing up his truck. Moving the diner to a new location could actually be in the cards for the struggling business. He pulled out onto the road, contemplating the fact that as soon as one aspect of his life started to run smoothly, another one began to tank. He had been certain of the signals Annie was sending, but then...

He brought his attention back to Joyce, who continued their conversation from the passenger side. "I still think you should have worn a suit, but it didn't seem to matter none."

"I wore a tie."

Joyce rolled her eyes. "Well, times have changed since I last applied for a loan. But luckily I have you to help me navigate. What was the part he said about inspection?"

"The bank has their own inspection guidelines we need to meet. It's so they can protect their investment."

"And their investment is us!" Joyce bubbled. "I must admit I thought you were overreaching when you first pitched the idea of moving Pop's Place, but, sweetie, you've pleasantly surprised me."

William glanced at his mother. "Overreaching? I thought you were eager to move."

"Well, truthfully, no. I was willing to do whatever you wanted, though. I still am."

William readjusted in his seat. "What exactly do you mean?"

She patted his arm in several quick flutters. "New ownership usually translates to new ideas, is all."

William hadn't wanted to have *this* talk today, but his mother's giddiness was forcing his hand.

"I can't do this with you," he told her, bracing himself for her bitter disappointment.

"Do what, dear?"

"Run Pop's Place."

"I don't understand."

"I can't stay here."

"Here?"

"Chinoodin."

"But, William, it's your home."

"No," William interjected, giving a brisk shake of his head. "It isn't."

Joyce's brow tightened in a streak of lines. "Is this about Dennis?"

William groaned. "No, Mom. This doesn't have anything to do with him."

"Because if his ghost is keeping you from staying here and building a life—"

"I can't stay for my own reasons. I have to move on soon."

"But the new property... I don't understand..." Her voice cracked as her fingers slipped into her handbag and emerged with a tissue.

"Since I've been away, a lot of things have become a lot clearer to me. If Pop's Place continues the way it's going, you'll wither away and..." He caught himself, readjusting his hand on the steering wheel before saying any more. He knew how high the stakes were for his mother if Pop's Place failed, but he couldn't bring himself to utter the word. It was too much responsibility to yoke on his shoulders.

It wasn't fair. He'd do the best he could to get her on the right track, to get Pop's Place on the right track, within his limited time frame. "I can help you get back on your feet before I leave, but I do have to leave."

"How nice of you." He strained to decipher any trace of sarcasm in her voice but found her sweetly sincere. It only made his heart twist with guilt. He waited for her to mention the cancer, to tearfully drop it into the conversation as a reason to hold him here. She could sob about how she was sick. She could tell him she had been fighting for her life. She could twist the knife and remind him that if Pop's Place disappeared, she wouldn't be able to afford her treatments. Cancer, bankruptcy, desperation. She had all the cards to lay on the table and force him to stay, and she could play them all.

But she remained quiet.

They rode silently for a few minutes until he pulled up to Pop's Place and threw the truck in Park.

"Mom…"

"When?" she whispered, dotting her eyes with her tissue and swallowing the lingering emotion before returning to work.

William shook his head. "I don't know. Soon."

"It's too bad, really." She sighed, her hand placed over the door handle as she added a parting thought. "I wasn't the only one happy to have you back."

WILLIAM CAREFULLY STUDIED the payroll sheets in the office. Line by line of numbers were making his eyes glaze over when something caught his attention out the window. He would have sworn he had spotted Annie's beat-up Malibu roll by, and the prospect of seeing her made him jump to his feet.

Without hesitation he moved to the back door. She was there, climbing out of her car, but as soon as her gaze met his, her face dimmed. She tore across the parking lot like a lioness stalking a gazelle.

"Annie," he began, offering an inviting hand, but she smacked it away and grabbed his other one.

"This," she demanded, pointing at his tattered knuckles. "Did you get this fighting?" William stiffened as her eyes read exactly what she needed to know from his silence. "And the other night when your face had been bruised... Did you get it fighting Sean?"

"How do you know about that?" he asked, inwardly cringing at his weak response.

"All that matters is you didn't tell me about it." She dropped his scarred hand and returned to her car. William jogged to catch her, and did, but found her eyes fierce. His breath caught at the sight of her. "What else haven't you told me? How do you expect me to trust you if you keep things from me?"

"Yes, okay," he sputtered, out of a desperation to try to reach her. To make her understand.

"Yes, okay, *what*? You lied to me, and now I'll lose James. Go!"

But she was the one to step backward and then ran the rest of the distance to her car.

"Why did you come here?" William called after her. "What did you want me to say?"

"Say why you did it!"

"Why I fought Sean? Because he was asking for it!"

"Ha!" Annie cried, her eyes moistened with tears. "Do you know how many times over the years other people have wanted to do the same and didn't?"

"But it's true," he insisted. "Ask Brandon."

"I'm asking *you*."

"Then believe me. He came itching for a fight with me that night."

"And that?" She pointed again to his hand. William hesitated, recalling the night he now regretted more than ever. "Well?"

"*I* was itching for a fight." He walked toward her.

Annie shook her head. "You have to give me something better if you want me to understand."

"I can't right now."

"If not now, when?" She squeezed her eyes shut, turning her face to the heavens as William edged nearer. "I don't want to fight anymore."

"This isn't a fight."

She frowned. "I don't mean with you."

William's eyes narrowed. "What happened with James?"

"Do you really care?"

"Of course I do," he answered without hesitation. He loved the little guy. "I care about the both of you. And Betsy, too."

"Sean served me with papers. He wants full custody of James."

"On what grounds?"

"You."

"Me?"

"He said you attacked him at The Grove, and you have a criminal record—"

"But I don't. He's just throwing out accusations to see which ones stick."

"Even so. If I fight him on the full custody, he might walk away with partial and... I can't let that happen."

William wrapped her in a crushing hug as he silently pledged himself to her and the children. They stirred a desire in him he'd never experienced before. It was a need to look out for them at any cost, to be there for them and...love them? He buried his face into her crown of wavy hair and breathed her familiar scent of chamomile, and caught himself considering the possibility he loved her and couldn't let her go.

"I won't let that happen," William echoed her words.

"No," Annie said, abruptly pulling away. "I'm the one who has to take care of this, William."

"Not by yourself."

"Yes. I came here to tell you... I can't see you again." Hearing her was like a vise wrenched on his heart. "Please don't make this any harder than it has to be."

"Sean's an excuse, Annie. Don't be scared of this."

"Of what?"

"You're falling in love with me."

"What?"

"And you're scared of what it means."

He searched her eyes for confirmation that he spoke the truth. It was the first time he had let the thought cross his mind, let alone uttered it aloud. And as soon as he had, he found himself wishing it would be true.

"William, I can't be with you, because Sean is going to use your history against me."

"He can't win, Annie. Don't pull away from me now."

Annie straightened and blinked back more tears. "I have to protect James. Please tell me you understand and you won't try to…"

"Kiss you? Hold you? Take you in my arms?"

"Don't get involved, William. Please. It will only cause more trouble."

"Annie."

"William, *please*." He searched her face for any indication…of what? That she really was in love with him and didn't want him to listen to her protests? Did it really matter if she had grown to love him? Falling in love with her was the worst thing he could do, as he was leaving town again to escape Denver and his past.

He wanted to avoid causing her any pain, but he needed to know she loved him as much as he loved her.

"Kiss me," he breathed, slipping an arm delicately around her waist.

"I can't."

"Kiss me goodbye, and I'll leave Chinoodin tonight."

"But Joyce..."

"All will be fine, as it should be. Folks'll help her get reestablished and the new location should excite new business. With time—"

"You'd walk away? After all that's happened?"

"Between us?"

Annie blinked. "What us? You won't even tell me the truth about your past. About why you're leaving."

He tucked a strand of hair behind her ear and cupped his hand at the nape of her neck. "Just trust me enough to believe I have to go, and I might as well go now if it'll make it easier for you...for both of us. Please kiss me goodbye, Annie."

He tilted his head, and she pressed her lips to his, telling him exactly what he needed to know. When she melted against him, a soft moan coming from her, he smiled and savored one last moment before she pulled away, her eyes fluttering open.

"Talk about someone who's scared," she murmured, her pout still puckered and poised inches from his. "I won't give you the out you want, William. If you hightail it out of town and leave your mother twisting in the breeze, then you take responsibility for it. Don't blame it on me, because I'm not asking you to leave. I'm only asking you to leave me alone." She brushed her fingertips to her lips. "And promise me we won't do that again."

William knew she was right and looked beyond her to where a weeping willow tree soared. He had nothing to say, nothing to counter. But he couldn't stand how she stared at him with sadness in her eyes. As he stayed transfixed on the graceful giant, its sweeping branches swaying with the wind, Annie eventually made her way to her car, and as best as he could assume, drove out of his life forever.

CHAPTER SIXTEEN

ANNIE MOTIONED FOR Karrin to follow her behind the kitchen doors before beginning her morning shift. As if ordering William out of her life the day before hadn't been bad enough, the events later that evening still had her shaken. She needed a trusted confidante and hoped Karrin would be up for the task.

"Hey, girl," Karrin whispered, studying her friend. "What's going on?"

"James knows about Sean wanting custody."

"What?" she said with a gasp. "How did that happen?"

Annie hung her head. "It was my fault. I thought he and Betsy were getting ready for bed, but they overheard me talking to Marjorie. He's really shook up about it, K. I'll fight tooth and nail before I ever let Sean take him."

"We all will," Karrin replied, squeezing her shoulder. "Do you need to take today off? I can cover the morning rush."

"No. I need the distraction. My mind can

only reel over Sean for so long." The truth was, she didn't want William to think she was hiding from him. That is, if he was still in Chinoodin Falls. She'd told him to stay away from her, but her heart had ached with each forced syllable. How she'd wanted to seek solace in his arms, but she'd never do that again. She was sure Sean had plotted it all: a selfish attempt to keep her within his reach. Even though she knew she was playing right into his hand, she'd do it because as much as she had fallen in love with William, she loved James more.

"Morning dare, Annie," Danny called out.

"Good morning," she said and poured him a cup of coffee.

"Oh, not lookin' too good, though, is it?"

"Why do you say that?"

Danny leaned across the table toward her. "There's something going on around here. I can feel it. Yous know what it might be?"

Annie attempted a casual shrug. "My morning's been fine. Thanks."

"Fine, eh?" Danny said, straightening up and taking a sip of coffee.

"Why don't you give me something else to think about, all the same?" Annie pulled out her order pad. "Earl? What can I get you?"

Earl studied her silently from underneath his Kromer hat before shaking his head and returning to his newspaper with his typical harrumph.

"What's with you dis morning, Earl?" Joe frowned as he and Danny shared an inquisitive look. "Just the usual for me," he continued.

"You, too, Danny?" Annie asked. He nodded. Her eyes suspiciously darted around to the three of them before moving on to place their orders. Miles poked his head out of the kitchen.

"Is William coming in today?"

"I don't think so."

"I needed to talk to him about a strange call I received last night."

"What call?"

"Oh, it was probably nothing. Never mind."

Annie left the window, swerved around the corner and barreled up to Miles. "*What* strange call, Miles?"

He paused, cracking his neck as he recalled. "Last night a man called, asking if he and I had spoken on the phone the other day. I didn't know what the heck he was talking about and told him so. He kept pressing, but when I said I had never talked to him and he must have the wrong person, he asked for Joyce."

"What did he want with her?"

"I don't know. She left right after she talked to him. She seemed kind of upset. Any idea what it's about?"

"I have a feeling I might know," Annie said under her breath. "Tell me if the guy calls back. I want to talk to him myself."

"Why?"

"Just do it, Miles."

"Whatever you say, Annie."

Annie returned to the dining room to take orders and serve breakfast platters, but her mind was on William. If he had left town last night, it wasn't because of anything she had said or didn't say. Someone was after him, and she worried what would happen if he was found.

ANNIE SLAPPED THE bill on the table and paused to listen as Danny teased Earl.

"It's going to be nearly eighty degrees today, Earl. You have to take your Kromer hat off sooner or later. What does Joyce think of you wearing it all the time?"

"She don't mind none."

"She's too nice for her own good. Sooner or later the beads of sweat streaming down your face will force it off."

"I'll swap it out for my hockey cap." Earl retreated behind his newspaper while Annie cleared away their empty plates.

"What are you reading that's so darn interesting, Earl?" Joe asked, swatting at the old man's newspaper.

"Ah, leave him alone," Danny said. "Earl likes to know the happenings in town, even if he don't repeat 'em."

Annie raised an eyebrow. "You're a good secret keeper, eh, Earl?" Earl lowered his newspaper and cleared his throat.

"Yous could say that," he stated, and rubbed a hand over his stubbly, gray chin. He then pointed a calloused finger to an article, asserting its importance with the thunk of his fingertip on the table.

"I'm not the brightest fella," he started, glancing up at her with his clear eyes.

"I coulda told yous that," Joe said, snickering.

"But," Earl continued, "I've been known to connect dots others might not see." Annie adjusted her weight to her other foot, the stack of breakfast dishes growing heavier in her arms.

"What are you mumbling about now?" Joe frowned.

"Somethin' funny is going on around here," Earl declared.

"Here?" Annie asked. "Pop's Place?"

"*Chinoodin.*"

She smiled. "There's always something funny going on, Earl."

"Not like this." He tapped on the newspaper article again, his eyes now boring into hers. "Not like the Heiress of Chinoodin."

Joe wafted a hand in the air in dismissal. "Nobody knows what you're talking about. Piece together more than six words, would ya?"

Earl refused to break his focus from Annie. "You can't get rich without the law on your side. And if the law ain't on your side, you hire someone to *get* it on your side."

"How do I get it on my side?" Annie chuckled. "You all know I could use the edge."

"Did you read another article about that land deal again?" Danny asked. "It's all you've been blubbering about recently."

"With good reason," Earl said in a huff. "No one could buy that preserved land without the help of a fix-it man."

Annie shifted the weight of breakfast dishes to her other arm. "A fix-it man?"

"That's right. He gets you what you want, no matter what it is you want. Someone who has access to the mayor's office. Someone with connections. Someone who doesn't mind breaking the law none. Perhaps he even thinks he's above the law. Now where could you find such a fella?"

Earl folded up his newspaper and motioned for Danny to let him out of the booth. Once he had finally pulled himself to his feet, he lay the newspaper on the breakfast dishes. "It's just a hunch, but you've got something on him, love. See if you can use it."

"Sean?" she said, barely audible.

"You're smarter than he is. The question is, are you bold, too?"

Then with a dip of his Kromer hat, he shuffled past her to the front doors. Annie stared after him, confused.

As she made her way back to the kitchen, she chuckled at how Earl had spoken more to her in that one conversation than he probably had in the three prior years combined. He was a bit rough around the edges but had showed his soft underbelly once Joyce had glanced his way.

Annie's eyes landed on the article he'd pointed to and her grin slowly faded. A company in California had bought up the preserved land—land that was never to be sold.

This wasn't news to her. The scandal had been the talk around town for weeks. But the article also asserted the Heiress's will had mysteriously disappeared weeks before the land had been purchased and then it showed up again with a built-in loophole. It was all speculation, but *The Chinoodin Chronicle* suspected someone with ties to the mayor's office had stolen and forged the will, so that the land could be sold and developed. Without a copy of the original, though, no one could prove it.

Annie stared out the window for several minutes as the dots began to connect in her mind, too. She transfixed on the way the mortar had cracked along the wall of the redbrick building across the street. The fracture formed a wandering line from the top to the flower beds below. She wasn't sure how long she had been standing in place or how long Karrin had been watching her.

"Annie? Are you sure you don't want to take off for the day?" the waitress asked.

Annie turned slowly, the hair rising off the back of her neck as she realized what she was prepared to do. "I have to call an old friend."

WILLIAM DREW THE shades in his motel room and cast a dingy hue over his bare essentials tossed onto the bed: cash, cell phone, toiletries, broken-in leather jacket, night goggles, bandana. The Econo Lodge on the outskirts of town was probably the first motel Denver would check after staking out his mother's house and Pop's Place. But his options were limited. He knew he could covertly park his truck there until Mike could meet him. As ticked as Mike had been before for calling off the sale, he'd quickly jumped when William called to offer him a greatly discounted price. The only caveat was he had to act *fast*. Luckily Mike had happily swung into the Econo Lodge less than an hour later with an envelope of cash.

William ran a hand over the five o'clock shadow he had been growing since yesterday when he'd overheard Miles talking to Denver on the phone. Without waiting to hear what came next, he'd taken off. It was only a matter of time before Denver made a beeline to Chinoodin Falls, and William had no intention of waiting around for him.

William slumped against the nightstand as he contemplated his options. Denver had most likely enlisted the local police to keep an eye out for him. He had to stay off their radar.

Once it was dark, he'd take a cab back to town to get Old Red.

He paced the tiny room while reassuring himself he wasn't doing anything wrong. If Annie and his mother had misinterpreted his extended visit to mean he was returning for good, it was a mistake. If they knew the whole story, they wouldn't second-guess him for a minute as to why he was leaving.

Although, he considered, if Annie knew everything about what had happened, she may not have fallen in love with him. And she was, wasn't she? In love? Hadn't he seen it flood her eyes when she'd first tipped her dainty chin up to meet his? Hadn't she kissed him back in the parking lot when they knew they were parting for good? The ache he felt when they were apart couldn't be one-sided. He was lovesick. Foolish and lovesick. And the only thing worse than feeling this way was if he stopped to consider the possibility she didn't love him back.

Flopping onto the bed, fully clothed down to his work boots, he had just closed his eyes to catch a few winks when his cell phone rang.

"William?" His mother's voice was in a panic, propelling him to his feet again. "Thank goodness you answered. I'm shaking like a leaf."

"Why? What's happened?"

"A man came by the house. He said you were in a lot of trouble. He said he was some sort of…of… Naval Criminal Investigator of some kind."

William kneaded his forehead with a knuckle. "Is he still there?"

"Heavens, no. I bolted the front door after he left."

"Mom, calm down. I'm okay."

"William, what's going on? He said he's been trying to get a hold of you, but you're evading an investigation. He said bad things could happen."

William pressed a cheek below the peephole on his motel door and ran a hand through his hair. "I'm okay, Mom. You don't need to worry. Did you get the make or model of his car?"

"Oh, no," Joyce cried. "I didn't. Should I have? He left a little bit ago."

"I can't explain who he is or what's going on right now, but you can't tell him where I am. If he visits again, say you haven't heard from me."

"I haven't heard from you. I went up to your bedroom and all of your belongings were gone!"

"I told you before I can't stay in Chinoodin. I'm leaving tonight."

"Tonight? My son! Are you even going to say goodbye?"

William closed his eyes as he replied. "Of course. Of course I will…"

"But?" His mother had sensed his hesitation. William waited a beat and then knew what he had to do.

"I need your help."

"What can I do?" she whispered.

"I need Old Red."

"Sure, but your truck?"

"Gone. I need wheels. I'll be back to get the bike in a little bit. Call me if you see that investigator again or notice anything suspicious."

"William." Her voice cracked. "What's going on?"

"Mom, I'll be there in a little while."

William shoveled all his belongings into his bag and ducked his head around the open motel room door, his eyes darting to every person within his sights. There was no time like the present. He had to go now.

ANNIE TUGGED AT the waist of her pantyhose just before she climbed back into the passenger side of Brandon's car. She breathed with a sigh of accomplishment. Glancing at her face in the vanity mirror, mascara-coated eyelashes and a sleek French-twist hairstyle greeted her. In a borrowed suit dress from Karrin and nylons she'd scrounged up in a hurry, she had to admit she cleaned up pretty well, even on short notice.

"How'd it go?" Brandon asked, steering out of the parking lot and onto the main drag.

Annie grabbed a granola bar from her purse and tore it open. Her mounting nerves had distracted her from eating lunch, but now in the safety of Brandon's car, they had instantly downshifted into a ravenous hunger.

"As good as can be expected. Thanks so much for driving me."

"I had the vacation time and needed to get out of the office. No worries."

"Are you positive the lawyer doesn't know Sean?" she asked. The hour-long drive to the next town didn't feel far enough from Sean's grasp, but she had limited options unless she wanted to travel several hours to Green Bay or Duluth.

"I'm not 100 percent positive, but he moved here from San Antonio and has only been practicing law a few years. Didn't you ask him?"

"Not...directly." It had been an awkward

meeting of sorts, considering Annie wanted to hire Kenneth Bailey to represent her for crimes she hadn't yet committed. She'd talked in circles long enough for him to get the gist that she was up to something, but he didn't seem to have the faintest clue as to what. She needed him to be her personal safety deposit box, but could she trust him to do what she needed when the time came?

"Does he have any experience in family law?"

Annie chomped down on a bite of granola and shook her head.

"Annie, you might not want to waste your time with someone lacking experience in custody hearings."

"Sean knows every lawyer in Chinoodin. He has his sleazy paws in everything. I can't hire anybody there."

"But you need someone specializing in family law. Right?"

Annie shoved another chunk of granola bar into her mouth and managed a nod. It was wise for Brandon to assume she had met with Kenneth Bailey to maintain full custody of James, but it wasn't correct. She had her sights set on the horizon. No more sleepless nights worrying about Sean creeping up her walk. No more watching the clock, dreading the minutes until Sean picked up James or finally returned him home. She and her family weren't going to live like this anymore. They deserved better.

"I know what I'm doing, Brandon."

He squinted at her as his gaze shifted from her to the road and back again. "Why do I have the feeling that you're not giving me the whole truth?"

Annie grunted under her breath. "You wouldn't want the whole truth."

Brandon swung off MI-28 and onto a gravel driveway. It led to a little house with a sign that read EAT secured in front. He put the car in Park and faced her.

"Try me."

She sighed. "It's best not to involve you, Brandon."

"It's *that* kind of talk that has me worried. You're not trying to win sole custody of the children…are you?"

"I need this to be over, Brandon. For James's sake. I'm making other…arrangements."

"James needs his mother, Annie. Promise me you aren't planning anything reckless."

"Me? Reckless?" Annie smirked, fumbling in her purse for her cell phone.

"You've been known to elicit raised eyebrows a time or two."

Annie scowled at her phone. She'd mistakenly set it to silent mode and had four missed calls from Marjorie.

"What's wrong?" she asked, phone sandwiched between her ear and shoulder as she motioned to Brandon to keep driving.

"Honey, James is missing," Marjorie said, her normally calm, buttery voice frantic on the other end of the line.

"Missing?" Annie sputtered.

"Yes. I can't find him anywhere."

"What happened?"

"I don't know, Annie. I am *so* sorry. I put the children down for naps, and when I went to check on them a little bit ago, the bedroom window was open and James was gone. Betsy is as worried as I am. I've called the police and neighbors and searched all over the house."

"Sean? Did you call Sean?"

"No, not yet. I wanted to get in touch with you first."

"Faster, Brandon," Annie demanded, grateful when he punched his foot on the gas without needing an explanation. "Marjorie, we'll be home in forty minutes."

WILLIAM SCANNED THE streets for any sign of Denver as he diligently instructed his cab-driver where to turn. Slouched in the back seat, his hood pulled up over his head, he eyed each parked car and stranger they passed.

"Slow down here," he said. "But don't stop."

As the cab crawled past his mother's house, William spotted Joyce pacing the driveway, clutching her cell phone in her hands. Her lips were moving, her body fidgety. She might as well have been holding a neon sign stating she was waiting to meet her outlaw son. William's eyes sharpened, searching for Denver or any-one else awaiting his arrival. Although nothing seemed amiss, he couldn't chance it.

As the cab continued to the far side of Lake-shore, William could practically hear the min-utes ticking away and his dollars along with them.

"Keep driving?" the large fellow with a disc-shaped bald spot on the back of his head called from the front seat.

"Cruise along the lake and then circle back," William replied. He knew it was time to leave, time to get lost and put distance between all the complications people came with. He'd got-ten used to living alone and taking care of himself, and that was exactly the kind of life he intended to return to. Life would be better again once he was alone.

Except for Annie.

Even once he staked a new life for himself, he wouldn't be the same person who had arrived in Chinoodin Falls. Annie's influence had seen to changing him, and he recognized it was for the better.

William squeezed his eyes shut, but all he could picture was her sweet, adoring face gazing back at him. He strained to remember the last time he had felt such an attraction to a woman, such a willingness to devote himself to one. As he cracked his window, desperate for fresh lake air to snap him alert again, he surrendered to the truth that his heart would most likely always belong to her.

But she didn't need him. Wasn't that basically what she had told him? No, it was even worse. She had made him promise to get out of her life, not because she didn't want him, but because he was a hindrance to her and the children. As much as he longed to protect her, all of them, she found him a liability. *I don't want you to leave. I want you to leave me alone.* Her words had been a sucker punch to the gut. The initial strike surprised, but since then the pain pulsed farther and deeper like ripples fanning out from him.

When he opened his eyes again, he concluded that the pain was exactly the reason why he didn't want to get involved with people. You couldn't get hurt if you were never really attached.

But the inconvenient truth was that he had become attached to Annie again. He hadn't been prepared for it, believing it was only their old flame reigniting before quickly fizzling. But as he tracked a lone seagull cutting lazy circles in the sky, he knew leaving Annie again might nearly break him. He'd survived some heavy blows in his life, but getting over her would prove nearly impossible. It was best to get out before he was pulled in any deeper.

The lake horizon blurred outside his window, a wash of dazzling blue glittering like diamonds on the surface under a cloudless sky. He'd sought refuge in the water before, staring out over a midnight blue mass as far as the eye could see while a million twinkling stars illuminated it from above. Nights spent on deck with no light pollution, no sound pollution, had hinted that this was the life he had been cut out for. Focus on the job at hand. Don't let anyone tie you down. Live for yourself. Take what's yours and get on with it. He'd return to that life. Perhaps not in the Navy again, but he'd carve out a life of solitude somewhere. He'd move past this short, confusing phase and return to normal. His normal.

A sight on the beach caught his eye. "Pull in here, driver."

"Here?"

"Yes!" The cabdriver had barely slowed to a stop along Lakeshore Boulevard when William had one foot out the door. He'd spotted the tiny frame and moppy brown hair through the tall grass that covered the slight ridge between road and beach. Was it the hair? The stance? If pressed he couldn't put a description on what exactly had snagged his attention. But it was something familiar. Something he knew. It had only been a flash, but as he jogged back down the beach, the sight of the little boy confirmed he'd been right.

William paused to glance in all directions for Annie or Sean. Once he was sure the little boy was alone, he quietly approached, watching the boy's weary walk along the sand.

"James?" he called softly, dropping to one knee. James startled and spun around at the sound of his name. His cheeks were red-hot and streamed with salty tears. He sprang toward William and collapsed into his waiting arms.

"Can I go home now?" he asked, relief clear in his tone and how he tightened his arms around William's neck. "I want Mom."

William kissed him on the head and tenderly stroked his back, an instinct he vaguely associated with his father. A faint memory of being held lovingly by a workingman's hands, his father's hands, had him holding the little boy the same way. As he carried Annie's son to the cab, he could feel his own heart emphatically whispering, *It's too late. You're already involved.*

ANNIE SPRANG FROM Brandon's car and raced to Joyce and James, who were cuddling on Joyce's front step. The churning pit in her stomach had only grown worse with each passing mile to Chinoodin Falls, but now that she could see James, see her child, she couldn't contain her relief.

"James!" she called, her heart pounding in her throat. She couldn't get to him quickly enough. Her legs felt like lead weights running through water. He was there. He was safe. He was hers. When she finally reached the steps and dropped to the ground in front of him, James buried his head in Joyce's side.

Joyce offered an apologetic wince, her eyes silently conveying she understood the pang of Annie's hurt.

"James?" Annie whispered, wrapping her arms around his hot, sweaty body in a desperate attempt to convince herself he was okay. "Come to me...please?"

James's body shuddered before he released his grip on Joyce and dove into his mother's tight squeeze. How was it that his body felt smaller than she remembered? She nuzzled her nose against the top of his head and couldn't let him go.

"He hasn't said where he's been," Joyce explained quietly as Annie rocked him back and forth. "William found him wandering the beach alone."

"William?"

"He brought him here. I guess Marjorie is at the police station with Betsy."

Annie paused to consider that William had been the one to find James. She had been so cold toward him before, and now all she wanted to do was fall over herself with thanks.

"Mom?" James asked, face buried in her shoulder. "I don't want to live with Dad."

"I know." She leaned back to get a better angle on his puppy-dog eyes.

"Promise me I can stay with you forever."

"You don't need to worry about such a thing."

"But I heard you talking yesterday about Dad taking me. Then you came home from work early, got dressed up and I thought…"

Annie held her breath. It was her only defense against the flood of guilt she could feel mounting up like a tsunami. "What?"

"I thought you left so Dad could come get me and take me to live with him. I don't want to."

"Oh, James."

James's face scrunched up as the tears fell hard like rain. "I didn't know where to go."

"Home," Annie whispered. "We're going home." She pulled herself to her feet with James still clinging to her. "Joyce, please tell William thank you."

Joyce's eyes shifted to the garage before sorrowfully shaking her head. "He's gone, sweetie. He won't be back now."

He'd left all right, but perhaps finding James was a goodbye gift of sorts. A last love song penned to her heart, even if he hadn't intended it to be. Circumstances had presented them with an intersection, fate crossing their paths for one last time. But Annie couldn't dwell on the hole he'd left in her heart. She had to focus on the future. She had toyed all day with doing the unthinkable, building up her confidence for her meeting with Kenneth Bailey, all the while not sure she had the guts to pull off her plan. But as she snuggled James against her, his teary smile building the longer she held him, she was ready to settle this situation with Sean—for good.

CHAPTER SEVENTEEN

ANNIE PACED ACROSS the kitchen linoleum, the warm light from the fixture dimly illuminating all but the darkest corners of the room as Sean hollered through the phone receiver. Several times she had checked to make sure the children were still soundly sleeping through the ruckus.

"Where were you? And why didn't I hear about this when it happened?"

"He's safe and sound now, Sean. His boyhood fantasies of striking out on his own were short-lived, and he made his way home." Annie could barely get the lie from her lips with enough conviction to make it believable.

"Striking out on his own? Are you kidding me?"

"I know it's somewhat out of character for him—"

"That kid doesn't wander across the yard without you or Betsy, but I'm supposed to believe he ran away from home on his own?"

"Are you calling me a liar?" Annie stopped herself.

She knew she had to bide her time if she were going to rectify things perfectly. "I'm as surprised as you are."

"*Are* you? I'm not so sure."

"What does that mean?"

"You know what I think? I think you lost him, and you're afraid of the implications in court. That kid is going to be all mine before you can even blink."

"I didn't lose him, Sean. Marjorie had put them down for early naps when James snuck out."

"And another thing. *You're* his mother. Why is that old lady always watching the kids? Where were you? I checked at the diner, you know. You didn't finish your shift this morning and left without a viable excuse."

"Now you're checking up on me?"

"Somebody has to."

"It's none of your business where I was."

"When you lose my kid, it is my business. Something fishy is going on here, and I'm going to sniff it out."

"I can't do this now, Sean—"

Before she could finish, the line went dead. Annie gently placed her phone on the kitchen table and took a few calming breaths. She reminded herself that soon she and the children would begin a new life and a fresh start out from under Sean's thumb. Squeezing her eyes shut, she pictured the life she wanted—happy and peaceful, a little yellow house with white gingerbread trim, a tire swing swaying from a century-old oak tree, a golden retriever that answered to the name Honey. Simple pleasures, simple joys. She'd build a new future for her family...

But as hard as she tried to limit her vision to just Betsy and James, it was William's face that kept appearing before her. He was there, walking ahead of her, holding the children's hands and smiling at them. His face brightened as he turned back to grin at her, eyes wrinkling in satisfaction. He was kind and understanding and the addition to their family she yearned for. As her shoulders sank, her heart ached for what they might have had together so many years ago.

It was a creak on her back porch that dissolved the fantasy in an instant. She had assumed Sean had been at the office when they spoke, but as her nerves jolted, she second-guessed herself. Easing slowly to the back door, she flicked the kitchen light off. She hadn't heard anyone pull into the drive, but as a shadow moved past the door, it confirmed she wasn't alone. The ding signaling a text message on her phone startled her for only a moment. It was William. He was outside.

"William," she breathed after pulling open the door. Dressed in a black hoodie and blue jeans, his eyes rose slowly to hers. She hesitated in the doorway for a moment, all the while aching to pull him into the kitchen. As she eased the door open wider, he stepped inside and glanced around. "They're sleeping," she whispered, quietly latching the door.

He pushed off his hood and stood in the middle of her kitchen with the commanding presence of an oak tree, her imagined oak tree, with muscled roots sunk through the floor. Her heart had leaped at the sight of him, but now, alone with him in her dark kitchen, she found herself searching for the right words.

She wanted to tell him she could never repay him for finding her son and bringing him back to her. If only she could explain that she wanted him to be a part of her life again. Could she admit how most thoughts she had over the course of the day were of him, and how they drove her mad? She wanted to confess she was scared of what she was going to do about Sean, but she loved James so much, she'd do anything at this point to look out for him. If William would only say he'd done terrible things in his past, too, and understood how she felt, all the while convincing her it didn't make her a terrible person, perhaps it would give her the nerve to carry on. But mostly she wanted to tell him to stay.

"You're here," was all she could whisper.

"I needed to know you were okay."

Her breath hitched as she found his eyes beneath knitted brows. "I'm not okay."

He nodded, as if sensing all she held back behind her admission, and came to her, sweeping her into his arms and lowering his face to hers. His delicate kisses slowed to longer, deeper ones.

Annie could sense their near future. Clothing strewn, bodies clasped together as she made another impulsive mistake with a man, albeit a man she loved.

"William?" she managed between breaths, pressing her hands to his chest. "Did you come here tonight for—"

"You?" he whispered, eyes twinkling in the low moonlight that slipped through the window sheers. She nodded. He pressed his forehead to hers. "I can't stay away from you."

"But you're still going to?"

He nodded slowly. "Someday I'll be back, Annie. I swear it."

"Then tell me now, William, why you have to leave? What is it you've done that's so bad?"

As he began to lean back, she wrapped her arms around his waist, forcing him to face her.

"You'll think differently of me."

"We all have dark secrets within us."

He ran a finger down the slope of her nose. "Not all of us."

"You'd be surprised at the dark thoughts I've entertained recently."

"Really?"

"About Sean," she confided.

William stroked a wisp of hair off her temple as if building his resolve to tell a story.

"The difference is I acted on my dark thoughts, and you never would."

Annie mentally wrung her hands as she thought about what she was preparing to do. Her confession was nearly to her lips when William drew a weary breath and began one of his own.

"I was working in the Navy and had settled into a good life there. I'd grown to appreciate the structure, the discipline that it offered. But as much as I tried, I still had this anger inside me. For periods of time I'd feel fine and then something would happen to trigger me. It was like I was fighting my old man again."

"Dennis?"

"Yeah. I hated how I left home, washing my hands of him and Chinoodin and all of it, and taking off on my own. I enlisted in the Navy and never looked back, which meant I never had the chance to face him as a grown man. I'd always been a kid fighting him, or more like a kid defending myself against his rage. On the ship or at port, the smallest thing would suddenly bother me, and for all the discipline I embraced over the years, the unpredictability of my feelings made me feel...weak."

"I haven't seen any of that since you've been back."

"I never want you to see it." He cupped her face in his hands. "Or the children."

Annie's expression softened. "You care for them?"

"I care for all of you," he replied, quickly serious.

She smiled inwardly. "Go on."

"We were docked for a few days near Greece. I'd gone ashore and gotten drunk. Not one of my finer moments. One of the buddies I was with was a guy I didn't know very well named Bart Miller. He had signed on about a year earlier, and he'd started hanging around my friends. The first night had been fun and lighthearted. We'd met some locals and toured around town a bit. But the second night I caught him red-handed trying to lift my wallet. He still denied it and blamed a local who had been hovering near us all night. It started a huge fight, and I had no intention of leaving until I'd pummeled Bart's face." He paused to read her reaction. "I told you I wouldn't come off as flattering in this story."

"Continue" was her only reply.

"I made it back to the ship, along with my friends, but Bart got picked up by port authorities and our superiors raked him over the coals for fighting. The bar wanted to press charges and sue for damages. It got ugly. Bart was furious. To save his own neck, he gave me up as the one who instigated the fight. It stunk, but our superior wouldn't drop any of the charges against him, even after I admitted to what had happened. Bart was enraged. He didn't want a bad mark on his record and he blamed me.

"One night, when I was coming back from upper deck, he attacked me with a knife. I fought him off, but he ended up getting stabbed. I didn't intentionally do it, Annie, I swear to you, but during the struggle, he took a bad one to the gut."

Annie covered her mouth with her hands. "You killed him?"

"Almost," William replied. "I felt awful, Annie. I couldn't believe it. He came close to death. The way he was bleeding..."

"Is that why they're after you?"

"During Bart's surgery, he slipped into a coma. I had explained to my superiors what had happened, but between the bar fight and now having a fellow sailor in a coma because of me, they discharged me from the Navy."

"Discharged you?"

"It was my darkest day. I had nothing, Annie. All I had worked for over the last decade was finished in one brief moment. I demanded my file be reviewed again and when they refused, I lost it. I was pretty much carried off the ship."

"So that's it? That's why you—"

"Let me get this out, would you?" William pulled away and moved toward the window. "It took me a few days to get my bearings and wrap my head around what had happened. I decided my temper had taken the career I'd been working for my entire adult life, and I needed to rectify it. I had just made up my mind to return to Chinoodin, to piece together where my life had first begun to go wrong, when I got word from a friend that Bart had woken from his coma and claimed *I* had attacked *him*. He actually said I had threatened to kill him with the knife."

"But you didn't do it," Annie interrupted, charging over to him. "It was self-defense."

"It's not only the fight with Bart, Annie. I had been in fights before. My track record..."

"Would lead them to believe Bart," she supplied.

"Yeah. It was my word against his."

"So what did you do?"

"What could I do? I ran. I took off before they could arrest me. By the time I hit Tennessee, I had a Naval investigator brought in for special assignments, calling me to turn myself in, but I couldn't. I *wouldn't*. If I go back I'll most likely get arrested and charged with attempted murder, and I'm not going down for something I didn't do."

"William," Annie said, running her hand up his shoulder, "eventually it will all catch up with you, and you'll look even more guilty. Being on the run isn't the kind of life you want to lead."

"I want a life here," he replied, turning to

face her. "With you and the children and Mom. But I can't live that kind of life sitting behind prison bars. I can't make money to send for Mom's cancer treatments while wasting away in a cell. She needs a son who can take care of her, and if I can't be here physically to help her, the least I can do is send her the cash to survive."

Annie buried her face into William's chest. All she wanted to do was hold him close to her heart and never let him go, but she could see now that loving him fully meant giving him up. For how long, she could never know the answer, but judging by the despair that had begun to wrap its icy claws around the most tender part of her heart, she could only guess it would be much longer than she could bear.

"You have to go, William." She spoke so softly. "You have to go for Joyce."

William grazed his hands over her as she peered up at him, her eyes damp while fighting back tears.

"If things were different, Annie…"

"But they're not," she replied. "Fate slid us a loser hand *twice* now, it seems. We both have to do things we don't want to do, William, but we'll get through it in the end. For James and Betsy…and Joyce… I have to believe that."

William stroked her hair off her forehead, his topaz-blue eyes narrowing to darkened sapphire as he studied her. She had to be solemn, put on a brave front for him to leave her again.

"Come with me," he whispered.

"What?"

"Pack up the children right now. I heard about some jobs in the Pacific Northwest. Come with me, Annie. There isn't anything for you here."

Annie slid her fingertips along the chiseled contour of his jaw. "I'm tired of being afraid."

"Then come with me. We'll be safe together, you and the children. Sean will think twice about—"

"No," Annie stated. "I don't want that life for my children. I can't take them on the run."

"Wouldn't it be better than staying here and fighting Sean day in and day out?"

Annie stepped back as William gently reached to keep a hold of her. "I know what I have to do for them, William."

"Annie…"

"You should go," she said, clasping his hand. "Marjorie said someone was circling the house earlier. You should leave while you still have the chance." It was a lie, but she had to end it while she was still thinking clearly. He shouldn't detour any more than she ought to right now with so much on the line for them both.

"I love you." William said the words sweetly, like a nostalgic love song he'd been humming along to happily all day without realizing it. Never had another's voice soothed her anxious heart so much. When her eyes widened, he offered a whimsical grin and lowered his head to kiss her. When it was over, she found him smiling. "I suppose that means you love me, too, huh?"

"I always have," she agreed. He ran a thumb across her dampened cheek before drawing away to the backdoor. As he slipped out into the darkness, she whispered to the night, "And I always will."

CHAPTER EIGHTEEN

ANNIE CHECKED HER lipstick in the vanity mirror one more time, running a shaky finger along the edge of her lip before hastily flipping the visor closed again.

Marjorie was staying at her house for the night to babysit the children. She imagined them playing board games and eating sloppy joe sandwiches for dinner. They were so easily excited. It was exactly what she hoped to preserve for them.

Before she'd departed the house, Marjorie had made one last-ditch effort to keep her from leaving.

"I don't know what's gotten into you, sweetheart," she said, eyeing Annie's outfit. "Why are you meeting him dressed like that?"

Annie had kissed Marjorie on the cheek and assured her it wasn't at all what she thought. But as she climbed out of the car and smoothed the red halter dress over her hips, she prayed she knew what she was doing.

"You liked it the last time I wore it."

"You've made some changes since then," she scolded with a cluck of her tongue. "First you ask me to be the children's legal guardian if anything happens to you and now *this*?" the old woman had said, reaching to pull the front of Annie's dress up to hide her cleavage in a fussy maneuver only a mother would attempt. She supposed it made sense, as she loved Marjorie like a mother. "How much do you expect me to buy on faith? I'm worried about where your mind is at."

"I can't talk about it now," Annie replied, glancing past Marjorie to the children, who were giggling and eating popsicles on the porch steps. "Please trust me."

"Don't make a deal with the devil," she muttered, bringing Annie in for a tight hug. "He always wins."

Not this time, Annie thought as she headed down the walk. She couldn't bear to look over her shoulder for fear the children's happy faces would have her doubting herself.

"Annie? Where are you?" Brandon had asked after she'd driven to Sean's apartment complex. His voice burst through her cell phone as urgently as Marjorie had hugged her minutes earlier.

"I can't talk now, Brandon. I just wanted to thank you for all you've done for me and the children over the past few days."

"Annie, meet me somewhere or let me come to you. We can talk about this."

"There isn't anything to talk about, Brandon. Nothing is wrong, so please don't worry about me."

"Whatever you're planning—*don't*."

"Brandon…" She bit back what she wanted to say. Sometimes justice needed a little nudge. Working at the mayor's office, Brandon should already understand that.

"Annie, I don't know what's gotten into you lately, but you have to think about your children."

Annie rolled her eyes. They were all she thought about. The realization Sean could whisk James away and upset him on his own leisurely schedule had left her feeling gutted and raw. The only way out of this mess was, unfortunately, through it.

"You've been a good friend, Brandon," she whispered before hanging up and switching her phone to vibrate. Immediately, it began to pulse in her purse and wouldn't stop as she approached Sean's apartment. She pressed the buzzer and waited, each second ticking by in agonizing silence.

"Who is it?" Sean's raspy voice barreled through the air, almost too forceful for the tiny speaker box to tolerate.

"Annie," she told him, summoning the last of her courage.

"What do you want?"

"We need to talk."

"Talk?"

"I brought wine."

The agitated buzzer reminded her that she only had a few seconds to change her mind. She'd be in too deep once she was at his door.

As she climbed the stairs, her mind slipped back to the last time she had worn the silky red fabric she had on now and had slow danced in William's arms. Her gut wrenched at how happy she had been for a brief instant and how blissfully unaware she had been of what was in store.

She turned the corner to Sean's apartment only to discover him leaning against the door frame, watching her.

"What do we have here?" he whispered.

Annie plastered on the most pleasant smile she could muster. She hoped it would pass for genuine.

"I wasn't sure you'd let me up," she lied.

He snorted and ran a hand over his mouth in response. "You and I need to bury the hatchet once and for all, don't you think?" she continued.

"Really? What did you have in mind?"

Annie pouted her lips. "I thought we could have that date. But first I brought wine!" She breezed by him into his apartment and quickly eyed the place.

"How did you know I'd be alone?" he asked, shutting the door behind them.

"I took my chances. Why? Are you expecting anyone?"

"I'm happy to say I'm not," he replied, running his tongue over his bottom lip.

"Give me a hand, would you?" she asked, struggling with the corkscrew.

"In a minute," he muttered, grazing his lips over the back of her neck.

"So, where would you like to go? Dominic's is always good and it's easy to talk there," she said, forcing the bottle into his hands. "It's quiet and…romantic, too."

Sean shrugged and twisted the top of the cork, breaking a chunk of it off. In frustration he chucked the corkscrew into the sink and pushed the cork into the bottle with a forceful thumb and a deep-throated grunt.

"I'm sure we'll finish the bottle." He winked and handed the wine back to her.

"Perfect," she replied, forcing a giggle. "Why don't you put on some music while I pour the wine." She gauged his reaction and imagined her entire plan unraveling in an instant before her eyes. She was executing a delicate dance with a wild bull that could gore her at any moment.

Sean cocked his jaw and smirked.

"Sure," he finally mumbled before easing out of the kitchen. "Any requests, baby?"

"Surprise me."

As soon as Sean was out of sight, Annie yanked two wineglasses from the cupboard and poured him a tall glass.

As soft music wafted through the air, Sean was back at her side. She swirled his glass and handed it to him, studying him from over the top of her rim. Taking a dainty sip of her own, she breathed a sigh of relief when he downed it all.

"Don't you want to have a shower and get ready if we're going out?" she teased, reaching for the wine bottle, but her body stiffened when he moved in for a kiss instead.

"Patience, patience, maybe you'll get a good-night kiss if you're lucky," she told him, giggling. On the inside, though, she was starting to lose her nerve. "But first I need to freshen up a second. Why don't you pour us some more wine? I'll be right back."

Sean hesitated, his eyes squinting in discernment, but before he could say anything, she had ducked from his embrace and scrambled to the bathroom.

Behind the door, she trembled and broke out into an instant cold sweat. She had come here in the stupid dress that William had loved, but she now despised it. If William could see her now, he'd be repulsed just as she was repulsed with herself. Promising herself she'd burn the dress as soon as she got home, she waited.

She tried to imagine William riding west into the sunset, the sun highlighting the flecks of gold in his hair and the bronze of his skin. In another life she'd be right there with him, clutching him around the waist as they journeyed off to happily-ever-after.

"Oh, William," she whispered. "If you had known what I was planning, you would have never left me last night."

"Annie, if you want me lookin' my best for our big date and whatever's to come, you'll have to let me in there." Annie's heart thudded as fast as a sprinting jackrabbit.

Holding her breath in absolute silence, she eased open the door. She half expected Sean to jump out in front of her, wise to her deviousness. His treacherous mind two steps ahead of her. But—nothing. He came toward her, gave her a big wink and shut the bathroom door closed behind him. She took several calming breaths and scanned the apartment again. She zeroed in on Sean's desk but froze.

What was she doing? What was she thinking?

All she wanted to do was run away—far, far away—and never look back. Perhaps William had the right idea. Maybe she should pack up the children now and follow him across the country. The law would be after them, but at least they'd be together and have the children...

Betsy's beaming face materialized at the forefront of Annie's mind, her daughter's rosy complexion and dancing eyes as warm and sunny as a summer day. And James's shy smile, as he peeked up at her from the living room floor with ships scattered around him, was as clear and real as if he were truly before her right now. She wanted to clutch their little faces between her palms and smoosh her face against their cheeks. She wanted to drink in their innocence and reassure them that their total dependence on her was solid. Whisper again and again in their ears as they slept that she loved them and would protect them from every bump in the night.

The panic began to lift as Annie raised her head to stare at her reflection in the living room mirror. Her children needed her to be bold now. Bold, brave, unwavering. No matter what anyone might say about her, she would do what it took for their best interests. She had come here with a purpose, she decided, and she wasn't leaving until it was done.

"Come on, Heiress," she muttered, her fingers wildly skimming through papers in Sean's office. "Help me find it."

Once Annie had found what she was hoping for, she called out to Sean, still in the shower, her excuse at the ready.

"You'll have to give me a raincheck on that date, Sean. Marjorie's just phoned to say James has a stomachache and I've got to go. You know what you're always telling me about how I should be a good mother."

Less than a beat later, Annie was zooming

down the stairs, but she was sure she could hear Sean cursing her name.

WILLIAM ROLLED UP beside a gas pump and surveyed his surroundings before cutting the engine. The farther west he traveled and the smaller the towns he passed through, the more likely someone could remember him or at the very least remember Old Red. As he filled the tank, he checked the number of miles until the next stop. He had slept a few hours in Duluth before hitting the road again and cruising west along Route 2 for what he knew would be hundreds of lonely miles.

There was no plan, no solid destination. He'd keep his eyes open for places to rest and do his best to keep his nose clean, thus avoiding any encounters with the law. When a place seemed right, he'd stop and find work. Before the end of summer, he'd maybe head southwest, making his way south of the border.

North Dakota was breathtaking in the summertime. He was thankful for the distraction, though the natural wonders would never unshackle the emotional chains from Chinoodin Falls. Between the Black Hills, roaming buffalo sightings and stretches of wide-open spaces unfolding before him, he had plenty to admire, but never in his life had he felt more trapped. Each mile constricted, and all because of a pining for the woman he'd left behind. He feared no amount of mileage could outrun the hold she had over his heart or soul.

William slid money across the counter to the old man for gas and beef jerky and had no sooner turned to leave when his cell phone rang.

"Brandon?" he asked, heading out again into the early-morning sunshine.

"Will."

The seriousness of his voice cut through the line, so unfamiliar from Brandon's usual comic flare. Throughout their friendship, William had never heard Brandon begin a conversation without a quip or quick joke. The mere sound of his own name made William stop short in the parking lot.

"What is it?"

"It's Annie."

The words nearly knocked him out cold. With his heart suddenly a lump lodged at the back of his throat, William waited for Brandon to continue and when he didn't, William scrambled for words of his own.

"Out with it!"

"Something is seriously wrong."

"With Annie? *What?*"

Brandon groaned into the phone. "She's talking crazy, man."

"Spit it out, Brandon."

"I took her to see a lawyer a couple of days ago. I thought she wanted to hire one since Sean filed for full custody of James. But the lawyer she met with doesn't specialize in family law. He's a criminal lawyer."

"Okay."

"She was saying all these things about taking control of her life and protecting James and…"

"And?"

"She had called me after seeing an article in the paper and asked me all these questions about what Sean does at City Hall and who he hangs out with. She wanted to know what kind of professional reputation he has. I had foolishly spouted off about things I suspected about Sean. It just fueled her questions. I don't remember everything she said, but one thing sticks out pretty clearly now."

"What?"

"She said someone has to make Sean pay."

William scowled. "What's that supposed to mean?"

"She was serious, man. I tried getting her to

talk last night, but she had an eerie calm about her. She's resolved to do something, but—"

"What?" William paced the parking lot, oblivious to the car pulling past him until he nearly smacked the front fender. He chucked his beef jerky at the fleeing back windshield before hustling back to his bike.

"I have a sick feeling about it, man. I stopped by her house this morning, and she didn't come home last night."

"The kids?"

"With Marjorie."

"Did she know where Annie was going?"

Brandon hesitated for a moment before muttering, "Sean's."

William strained to recall anything out of sorts the night he had said goodbye to Annie. He replayed their conversation and searched for an inkling that she was preparing the unthinkable. He had been drawn to her heart, her goodness, the love bubbling inside her. But he also knew the love she had as a mother might push her to the brink. He had to get to her before she maybe did something reckless.

"She isn't answering her phone," Brandon went on. "She's so worried about James, I'm not sure she's thinking clearly."

"I'm on my way," William told him and

shoved his phone in his jacket pocket to fire up Old Red. Swinging back down the lonely highway he'd just covered, he punched the gas without reservation. He knew he wouldn't make Chinoodin Falls until the evening if he drove straight through and even to do that, he needed to fly. He just prayed he wouldn't be too late.

CHAPTER NINETEEN

WITH THE SUN at her back, Annie arrived in Chinoodin Falls a new, albeit exhausted woman. She rubbed her tired eyelids and rested her head against the seat. One yawn accompanied another as she closed her eyes for a few quick winks. But as much as her weary body tried to sleep, her mind was restless. Peeking open a mascara-crusted eye to study her cell phone, she dialed Marjorie.

"Good mornin', sunshine." Marjorie's voice reassured with each lovely lilt. "Are you okay?"

It was too much effort to keep her eyes open as she pressed the phone to her ear.

"I'm good," she murmured.

"When will you be home?"

"Later today. I have one more thing to do."

"Honey, I've been so worried about you, I haven't slept a peep."

"I'm fine. Really. I crashed at Karrin's and was up early this morning to take care of some out-of-town business."

"The children woke up asking for you, and I've been stalling."

"Put them on the line, would you?" Annie smiled. She had attempted to come home after leaving Sean's, but a suspicious car had been parked in front of her house. If the man inside was the one after William, she couldn't afford to get involved. Not until she was finished. This was the only insurance policy she had, and she couldn't let anything detour her plan. Luckily, Karrin had made up her couch for her, no questions asked.

"Mommy?" Betsy asked. "Where are you?"

"I'm running some errands, sweetie. Did you eat breakfast?"

"Marjorie made us French toast and strawberries."

"It sounds delicious." Annie wanted to reach right through the phone and squeeze her in the longest hug Betsy would afford her. "How's your sidekick?"

"He's playing with his boats again. Do you want to talk to him?"

"Hold the phone to his ear."

"Hi, Mom," James mumbled. "When are you coming back? I miss you."

"I miss you, too, sweetheart. I'll be back later today. Be a good boy for Marjorie, okay?"

She could hear a shuffling as Marjorie returned to the phone.

"Annie," she whispered, "everyone has been calling for you."

"Who?"

"Joyce. Brandon."

"I'm fine, Marjorie. I'll be home later today. I have to go." She hurriedly said goodbye to Marjorie as another call interrupted them. She drew an excited breath as she answered it. "William."

"*Thank you* for answering your phone," he breathed. "I just pulled over in Duluth."

Annie sat forward. The choppy lake water tossed with a gray, dismal hue. It matched the sky for miles, but all she could see when she stared out over it was William's perfect face.

"Why are you calling, William? Are you okay? I thought you'd have made it farther than Duluth."

"That's what happens when you start driving back the way you came."

"You're coming back? You can't."

"Brandon said you wouldn't answer your phone, Annie. He thinks you're talking strange. What on earth is going on with you?"

"It's none of his business," Annie huffed. "And I'm *fine*."

"Then tell me you didn't see Sean last night."

"What?" she replied, nearly laughing from nervousness. "I…I had to talk to him about James. What's gotten into you?"

"Me? I've been doing eighty for the past few hours, all the while sick with worry about you."

"William, turn around. If you come back to Chinoodin, you'll be arrested. We made our clean break the other night, and it was beautiful. Let's leave it at that."

"Whatever you're doing, I can help, Annie. You don't have to take matters into your own hands."

"Oh, but I do," she whispered. "I love you, William. I always have. My feelings have never waned even after all these years. And that's why I'm begging you to turn around now. The man after you is parked outside my house. I'm sure of it. You can't come back here without him finding you. *Please*."

"Denver is there?"

"Who else could it be?"

"I'll meet you somewhere else."

"Goodbye, William. I know you're a good man, and you'll make the right decision. Take care of yourself."

Annie stared at the phone in her hand, releasing her finger from the darkened screen. How she willed herself to compartmentalize her feelings. To hide. To bury. To postpone. She couldn't mourn the loss of William today. She could lose herself in a frenzied oblivion tomorrow. She could dive beneath the covers and sob until the places in her soul that mourned his loss were exhausted.

Today she had to finish fixing her Sean problem. Her plan wasn't over yet, and the last part would be the most challenging thing she'd ever have to do.

ANNIE FIDDLED WITH the stem of her water glass, running her fingers along it as she rehearsed her speech in her head. To be convincing she couldn't sound rehearsed. But reminding herself of the key points ahead of time couldn't hurt, either.

The waiter returned to her table, glancing at the wine menu she hadn't yet touched.

"Still waiting on your companion?"

"Yes."

"May I place a drink order for you?"

"No, thank you." Annie returned her gaze to the front entrance as the waiter moved on to his next table. She couldn't allow herself to sip a glass of wine no matter how desperately she craved it to calm herself. She needed her wits about her completely.

Her thoughts drifted to William, offering his help to her and nearly pleading for her to accept it. She wished she could, but she had to protect him the best way she knew how and that was by not involving him at all. She was alone on this one, but nothing had felt lonelier than the night before, snooping around Sean's apartment. It had been eerily silent, except for her shuffling among his papers and files. The memory made her shudder as she glanced around at nearby patrons, grateful to have their company.

She glanced down at the red halter dress still clinging to her body. Denver had been outside her house, and meant she couldn't return home until this deal was done. First she'd hug the children, then she'd scrub away the last twenty-four hours and let it circle the drain.

"Are you ready for that raincheck?" A familiar voice snapped Annie alert again. She cringed as Sean kissed her on the cheek and tickled his fingers down her back.

"What makes you say that?"

"Your dress doesn't lie."

Oh, but it does, she thought as Sean took a seat across from her. He immediately motioned for the waiter and ordered two whiskey sours.

"Thank you for meeting me, Sean."

"I got your text, but I would have preferred an invitation in person." He leaned back in his chair, arrogance saturating his large frame. But from the softness in his eyes, she knew he wasn't certain about what was really happening here. It was a bluff.

"You and I didn't get a chance to discuss James last night," Annie began, sitting straighter in her chair.

He smiled through hooded eyes. "We were a little distracted."

"I don't know if you've noticed recently, but he's been withdrawn."

"That's just who he is. He needs a man in the house." Sean shrugged, reaching for his first glass of whiskey and sour. Annie fiddled with the frayed edges of her dinner napkin as Sean slugged back half the glass. "We should talk about that, baby."

"I can take care of James and myself," Annie replied with an eye roll. "You're the last thing I need in my house, Sean."

"So what was last night? What's this all about?"

Annie readjusted in her seat, inclining her head. "Testing the waters."

"Really?" Sean chuckled.

"I have no intention of ever getting close to you again, Sean. In fact, I'm planning on burning this dress as soon as I get home."

Sean shot a look around the crowded restaurant as if to spot whether anyone else was listening.

"Is this some kind of tease, Annie? Because I don't think you want to play with me."

"I've done nothing but try to make things work with you, Sean, for the sake of all of us, especially James. But all you do is bully me and torment him. Do you get some kind of pleasure out of it? Because you're breaking his heart."

"Is that what we're doing here?" Sean scoffed, tossing back the rest of his drink. "Were you trying to butter me up last night? You should have tried a little harder, Annie." Sean leaned heavily on the table, his whiskey breath easy to smell. "Maybe I take that job in California, huh? You'll see that kid twice a year if you're lucky *and* if you can afford to buy the plane ticket. Though you probably won't be able to without my child support keeping you afloat."

"I'm his mother. How could you do that to me? To *him*."

"Nobody pushes me around. You think you can parade about town with that swabbie and then cuddle up to me to get your way with the kid? Have fun paying a lawyer without my money comin' in every month. You're *finished*. James will be asking 'Mommy who?' before I'm done with you."

As Sean pushed back his chair to leave, Annie took a manila envelope out from beneath the table and placed it on his bread plate.

"I wouldn't leave without this, if I were you, Sean. You wouldn't want it falling into the wrong hands."

Sean's eyes sharpened as he stared at the envelope. "Tell me what it is."

"No."

"What's gotten into you?"

"Get on with it already," Annie ordered, drumming her fingers on the finely pressed tablecloth. She was grasping for anything she could think of to help her keep her cool. Sean had to believe her and believe her enough to be scared. No. Not scared. Utterly terrified.

Sean pulled the manila envelope closer. After taking a swig of his second glass of whiskey sour, he peeled open the top of the folder and peeked inside.

"It's not going to bite you," Annie said calmly. "It's like ripping off a bandage."

"I like watching you like this." Sean smirked. "You're trying so hard to be...what? Mysterious?" He laughed, making her draw a sharp breath. "You're not in control, baby. I appreciate this act you've put together for me, although I don't really know why. Maybe you're having regrets about us at last?"

"No, that's not it at all, despite how this may look to you."

"I'm not so sure about that." He waved the envelope at her. "I think you wanted to work out an arrangement because you're getting desperate. Do you really think you can keep James from me? Nobody in this town would ever cross me." Sean guzzled the last of his drink, his face slowly reddening from his neck up to his cheeks and oblong nose. "You had better think long and hard about crossing me, baby. You're nobody in this town."

Annie's eyes narrowed. "I'm James's mother. And given you're his father, I'm the most important person in his life."

Sean laughed. "Your father left you. Your loser boyfriend bailed when he found out about Betsy. I'm the best thing that's ever happened to you, and perhaps—" he looked thoughtfully off into the distance "—I'm the best thing for James now."

"I'm his *mother*. You know I love him more than I love myself."

"You're barely holding it together!" Sean scorned her. "I'm a professional, a citizen in good standing, and I can provide him with a life you could never dream of. A private school, a beautiful house on the beach, every opportunity available.

"Look at you. You have two children to two different men, a job that doesn't come close to paying the bills without my financial support. Heck," he mocked, "you don't even have another dress to wear."

"What are you saying, Sean?"

"The job I was offered in California was too good to pass up, and I already filed the paperwork for James. When you showed up on my doorstep last night, I figured I had played you all wrong. I thought maybe I could reconsider a custody hearing. But now it's time to teach you a lesson. Consider it a done deal."

"How low of you, Sean," Annie replied, shaking her head steadily.

He shrugged, his face smug. "It's the way of the world, kid. Eat or be eaten."

"Apparently." She nodded before drawing a

breath. "Well, if that's the case, I want to thank you for making this so easy for me. I realize now, more than ever, how much James needs me to protect him from you. I was busy last night, and perhaps a little…naughty.

"*But* as it turns out, not nearly as naughty as you. Inside that envelope, which you are too busy gloating to open, is evidence that can be used to incriminate you for forgery." Sean's patchy red complexion, which had grown warmer from the whiskey, now became a grave white.

Flipping frantically through the papers, he asked, "Where did you get these?"

"The original will of the Heiress of Chinoodin? I should ask where *you* got it."

"I… I… You couldn't have—"

"Tsk, tsk. Try to keep up, darling." Annie felt a surge of fiery brazenness fill her. Terror splashed across Sean's face as he thumbed through the documents. His grimace told her all she needed to know: her plan was going to work.

"Would you like to hear the specials?" their waiter asked, suddenly hovering over their table.

"It turns out we won't be staying," Annie replied.

"These are all copies," Sean growled. "Where are the originals?"

"Which originals do you mean, Sean? The original will you forged so that company out west could buy the land preservation and pay you a very handsome finder's fee? Your new BMW and motorcycle make a lot of sense now."

"But…but—"

"Here's what's going to happen, Sean. Listen carefully, because your freedom depends on it. You're going to accept that high-paying job in California and begin immediately. You're going to drop the custody suit for James. You will continue to make child-support payments on time every month because he's your only son and you care about his welfare. And most importantly you will have no further physical contact with James unless *he* chooses it. You may mail birthday cards, Christmas cards, thinking-of-you cards… I don't care. I'll make sure he gets them. But all other contact in person or by phone will be up to him."

"Do you think you can threaten me with this and then waltz out of here scot-free?" Sean demanded.

"I'm counting on it. Because if you don't comply, bad things will happen to you. If you threaten me or the children in any tiny way, my lawyer—"

"Your lawyer?"

"Mmm-hmm."

"Who in this town would take your case?"

"My lawyer will access the originals and hand deliver them to the authorities."

"Why wouldn't you do that now?"

Annie paused, thoughtfully contemplating her answer. "I have my reasons, I suppose. One of them revolves around James and the legacy you'd be leaving him as a man and a parent. Whatever my reasoning, you'd be wise to take advantage of it, Sean. It's the one and only chance I'm offering."

"So you think you can leave me with *nothing* and get away with it?"

"I wouldn't call your freedom nothing. And I'm still offering you an opportunity to rebuild a relationship with your son, albeit on his terms." As the waiter returned with the bar tab, Annie stood, gathering her purse. "You can leave the bill with him." Shoulders back, chin tilted, she faced Sean with a confidence she had spent years grasping to find. "I would say I'll see you around, but we both know it's in your best interest that I don't."

Sean glared at her. "This isn't the end, Annie," he whispered.

"It is for me." And with a swelling pride, she strode out of Sean's life, and her nightmare, for good.

CHAPTER TWENTY

WILLIAM SAT BACK on the leather seat and took in the familiar landscape. His hands throbbed from gripping the handlebars and throttle all day with no more than a few minutes' break between long stretches on the road. He brushed bugs off the front of his jacket and noted that buying a larger windshield would have served its purpose. He'd put more miles on Old Red in the last two days than Dennis probably had in the fifteen years he'd owned her.

He reached into his pocket as his cell phone rang. Smiling at the caller ID, he crooned into the phone.

"I knew you couldn't stay away for long."

"William," Annie breathed, a hearty laugh following. "It's over. I've beaten Sean at his own game."

"Are you okay? Are you *safe*?"

"Yes. I'm on my way home."

"Good." William nodded, running his hand

through his hair. "You didn't push him off a cliff or anything drastic, did you?"

"*No,*" Annie asserted, laughing harder. He could tell the stress she'd been harboring had finally found a release valve and was steaming out of her in bursts of giddy laughter. "But I did it. I actually did it, and James is going to be okay. He's going to be more than okay. He's going to be wonderful! Oh, William, I wish I could see you right now and tell you all of it. You wouldn't believe what I've done. *I* can hardly believe it!"

"Where are you now?"

"Turning onto my road." He smiled wider when he heard her gasp into the phone. "Is that *you*?"

He swung his leg off the bike and met Annie at her driver's-side door. She had barely managed to cut the engine when she sprang from the car and flew into his arms.

"Surprised?" He grinned as she tightened her hold around his neck.

"What are you doing here? Denver will get you! He'll arrest you right here in my driveway!"

"I needed to know you were okay."

"William, no." She kissed him, pressing his face between her palms as tears glistened in her eyes. "I'm so happy to see you, but Denver…"

"I'm meeting him next."

"You're what?" Annie gasped, gripping the collar of his jacket to give him an abrupt shake. "No, William, I won't let you!"

"Annie," he said, as calm and peaceful as a Sunday morning. "I've been thinking about it on the ride back here. Hours on the road give you plenty of time to think and assess your life. You told me I was a good man, and I'd do the right thing. And I'm actually going to. Thanks to you. I've already decided, Annie, and I know now that this is what's best for us."

"Us?"

"I'd like to believe there's an us in our future."

Annie kissed him quickly before pulling her face away again in protest. "But, William, if you meet Denver…how will you… What will he…"

"I know what I'm doing, Annie. I told Denver I'd meet him at the diner to turn myself in. When I was running, it felt wrong. It was wrong. I felt like I was delaying my real life from the beginning. If accepting whatever punishment they throw at me is what it takes to have a clean slate and a new life with you, then that's a far better trade than years being free, but on the run alone. I know the life I want now. It took me forever to figure it out, but now that I have, I'm going after it with everything I've got."

Annie smiled beautifully. And he warmed from the tips of his ears to the tips of his toes just from being near her in all her radiance.

"When do you meet him?" she whispered as he kissed her on the forehead.

"Now."

"Now?"

"It will be all right. Go hug your babies. It's the start of a new life for all of you."

"*Wait*. I have to tell you what happened with Sean."

"Whatever happened, I just wish I could have seen the look on his face." He fired up the bike, but before pulling onto the street, he stopped to study her. "Is that what you wore?" She shrugged, a wry grin on her lips. William rolled his eyes. "That poor sucker never had a chance."

ANNIE SLIPPED INTO the house, dropping her purse on the kitchen table. Through the window she could spot Marjorie and the children in the backyard, huddled around something in the grass. Whether it was a bug or flower, it had the children fascinated.

It's the beginning of a brand-new life for all of us, Annie told herself. She wanted to declare it to anyone who would listen, but she had to take care of first things first.

Annie raced up the stairs and ducked into the bathroom, delighted to finally wash the last two days off her. She peeled the red dress from her body, dropped it in the backroom sink and paused to stare at it. In the light of day, her meeting with Sean over, her pledge to set the garment on fire now seemed foolish. Mia wouldn't be too thrilled to learn about it, considering it was her dress. Perhaps a long, hot shower would be all she needed to recharge.

But as she recalled how she'd felt wearing it the night before, she reminded herself she was always a person to err on the side of, well, symbolism. She would never wear it again, and she wouldn't let Mia be caught dead in it, either. It had to go. Now.

Rifling through the medicine cabinet, she found a matchbook from her wedding reception. Finding it appropriate, she flung three lit matches into the sink. They singed a hole in the center of the crumpled garment before the flames quickly fanned to consume the rest. Extinguishing the flames with water from the faucet, she assessed the damage. It was gone now. Gone and soon to be forgotten.

The shower was steaming within minutes, and Annie felt grateful. Hanging her head, hand planted on the shower wall, she exhaled slowly. She released the tension she'd been holding for more than the past two days, as the hot beads of water pelted her neck. She'd fought for years. Years. But her plan had worked, and Sean would be flying to California shortly without her sweet James. She let out a little yelp at the thought of it.

"Oh, William." She chuckled. "Things will be okay now. I know it. Someday you'll be home with us again and this period of my life with Sean will be as forgotten as that dress."

Annie smoothed her hands over her face as she eased her head back into the water and replayed his parting words to her: "This isn't the end, Annie." She'd been so self-assured at the time, it hadn't phased her. It was the sort of thing she would have expected him to say. He hated to lose, to be called out, to be in the wrong.

But it had been the end in her mind. The final chapter. Any rational person would pack his belongings and hightail it out of town before she changed her mind and notified the police. Sean wouldn't be able to stand being caught and arrested.

She shut off the water and stepped out of the shower, just as a terrifying thought crashed over her. Sean wasn't a rational person. He was unpredictable.

Instantly, the urge to get to her children hit her. Cinching a towel around her petite frame, she hustled from the bathroom and down the stairs, leaving a path of wet footprints behind her. Marjorie met her at the foot of the staircase.

"What's wrong?" Annie gasped, reading the concern on her friend's face. "Is it the children?"

"The children? No," Marjorie said as Betsy and James ran into the hallway.

"Mommy! You're home!" Betsy shouted, springing for her mother's arms. "When did you get here? Wait a minute…were you taking a shower?" Annie squeezed Betsy and James all the while never taking her eyes from Marjorie.

"I answered your cell phone," Marjorie explained, holding it out for Annie. "She said to get to the diner immediately."

"Who?"

"Karrin."

"Really? Why?"

"She said immediately."

"*Why?*"

Marjorie shook her head and clasped her hands at her chin. "Now, Annie. Go *now*."

WILLIAM CRUISED UP and down the Chinoodin city streets, stretching out his short ride to the diner for as long as he could. A calm had swept over him as soon as he'd made the decision to call Denver. Even though he could be heading to prison, he somehow already felt like a free man. He knew what he wanted from life and saw the path needed to get it. Perhaps the system would go easy on him. Perhaps not. But he didn't want to fight any longer when he had people who needed him.

As he drew closer to Pop's Place, things didn't seem right. People milled around on the sidewalk, many straying out into the street. The thought of a party letting out of the dinky diner was the only explanation his drained mind could muster, but even in his exhausted state, he knew that notion was ridiculous. It wasn't until he got closer that his mind could even accept the full severity of what was happening. The sudden shock of it all.

From the roof at the back of the diner, smoke billowed. It was more smoke than he had ever seen. The sliver of moon, a clipped fingernail rising higher with each passing minute, flickered in and out of view beyond it. Nearly dumping the bike against the curb on the opposite side of the street, he gasped up at the sight in horror.

Before him was a monster, a fiery locust engulfing every inch of his mother's diner with uncompromising destruction. The near-white flames edged with goldenrod yellow, spouted from the roof before coiling up, rising in an intricate dance of nature's most primal and demolishing element. Smoke illuminated red and orange by the flames climbed several hundred yards into the air before camouflaging the sky. He imagined the trail of smoke stretched for miles and perhaps would still be visible by morning, although Pop's Place would most definitely not be.

Seconds ticked by, and the trees and hedges around the diner flew up into singed ash. The Pop's Place sign crashed to the ground with startling calamity, the bubbling, sweltering paint easily visible. The awning had dissolved into nothing more than a black rib cage while the roof at the front had sunk in like a charred wooden spoon. The brick building was blistering into a pile of wreckage before him, and like the surrounding crowd, he couldn't tear away his eyes.

Onlookers stood aghast, unable to find their feet. Cell phone cameras emerged, the sporadic glow of screens flickering like fireflies to capture the sight. Perhaps it was the only thing a person could do when there wasn't anything left to do. But they startled and fled when flames burst from the windows, shattering glass across the sidewalk like a million tinkling diamonds.

William shielded his face with an arm as he ran through the crowd and toward the blaze. His only thought was of his mother. Was she here? Had she made it out safely? Peeking out above the crook of his arm, which had warmed from the heat, he wafted a flailing hand in front of him, weakly probing to find his way. The wind had shifted a cloud of smoke over him, encompassing him in near darkness. It consumed his lungs. Choking and sputtering for any pocket of fresh air, he yanked his shirt over his nose, a makeshift filter that was weak at best. His eyes scratched with each blink, tiny fragments of debris saturating the air swirling around him.

The wail of dueling fire engines gaining in the distance cut through the screams and shouts reverberating around him. Their piercing sirens both relieved and terrified him as the trucks arrived on scene. Firefighters scrambled to their stations. The rev of their engines rumbled in jarring shifts as they hooked up hoses and lifted a ladder to tower over Pop's Place. Police cars swarmed from every direction, their flashing lights no competition for the raging flames, which picked up velocity by the second.

He pushed on, around the side of the diner, where the curtain of smoke lifted. Pressing through the crowd that had sought cover alongside the barbershop parking lot, he frantically searched faces for the familiar one he had to find.

The first familiar face William spotted was Bobby, who had pulled his apron up over his nose to breathe. As he locked eyes with William, he flagged him to keep going.

"Joyce is around back!" he shouted.

William tore through the crowd to the back, where Karrin was comforting his mother. Her eyes were swollen red slits she could barely pry open between harrowing sobs.

"Will!" she screamed as he joined her. "It's awful! Dear God, it's awful!"

William threw his arms around his mother, clasping her tightly as she buried her face in his chest. "Miles!" he called. "Is everybody out?"

"Yes, but I don't know how it started. It wasn't from the kitchen."

"Somewhere from the back!" Karrin yelled over the sirens piercing through the deafening roar of the fire. Another fire engine had arrived in the back parking lot, sending people scattering like ants in all directions.

"How could this happen?" Joyce wailed. "What will I do?"

Another explosion sent people scrambling for protection, and William used his body to shield his mother. When he looked up again, he spotted Denver at the far end of the lot, hauling Sean off the ground in handcuffs. William blinked, straining to decipher if his eyes were telling the truth. But it only took him another moment to understand exactly what had happened.

"Mom, we have to get you home," William

coaxed gently in her ear while leading her toward to the barbershop.

"Karrin called Earl for me. He'll be here any minute. If I leave, he'll be upset, William. I have to wait for Earl!"

The spray from the firefighter's hose was forceful, but futile attempting to extinguish the flames. The firefighters would have to prepare themselves for a long, hard fight. One that would probably last through until early morning. He couldn't leave now. He had to stay. To see. He had to bear witness to the end of Pop's Place. The end of it all.

William's eyes shifted across the gravel lot to where Denver had loaded Sean in the back seat of his car and slammed the door shut. He stood beside the vehicle, heaving labored breaths. William knew he'd be next. The man was staring him down, seeming to gauge his next move. William didn't know what to do anymore. Glancing at the thundering inferno combusting before his eyes, he squeezed his mother to his side. How much did he have to pay for past mistakes? Because as it turned out, it was the people who needed him the most who would be stuck paying the price. Deep in his heart, an ache nearly caused him to hunch over in pain.

He lowered his head and found his mother gazing up at him.

"Do you have to go now, sweetie?" Her eyes glistened with tears, but her mouth turned up in a forced smile.

He furiously shook his head, unable and unwilling to abandon her. "Not until I know everyone is okay."

"We'll be fine," she assured him. "Everyone escaped with plenty of time. Go on now, sweetie." She glanced past him to Denver. "I know you have to go."

"But I need to take care of you. I can't leave you like this."

"Joycie!" Earl cried, moving as quickly as his stout, stiff legs could carry him. He pushed past a police officer and dodged around a taped-off barrier with astounding speed for a man who could barely climb in and out of a booth. "Joycie, love! Are you hurt? It's okay, love. I'm here now."

William relinquished his mother into Earl's arms as masses of molten embers sparked and twirled above their heads. He fell silent as the couple swayed back and forth, their shadows clinging, one unwilling to proceed without the other.

He found himself releasing a sigh of relief.

Earl held his mother, and William knew the old man would never let her go. Backing away, he strode across the parking lot to face Denver and the next phase. He could only guess how long that would last.

"I wasn't sure you'd show, Mr. Kauffman," Denver said, his voice deep and crisp.

William held out his wrists for handcuffs. "I'm a man of my word, Mr. Corrigan."

Denver waved him off. "You're not under arrest, son. For the time being, anyway. The authorities do want to question you, and we can go from there. Think you can behave yourself?"

He nodded and followed Denver around the back of the car, pausing to check the progression of the fire. It was dragging the fifty-year-old building to its knees with unapologetic force, and there was nothing anyone could do about it. He imagined Dennis there, somewhere in the crowd, suffering the kind of gut-wrenching loss William had always wanted to inflict on him. But even after years of fantasizing about such a thing, William took no delight in the thought now. He wouldn't spend any more time harboring anger toward his stepfather. The old man's hold over him would perish along with the brick and mortar.

Once he'd slid into the back seat, he brushed ash from his hair and the tips of his eyelashes. The singed aroma wafting from his clothes, which usually elicited memories of summer cookouts and late-night bonfires, now made his stomach turn. He could sense Sean's eyes boring into the side of his head, watching his every move.

"Why did you do it, Sean?" William asked with forced calm before glancing at him. "Why did you destroy it?"

Sean huffed in defiance. "You're right here with me. I knew you were dirty, swabbie. I knew it from the moment I laid eyes on you that day in the diner. We're alike, you and I."

A tightness crept up William's jaw. "We're nothing alike, Sean. You destroy whatever you touch."

"Is that right?" Sean chuckled. "And you don't?"

William cast his eyes out the window, listening to Denver radioing to local police, considering Sean's words. Perhaps he had destroyed everything he had touched, too. He had tried to rectify his mistakes, but where had it gotten him? He'd just taken a longer road back to this very spot, stuck in a car with a man he not only despised, but a man who'd commit a felony because he didn't get his way.

"Why would you destroy it, Sean?" William muttered. "It was her home." Sean would never answer him. He would never admit to arson even though Denver must have caught him red-handed. In Sean's world, taking responsibility for his actions was out of the question.

"I hope your mother is well insured," Denver said, sliding into the driver's seat. "Once it hit the broilers, there was nothing the fire department could have done. It'll still be cooking by daybreak."

The car slowly crept forward, out of the way of bystanders, and maneuvered onto the street. It was then that William spotted Annie, sprinting past his window unaware she was so close to him. Her face was pinched with worry, her hair wild and highlighted with gold flecks from the firelight. He waited for her to turn and spot him, the love between them acting as a conductor and pulling her gaze to his. Surely she would sense his presence and turn.

She was a vision. An angelic vision against the hellish raze they'd been thrown into. He pictured her learning about what Sean had done. He pictured her grappling with how to tell the children. How could she summon a feasible explanation for Sean's destructive act? His skin boiled knowing he wouldn't be there to comfort her or to sit by her side as she explained the unthinkable to Betsy and James. He wanted to break out of the back seat. He wanted to throw his arms around her and promise to stand by her through each difficult conversation, every tough decision that would have to be made. He wanted to tear across the parking lot and hold her until she couldn't cry anymore. But he couldn't. He couldn't, and it made his heart twist with anguish.

All he could do was slump in the back seat and watch her float through the crowd while a lump rose to the back of his throat. His eyes moistened as she turned and disappeared into the crowd, lost to him yet again.

"She came," Sean mumbled as Denver drove down the street.

William shook his head. "How could you destroy it all in an instant?"

"You wouldn't understand."

"Probably not. But tell me anyway."

Sean pressed his forehead against the windowpane and closed his eyes. In a voice barely audible, he whispered, "Because…I love her."

William let his eyes glaze over as the passing buildings blurred against the darkness. Aside from the occasional static break on Denver's radio, the silence in the car was a comfort now. He needed to rest. He needed to reflect. He needed to get back to Annie.

William lay his head against the seat. He'd think of Annie. Of someday being home with her, and Betsy and James. With a resolve earned only after years of pursuing the wrong things and gaining wisdom along the way, he replied, "I love her enough to rebuild."

EPILOGUE

Annie refastened the sprigs of baby's breath in her hair, patting them lightly before grazing her hand lovingly over her belly. She hummed happily to herself. She wasn't showing yet and could keep her secret until the festivities were over. Today was about the wedding. There would be time enough for celebrating babies.

James darted between guests, his cheeks sweaty from playing in the hot sun after the ceremony.

"Come here, scoundrel." She laughed, reaching for him, but he yelped with delight and jumped out of the way. He had probably changed the most out of anyone over the last year. As she watched him dive and dip among the guests, chasing other children with a new-found confidence, she had finally felt she was getting to know the real James now.

Guests filed into the diner, their boisterous voices bouncing off every inch of the soft white-and-cornflower-blue-colored walls and warming every corner of Annie's swelling heart. Wherever she turned, smiling faces greeted her. The family she had once longed for, once desired, had manifested itself over time and had been all around this greasy spoon.

Joyce's peachy cheeks had rounded into permanent fixtures from a series of giggles and chuckles that hadn't stopped all day. As sweet as a strawberry, her hair was fuller, falling in soft curls around her shoulders. The sight of her good health and happiness made Annie's joy all the more amplified.

"Honey," Joyce said, clasping her hand. "You really are stunning."

"And you look radiant. No corsage, though?"

Joyce giggled. "No. I'm sure Earl had other things on his mind. Like wrangling up a suit."

Danny winked at them both as Joe pecked a kiss on Joyce's cheek. They both donned dress slacks and ties, and even Earl had combed his hair and ditched his Kromer hat. Each man stood with pride that emulated from his freshly shaved jaw to his rose boutonniere.

"The new sign is beautiful, honey," Danny said.

Joe pecked a kiss on Annie's cheek, too. "Yes, you did a good job dare. It felt darn good to see it hung this morning. We went from one ceremony to the next."

Danny leaned in. "And how did yous pick the new name?"

"William picked it."

"Does it mean anything special?"

Annie bit back a smile. "Perhaps."

Betsy was a vision in pale blue. Her hair, piled on top of her head and crowned with flowers, made her look older than the grinning little girl Annie was trying to hold on to for as long as possible. Her daughter knelt beside a seated Mia, nuzzling Mia's chubby-faced baby girl, and knew there was no reason their daughters couldn't grow up together. The next generation of friends like family she could enfold into their lives.

William slipped through the crowd to her and brushed a delicate kiss along her ear.

"This suit jacket will be the death of me," he breathed before peeling it off his shoulders. "Whose idea was it again to get married in August?"

"The ceremony is over. You can relax now," she crooned, spinning her gold wedding band around her finger and drawing pleasure from feeling it there.

"It looks good on you," he mused, catching her hand in his and pulling it to his lips for a kiss. "And you are absolutely glowing." She beamed. He'd learn the reason why soon enough.

It had been a year of surprises for the both of them and piling on another happy one made her already grateful heart swell.

After the fire, Annie had solicited Kenneth Bailey's help to deliver the Heiress's original will to the police. The authorities were willing to ignore how she had uncovered the Heiress's will given that she would testify against Sean. And with her family by her side, she had. The company in California was brought up on charges for collaborating with Sean, and the land preservation would remain just that—preserved.

"Should somebody check on the food?" she asked.

William nodded. "The wedding coordinator just did. She is worth her weight in gold."

"If you hadn't hired her, your mother would be doing everything."

"After the year she's had, I just want her to relax and celebrate. She deserves that."

"We all do."

William grazed his fingers along her jawline as his face broke into a grateful smile. She knew he felt like a new man once his name had been cleared. Bart Miller had thankfully admitted to starting the knife fight with William once another sailor told police he'd spotted Bart wielding the knife and gunning for William.

"I feel like I should make an announcement. There's so much to be said."

"Another one? I don't know if you can top the one from this morning."

"Revealing your new sign for the diner turned out to be more exciting than I thought," he said, squeezing her close. "It's the start of a brand-new chapter for us."

"Then get up there and say so!" She laughed, and he leaped on top of a bench and clinked a coffee mug with a spoon.

"Family and friends!" he called, as seventy pairs of eyes latched on to him.

"Shouldn't the best man be making da speeches, William!" Danny shouted as everyone laughed. William smiled and started again.

"I can't let this moment go by without thanking all of you for your love and support. This past year has been difficult on us, but it was hardest on my mother. Isn't she a beauty?"

Joyce beamed as Earl wrapped his arm around her and nodded in agreement.

"So many of you helped us rebuild this place and were witness to her courage and determination. She's set herself apart as an example to us all." He paused, his face erupting into a smile as he waited for the applause to quiet down. "This business was worth fighting for because it isn't only a restaurant. It's a place where friends come to visit, families enjoy each other and—" He reached down to take Annie's hand tightly in his. "People fall in love even after so many years of thinking they'd missed their chance at happiness. This is why it's so fitting today to celebrate not only the reopening of our diner under its new name, Moon Over Main, but to celebrate the marriage of two of our own. Please put your hands together in a big welcome for Chinoodin Falls's newest bride and groom—Mr. and Mrs. Earl Anderson!"

* * * * *

*For more great
Harlequin Heartwarming romances,
visit www.Harlequin.com today!*

Get 4 FREE REWARDS!

We'll send you 2 FREE Books plus 2 FREE Mystery Gifts.

Love Inspired® Suspense books feature Christian characters facing challenges to their faith... and lives.

FREE
Value Over
$20

MUST ♥ DOGS COLLECTION

SAVE 30% AND GET A FREE GIFT!

Finding true love can be "ruff"— but not when adorable dogs help to play matchmaker in these inspiring romantic "tails."

YES! Please send me the first shipment of four books from the **Must ♥ Dogs Collection**. If I don't cancel, I will continue to receive four books a month for two additional months, and I will be billed at the same discount price of $18.20 U.S./$20.30 CAN., plus $1.99 for shipping and handling.* That's a 30% discount off the cover prices! Plus, I'll receive a FREE adorable, hand-painted dog figurine in every shipment (approx. retail value of $4.99)! I am under no obligation to purchase anything and I may cancel at any time by marking "cancel" on the shipping statement and returning the shipment. I may keep the FREE books no matter what I decide.

☐ 256 HCN 4331   ☐ 456 HCN 4331

Name (please print)

Address   Apt. #

City   State/Province   Zip/Postal Code

Mail to the **Reader Service:**
IN U.S.A.: P.O. Box 1867, Buffalo, NY. 14240-1867
IN CANADA: P.O. Box 609, Fort Erie, Ontario L2A 5X3

Get 4 FREE REWARDS!

We'll send you 2 FREE Books plus 2 FREE Mystery Gifts.

FREE
Value Over
$20

Both the **Romance** and **Suspense** collections feature compelling novels written by many of today's best-selling authors.

Get 4 FREE REWARDS!

We'll send you 2 FREE Books plus 2 FREE Mystery Gifts.

Harlequin® Romance Larger-Print books feature uplifting escapes that will warm your heart with the ultimate feel-good tales.

FREE
Value Over
$20

READERSERVICE.COM

Manage your account online!

- Review your order history
- Manage your payments
- Update your address

*We've designed the
Reader Service website
just for you.*

Enjoy all the features!

- Discover new series available to you, and read excerpts from any series.
- Respond to mailings and special monthly offers.
- Browse the Bonus Bucks catalog and online-only exculsives.
- Share your feedback.

Visit us at:

ReaderService.com

RS16R